SLEEPING
GIANTS

—

SLEEPING GIANTS

A NOVEL

RENE DENFELD

HARPER

An Imprint of HarperCollins*Publishers*

SLEEPING GIANTS. Copyright © 2024 by Rene Denfeld. All rights reserved. Printed in the United States of America. No part of this book may be used or reproduced in any manner whatsoever without written permission except in the case of brief quotations embodied in critical articles and reviews. For information, address HarperCollins Publishers, 195 Broadway, New York, NY 10007.

HarperCollins books may be purchased for educational, business, or sales promotional use. For information, please email the Special Markets Department at SPsales @harpercollins.com.

FIRST EDITION

Designed by Nancy Singer

Library of Congress Cataloging-in-Publication Data has been applied for.

ISBN 978-0-06-301473-2

24 25 26 27 28 LBC 5 4 3 2 1

For Lulu, Dontonio, Markel, Tamira, Lihn, and Aria

SLEEPING
GIANTS

—

1

THE LITTLE BOY WENT CHARGING ACROSS THE EMPTY, HARD sand of the beach. The cliffs rose high to his right; the sea thundered in large, glassy gray clouds. Mist struck his face with force, and the wind tore at the institutional shirt he wore. His face was filled with anguish.

Behind him, signs littered the dunes by the beach road. WARNING: TREACHEROUS CURRENTS. WARNING: HIGH TIDES. WARNING: SHARP DROP-OFFS AND SNEAKER WAVES. WARNING: NO LIFEGUARD ON DUTY. NO SWIMMING. NO WADING. BY TOWN ORDINANCE.

Still he ran across the Oregon beach, all alone except for an eagle circling overhead. And a solitary man, leaving his battered truck and chasing after him.

The boy was very small against the sea. He was only nine, and tiny for his age. His name was sewn on the back of his shirt. The wind lifted his blond hair as he ran, and the sea rushed up to greet him.

The water was shockingly, breathtakingly cold. He had never been in the ocean before. He'd had no idea how icy the water would be, how swift and unmistakable its power. The first wave nearly knocked him down. The second flooded his pants and drove the air from his lungs. Soon he was floundering, and yet he pushed forward, out to the high pitted rocks where the sea lions roared; the glassy sea was now a sun overhead, a yellow curse that fell over them all.

His feet left him. One moment he could feel the sand underneath him, and the next he was out in the waves, being tossed like a cork. His shirt, sopping wet, was almost pulled off his body, and the sea seemed to want his sneakers. The current was so swift, so strong—the outgoing tide grabbed the boy in delight and spun him out to sea. His face bobbed in the waves. All he could taste was salt. All he could see was sun.

This is how I die, he thought. He closed his eyes.

The man running from the truck was large and long. At least his shadow was, as he pounded across the sand in battered work boots. The wind tore his cries from his lips. He dove into the ocean after the boy without hesitation. But the sea was so big, the waves a terrible force between the two capes, roaring at the empty sand. The waves nearly knocked the man down. The undertow sucked at his boots. He could not see anything. He splashed deeper into the churning waves, scanning the watery horizon, screaming the boy's name. Over and over again he screamed, thrashing in the surf, spreading his hands in the water, his calloused fingers empty.

Dennis! he screamed. *Dennis!*

Out in the waves, the boy gasped and sputtered. Salt water filled his mouth, and his eyes opened wide in surprise. He took a deep breath, and the water filled his lungs. It burned worse than anything he could have ever imagined, but it was not as bad as things that had happened to him before. He felt his body suddenly become light as his lungs became heavy, filled with water.

With a hard yank, the sea grabbed the boy and pulled him down under the surface, into a watery paradise of sparkling blue and rushing currents.

His body was never found.

TWENTY YEARS LATER

The shopkeeper's bell rang above the market door. The market in Eagle Cove reminded Larry Palmer of long-ago corner stores, the kind with a butcher counter and a produce section full of bins of dusty vegetables and unwaxed apples. There were aisles of detergents and soaps, boxed generic macaroni and canned milk, chocolate buttons, dry flour, a few rows of seasonings, and a case full of hot dishes like scalloped potatoes and ham, all cooked in the kitchen in the back. It was, in short, everything a man needed to live.

The teenage girl behind the counter was a local. She had frizzy hair, tied back from her face with a red bandanna.

"The spaghetti bake, please," he said.

The girl scooped it into a cardboard clamshell, then wrapped the container firmly with plastic wrap. She added a plastic fork, though he had told her before he didn't need any forks. His cabin was getting full of them.

"I'm good on forks," he said.

She put the fork down and looked away. She must see hundreds of people come and go, he thought. Travelers who came in whining about the cold and unfriendly beach, retirees like him who came here and then died. This was not a family place.

She handed him the warm parcel and then gave him an unexpected smile. Maybe, after so many months here, he was starting to be accepted. Or maybe she just felt sorry for him.

It had been his late wife, Marjorie, who had wanted to come here. *Let's retire to the coast, Larry,* she kept saying after he left the force. They had looked at real estate listings, quickly pricing themselves out of the more touristy towns with quaint names and taffy shops, and had finally chosen Eagle Cove, far away from everything, with an ocean so unruly that local ordinances had been passed to prohibit wading. They had found the cabin the week of her diagnosis, and for some reason, he had felt compelled to go through with it all. Now Marjorie was in an urn on his mantel, and he wondered what the hell he was doing.

He paid for the spaghetti bake and left. When he looked back, the girl was looking away.

HE TOOK THE LONG WAY HOME, BECAUSE HE HAD NOTHING BET-ter to do. The road was shifting with sand moved by the wind. The beach itself was empty, except for flocks of sandpipers racing on tiny legs.

He passed under the large metal signs dotting the low-lying dunes before the flat, innocent-looking spill of sand. He often mused about how he had moved to a beach town where the beach was dangerous.

He had never been so bored in his life.

He turned up the dune road, heading to his place. He could see the light he had left on, in the window. The other homes on the road were dark. Most were summer rentals and investment properties, for a wave of tourists that never came. His thighs began to ache with the climb. The air was heavy with the scent of the pines, bent backward from the wind, and the yellow primroses lining the road.

At the top of the dune was the local cemetery. He hadn't known it when he bought the place. Marjorie would have gotten a kick out of it, he thought. She was a big one for antique stores and Ouija boards. Her laughter would scare the devil, he had often joked.

How he missed that laugh now.

He stopped at the top of the dune, taking in the view. From here he could see the entire coastline, from the mountain that looked like a dog with its paws in the sea—crashing in anger at its feet—to the long curl of waves, white against blue; and, finally, the distant, shimmery horizon. About twenty miles down the beach was another mountain, its snout in the sea. The ocean clamored in between these two capes, raging and constantly in conflict with itself. In the distance, massive rocks rose from the sea. Sometimes, at night, he could hear the sea lions bellowing for their mates, and could imagine their slippery, cold, wet bodies.

His viewing done, he turned into the cemetery, thinking of his dead wife. Marjorie would have volunteered to take care of this misbegotten place. Marjorie this, Marjorie that, he thought. He couldn't stop thinking about her. The sandy soil made the graves look lumpy and unkempt. He wandered among the headstones, thinking that soon enough, there would be one for him. When he was young, the thought would have paralyzed him. Now it soothed him. Once you get to a certain point, death is the only thing that makes sense.

At the edge of the cemetery, overlooking the sea, was a small memorial. It was nothing more than a stone set on pitted concrete. But something about it called to him. Maybe it was the single name, carved into the rock. Maybe it was the epitaph. *Lost in the sea but not from our hearts.* He surmised from the epitaph that the body had never been found. Someone had scattered seashells over the ground, as if in offering.

Or maybe, he thought, it was the age of the boy who'd died. Dennis Owen, age nine.

There were no names of his surviving family, no quotes from his loving parents.

It was all a bit of a mystery.

2

MORNING CAME, A PALE SHAPE THROUGH THE BEDROOM WINDOWS. Larry was beginning to think he was going mad. He was aimless with boredom. He and Marjorie had never had kids, and the work had eaten away at his friendships as it so often did, so by the end, it was just him and Marjorie. Somehow, the miracle of her love was that it kept part of him pure. But only for Marjorie.

He bought his meals at the market because he didn't want to cook. He didn't want to clean. He didn't want to play checkers by himself. But he also didn't reach out to anyone back in Portland. He didn't think they cared.

Instead, he wandered, trudging up and down the beach until the spray coated his face with something like tears. You're grieving, his mind told him, but he didn't think that was true. A love as long as he and Marjorie had had couldn't be contained in one simple word. There really was no way to explain it.

HE WAS WALKING BACK UP THE DUNE WHEN HE SAW THE YOUNG woman. Her blond hair was loose, blowing over the shoulders of her parka. He thought of the weather alert he had heard on the radio that morning. Storms were set to sweep the beach. Batten down. It was a brave visitor, he thought, to chance getting trapped here during a spring storm. But then, strangers often had no idea of the storms' ferocity.

As he watched, the young woman walked away from her car, which she'd parked at the side of the road, and went into the cemetery. He followed her, curious.

SHE WAS LOOKING FOR SOMEONE'S GRAVE, THAT MUCH WAS CLEAR. He watched as she stopped and read the headstones. Getting closer, he judged her to be somewhere in her twenties. She had a smooth, freckled face, and her eyes were a very dark blue.

"Can I help you?" he asked.

She gave him a cautious smile.

"I'm looking for a memorial," she said. "For a boy. He died a long time ago. He was swept away in the sea."

He nodded, feeling the sandy air stir the hair around his ears.

"Right this way. I think I know where it is."

He led her to the memorial overlooking the ocean. When she read the name, Dennis Owen, her expression changed. Suddenly, Larry was looking at his own grief, in a much younger face. It was the grief of someone who has no idea what they have lost.

She turned her eyes from the memorial to the sea. It was thick and heavy looking that day, a deep, swollen blue reflected against a sullen plum sky. It was always this way before storms. It was like the ocean was gathering force, like a boxer coiling her mighty, frothy fist.

He wondered if he should leave, give the young woman some privacy.

"I wonder why they put it here," she said softly.

"What do you mean?"

"Here, where he can see the ocean."

"I don't think they actually found him, miss."

"You're right. I meant, why put his memorial here, in sight of the sea that killed him?"

Larry didn't have an answer to that. A strand of her hair blew into her face, and she brushed it away.

"I'm sorry," she said. "I'm being rude. My name is Amanda Dufresne."

"Larry Palmer," he said.

A sharp wind came suddenly, off the ocean. It rushed up the dune, startling them. The sea was gathering under the angry sky, and in the distance, he could see the thick dark clouds that warned of storms. Sometimes the storms were so bad, they turned into cyclones. The beach was a hazard then, and to stay outside anywhere was a risk. At best, the young woman would get doused. At worst, she was at risk of being killed by a falling tree or literally swept away.

"We got a storm coming in," he said.

"I heard that on the radio driving down."

"Are you staying in town?" he asked. There was a single hotel, an old ramshackle place right off the beach, with peeling clapboard and tiny, sandy rooms warmed by electric baseboard heat.

"No. I was only planning to stay for the day."

"You need to find a place to shelter during the storm."

"Is there any place in town?"

"There's a market, but it closes down in storms. Everyone goes home, locks down tight."

"Oh."

"You're welcome to come to my cabin," he said, hoping she wouldn't think him a creep. "I'm a retired police officer, but don't hold that against me. I'm okay. Really. I moved down here with my late wife, Marjorie."

Larry wondered if he was making a mistake. He was not in the habit of inviting strangers home. But he didn't want to leave the young woman out in the storm.

"You know what they say. Any port in a storm," he said.

A single fat raindrop hit her face, a warning. She blinked at the black clouds racing overhead. The ocean looked like it was poised to jump ashore.

"You don't want to be outside for one of our storms," he said. "Trust me."

"What about my car?" she asked, as if it were a dog.

"It'll be okay; you're out from under those trees."

"Okay."

She followed him down the road to his cabin, where for the first time, it felt like the light he had left on had made a difference. Once inside, he lit a fire, and when the wind howled the smoke right back down the chimney, he laughed and fixed the draft, saying he had been in the Boy Scouts, after all.

ALL HE HAD IN THE HOUSE WAS LEFTOVER SPAGHETTI BAKE AND scalloped potatoes from the market and some tuna fish to eat with crackers, all of which he offered her, feeling embarrassed. *I should have learned how to cook*, he wanted to say, but that wasn't true. When Marjorie was alive, he was the one who liked to tie on an apron and make dinner. There was something about the frilly white apron tied around his fat ass that made his wife laugh, and helped her shake off the day.

Amanda politely declined the food, but he thought she might be hungry, so he found a bag of Brazil nuts, and they sat in front of the fire, cracking those and eating them by the handful. To go along, they had icy cold beers, and for the first time in months, Larry began to feel human.

"You mind me asking why you came here?" he asked, scooping nutshells from his lap and tossing them into the fire, where they turned black and hissed.

She turned from the fire, her face glowing with the light. Outside, there was a sudden clap of thunder, and the eaves began to shake. The sky broke open, and the rain poured down. They could hear it on the roof.

"I was adopted as a newborn," she said.

He smiled encouragingly at her.

"It was a private adoption. Right after I was born, my mom disappeared. I have good parents—great parents. I never felt a reason to go looking for my birth mother. Then recently, I started wondering. What parts of me are me, and what parts are her? So I decided to look for her. I had her name, so it wasn't hard."

She looked at the fire.

"It turned out she'd died not that long after I was born. Alcoholism. But here's the surprise: Three years before she had me, my mom had a boy. He was taken away from her and ended up in foster care."

Larry reached into the nut bowl.

"His name was Dennis Owen," she said.

"He was your brother."

"Yes. My older brother."

She studied the fire. He could tell she had spent a lot of nights since finding out thinking about fate.

Larry cracked a nut. It fell into his hand, gleaming and white.

"Your parents were never told about him?" he asked.

"No. I guess this kind of thing happens a lot in private adoptions."

He grunted, brushing crumbs from his lap.

"I tried to learn more about him. This was all I found."

She reached inside her jacket and pulled out a piece of paper, folded in half.

Larry hesitated, then put down his nutcracker next to his beer. He wiped his fingers carefully on his trousers and reached for the paper.

It was a copy of a newspaper article from the *Coastal Herald*. "Boy

Swept Out to Sea." The article was very brief. Dennis Owen, age nine, was presumed dead from accidental drowning. He had been a resident of a place called Brightwood. Larry had never heard of it.

"I looked it up," Amanda said. "It was a home for troubled boys."

"It makes more sense now," he said. "The memorial."

"How so?" She looked curious.

"No parents listed. No quotes from loved ones."

"The home closed the year after he died."

Larry looked at the date on the article and did the math. Had he lived, Dennis Owen would have been twenty-nine. That meant Amanda Dufresne was twenty-six.

Outside, the thunder cracked, and the wind screamed. The sea itself was like a background monster, growling at the sand. It sounded like it wanted to climb up the hill to them.

"It's hard to lose someone you never met," he said.

He could see the emotions in her face.

"Is it normal to feel so sad?"

"Yes." He said it immediately, without hesitation, and Amanda Dufresne looked up, deep into his eyes. Larry looked away.

"What did you hope to get out of coming here?"

She stretched out her jean-clad legs in front of the fire. "I guess I want to know who he was. If he was okay. If he had any happy times. I want to know how he died."

THE STORM STOPPED AS ABRUPTLY AS IT HAD BEGUN. LARRY FOL-lowed Amanda outside, her shoes squishing in the wet sand, and they walked back down the road to her car. The car itself looked fine, but the road was covered with fallen trees.

"Jeez," she whispered.

He walked a bit farther down the road, toward the tumultuous ocean. The sea roiled as if considering its next move. The pavement was covered with large tree limbs. Down the street, an entire pine had collapsed, its needles shrouding the wet asphalt. The road was completely blocked.

"They'll send someone out to clear this," he tried to reassure her.

She glanced at the thick gray sky. Night came early on the Oregon Coast.

"How far is it to town?" she asked.

"It's not far. I'll walk you to the hotel. They keep a room or two ready for when this happens."

"Are they expensive? The rooms."

"Here? Not at all."

"Okay." She gave him a quick smile, reassuring herself. "I'll be fine."

"Course you will."

She grabbed a backpack from the back seat of her car, and he saw that she hadn't brought much. The ocean, not tired of playing games, howled up the empty roads and threw sand at their ankles. It lifted her hair around her face so it looked like an aura, and he couldn't help it, he thought, Poor girl.

HE WAS UP EARLY THE NEXT DAY, FEELING MORE EXCITEMENT THAN he had in a long time. The storm had left a strange afterglow, a bruised pink against the windows. When he stepped outside, the mountains seemed closer than before, the pine branches covered in white raindrops.

He skirted the fallen trees on the road, seeing how the one and only road crew of Eagle Cove—a man named Joe—was already out, drinking coffee from a thermos while he hurled branches into his flatbed truck. The air was hazy with the scent of fresh pine dust and the memory of Joe's chain saw.

The market was just opening, and the smell of boiling corn and hot mashed potatoes came out through the open door. The teen girl was sweeping in front.

He found Amanda in the cramped hotel office, pouring a cup of coffee from the pot and sniffing it suspiciously. She dumped in a bunch of the old powdered creamer next to the pot, and then some lumpy sugar from a box.

She turned to see him, and smiled, clearly relieved.

"I was just going to ask how long it might take to clear the roads," she said, in her soft voice.

"As long as it takes," the hotel manager said from behind his desk. Charlie was a tall, reed-thin man who was always grinning. No one knew why, and no one asked.

"I meant—"

"Maybe a day. Who knows?" He kept grinning. "Didn't you hear the warning when you were coming down?"

Larry felt for Amanda in that moment. She looked like she was longing for home, though part of him wondered just how at home she felt anywhere. She had a sense of differentness about her, as if she lived apart from others.

"What's the first thing you like to do in the morning?" he asked.

"Drink some coffee," she said.

"Well, we already have a start on that. Let's go out and sit on the beach. We can solve the problems of the world later."

THEY SAT ON A DRIFTWOOD LOG, OVERLOOKING THE OCEAN. THE sea rose in great dark swells that shattered like ice on the sand. Gulls ran along the shoreline, as if in celebration.

"You don't seem to get a lot of visitors here," she said.

"Summer brings a few tourists."

"What do they do?"

"Scream at each other. Fling seaweed around. Look for shells and watch for the sneaker waves. Most of the time, they end up in the market, complaining about the price of everything without wondering how much it costs a truck to come over the passes. Then they leave."

She smiled and sipped her coffee.

"You stayed," she said.

"I came here because . . . because . . ." He couldn't answer.

She was intuitive. "Was it your wife's idea?"

"Yes."

She fell silent, sipping. After a bit, she unwrapped a blueberry muffin from the hotel's free continental breakfast, which had consisted of a few stale pastries and rock-hard bagels. She offered him a piece, and he shook his head. The muffin made crumbs all over her lap, and an inquisitive seagull landed nearby, curious. She threw it a crumb.

"You shouldn't do that," Larry told her. "There will be a hundred of them in a few minutes."

Sure enough, they were soon surrounded by raucous gulls. Amanda picked up a stout stick and chucked it at them, surprising him. Afterward, she examined her fingers.

"What do you do for a living?" he asked her.

"I work at the Oregon Zoo. Today is my weekend."

"What do you do there?"

"I work with the polar bear, Molly."

"Really?" He was gratified. It seemed like a perfect job for her.

"Yes. I love it. I started working there when I was eighteen. Now I'm the lead keeper. Though I don't like that word. I'm more like a paid friend to Molly."

"I feel like I've heard of her."

"There were a lot of articles when we got her."

"I remember now. The world's loneliest polar bear."

"That's what they call her."

Amanda finished the muffin. The birds flew overhead. She folded the plastic wrap the muffin had come in into a tiny square and buried it deep in her pocket. She looked out at the ocean, her eyes dark.

"Maybe you could help me some more," she said.

"Sure."

"I was thinking about that center, Brightwood. Since I'm stuck here for a few hours, at least, maybe I could find it."

"We'll ask back at the market."

"Why there?"

"It's the place where everything happens here. Problem is, nothing happens here. I'll go with you. But first, I've got to use the loo."

She turned to look at the expanse of sharp seagrass tufting the low dunes around them.

"There's one on the path back," he said.

IN THE MARKET, THE TEEN GIRL WAS STOCKING ROLLS OF TOILET paper with rinds of dust on them. She wiped this on her jeans, making it look like she had been in a war with a million moths. She climbed down from her rickety step stool.

"I know about that place. Ma!"

Her mother appeared, a half shadow behind a kitchen door. Larry saw the shape of a spatula in her hand. He had never seen the woman, and had begun to suspect that she was severely introverted. Or depressed. As with much in the town, no one discussed it. At least not with him.

"Yes?" The voice behind the door was muted.

"They're asking after that old kids' home. Brightwood."

"Who's asking?"

"That old man. Sorry," she said to Larry. "The one who was a cop. And a woman who got stuck here with the storm."

"Joe should know better."

"He can't pick up trees before they fall."

"No, you nitwit. I meant he should put up that sign we've been talking about forever. On the highway. At the turnoff."

Her daughter sighed. She looked at her messy jeans. The subject of the sign was the source of a long-standing debate in the town of Eagle Cove. Some said visitors deserved a warning that they might get trapped in the town by falling trees. Others said Joe shouldn't have to risk his life just to hang a sign that the dumb tourists would ignore anyhow. If they didn't have the sense not to drive before a storm, they deserved whatever happened to them.

"I'd just like to know where it was," Amanda called to the shape behind the kitchen door.

Silence seemed to greet this.

"It's up Barker Road. About three miles. In the woods."

"That's on the mountain," Larry said.

"They closed a long time ago," the girl told them.

"Was it because of the boy who died?" Amanda asked, but the girl didn't answer.

OUTSIDE, LARRY WAS APPARENTLY GEARING UP TO GO WITH HER, checking the bottoms of his walking shoes and stretching his legs.

"Would you like company?" he asked.

"Yes, please," Amanda said, relieved.

"Lions, tigers, and bears?"

"More like I'm afraid of getting lost."

"Don't blame you. There's lots of old logging roads in these mountains, and some of them lead nowhere. It's easy to get looped around and lost."

"Don't tell me," she said with a shudder.

THEY WALKED UP THE OLD BLACKTOP ROAD. THE CLEANUP TRUCK clearly didn't make it out here often, as fallen pine trees, both old and new, littered the cracked pavement. The trees were deep around them, and they could hear sounds in the brush. Elk, maybe, or deer. Birds tittered.

Larry had the sense of climbing higher. Away from the clamor and wind of the beach, the air here felt balmy and soft. The salt wind whispered in the trees, and Amanda became aware of just how quiet it was, outside of the birds. A distant plane droned, but other than that, there was silence.

The three miles began to feel like ten, going uphill. Larry trudged quietly, taking care with his knees. He was starting to wonder if they had taken the wrong road when they saw a large building rising out of the trees. It looked like a dot of gray on a green felt background.

The sign at the front gate warned them.

BRIGHTWOOD, A PLACE FOR HEALING, it said. And under that, in newer letters, NO TRESPASSING.

THE GATE WAS RUSTED AND OLD; A BROKEN PADLOCK HUNG OFF A chain. Amanda pushed it open. A decaying drive greeted them, overgrown with tufted grass that had broken through the pavement.

The place was much bigger than Larry had imagined. A prison, not a home.

The front yard was snarled with wild manzanita bushes. Wild blackberries had grown over them in a crusted mantle. Larry and Amanda stepped carefully across a rotting porch to the front door, which was green with mold.

CAUTION. DANGER. UNSAFE BUILDING, said an ancient notice bolted to the door. Underneath, someone had written *Eat shit*. But most of the building was clean of graffiti, Larry noticed. Not enough teenagers around, he thought. As Amanda opened the door, Larry reached for a weapon, instinctually. His hand fell to his side, empty.

The door creaked, and a cold draft coiled down the hall and blew against their legs. The air was rancid. There was decay and mildew and something bitter, like swollen weeds.

"Careful," Larry warned her. "The floor could be rotted."

He went in first, taking the lead, Amanda following him as they walked down the tiled hall. There was a closed door that said OFFICE and one next to it that said DIRECTOR. Amanda cautiously pushed them open. The rooms were thick with darkness. Abandoned desks crouched in the corners, and the windows seemed furred with moss.

The smell got ranker the farther into the building they went. Larry proceeded slowly, feeling each step. The last thing he wanted was for them to fall through to the basement. He could almost feel it simmering below them, full of water from leaks and broken sewer pipes.

He looked at Amanda, wondering how she was feeling.

At the end of the hall was a narrow stairway. They took this, climbing carefully, to a landing where a broken window looked over the unbroken forest. The trees were like a serene blanket. Or a fence, Larry thought.

Down the hall of the second floor was a stretch of dormitory-style rooms, each impossibly small, with the black marks of cot legs on the floors. The windows were little more than narrow slots, and some rooms had no windows at all. Those rooms whispered of a darkness older than time.

The floor began to feel spongier, and Larry stopped. He signaled to Amanda, and they retreated back to the stairwell. There was no way of knowing which room Dennis had lived in. Larry was filled with questions. Why had the boy been at the beach that day? How had he gotten there? Hadn't he seen the warning signs? There was so much they didn't know.

They began to climb to the third floor. The stairwell felt narrower, and steeper. The ceiling was lower up here, and the bedrooms were even smaller and more cramped than those on the second floor, as if they had been built into what was originally an attic. Larry stopped Amanda, signaling that it was unsafe.

He led her down the stairs, breathing easier as they went. Back on the first floor, they explored, finding an institutional kitchen with cold metal shelves and a broken stove pushed on its side. Mice had eaten the insulation. The pantry was empty. There was a schoolroom, with broken-down chairs and desks piled in the corners and a blackboard so thick with mold it looked like wet felt. Nearby was a small gymnasium, the floor lined with rotting wrestling mats. Next to that was a massive bathroom, with industrial showerheads over a rusted floor. The bathroom stalls didn't have doors. The next room was a narrow dining room. The dining room led to a visiting room with decaying bookshelves. A single plastic flower was on the floor. At the end of the room was another door.

TREATMENT SERVICES, said the sign.

Larry pushed the door open, his heart suddenly heavy.

The hallway was long, and the doors were many. Amanda stopped to clear a dirty pane of glass on one. They were looking into a small rubber room. That was the only name for it. It was a padded cell.

The hall was lined with these isolation rooms. Larry had been in a lot of jails and prisons in his time, but few images were as haunting as this cold, empty hall filled with coffin-like cells. He could imagine boys inside the rooms pounding on the doors, begging for release. Or maybe they just sat and waited, hoping they would not be forgotten and left to starve to death.

At the end of the hall was another room, this one littered with tattered sheets and deflated, moldy pillows. A rolled-up rug lay in the corner, covered with mouse turds. That room smelled awful.

The final door had a sign that said CUSTODIAN, and Larry opened it to find a simple hallway closet, filled with old brooms and mops with stone-hard heads. He watched as Amanda backed away. She turned to leave, rushing until she was at a near run, and he followed her, concerned. She didn't stop until she was outside and below the narrow windows, with the trees all watching, and he wanted to reassure her, *There is no one here now.*

But there was, they both knew. There was.

BY THE TIME THEY GOT BACK TO TOWN, AMANDA LOOKED EMOTIONally spent. Larry studied her, thinking about the three- to four-hour drive back to the city, and on dark and twisty mountain roads, without any cell service.

The hotel manager greeted them, still grinning, saying the roads were clear.

"Should be able to get to the highway now, miss."

"Thank you," Amanda said, and went to fetch her backpack from her room. Her hair felt musty and her teeth furred. She longed for home, and yet she was dragged with guilt, as if she were leaving her brother behind.

Larry walked with her up the dune to her car, which was still parked near the cemetery. She decided to visit it one last time to say goodbye to the brother she'd never known. Larry wasn't sure if he should accompany her. He waited for her a few feet away, on the bluff. The sea below him lashed back and forth, like an angry cat drawing its claws up and down the coast.

"I'LL BE HEADING BACK NOW," AMANDA TOLD HIM, AFTER A BIT. "Thank you for being so nice to me."

She sounded so unexpectedly genuine, Larry was moved. He was suddenly overwhelmed with emotion and didn't know what to do. He took a couple of long breaths. Marjorie, he thought. I wish you were here.

Amanda waited patiently.

"Sorry," he said. "Sometimes it just comes over me."

She smiled at him, understanding.

"Come back, visit me," he said. "Maybe I could help you learn more about your brother."

Amanda turned to the sea. She looked over the swells as if she might still see Dennis out there, bobbing in the waves.

"I'd like that," she said.

3

AMANDA WAS BACK A FEW WEEKS LATER. SHE HAD CALLED LARRY the day before, but he wasn't expecting her so early. He was still in his old plaid robe, which he'd had forever and a day. He remembered wearing it on a cruise with Marjorie. It had been their one and only cruise. Marjorie had spent most of the time in their stateroom.

Homebodies, Marjorie had liked to say. *We're homebodies, Larry.* But the truth was thornier and harder to bear. There were reasons Marjorie had retreated from life, and now that she was gone, Larry was starting to think they were all his fault.

Now Amanda was standing outside his door, which like those on all proper cabins here faced away from the wind that blew perpetually off the coast. She wore the same parka, her blond hair blowing in the wind.

"Oh! I caught you too early." She looked worried.

"Sorry. Late to bed. Old habits." He smiled.

He let her in, then excused himself to change. In a few minutes he had joined her in the living room.

"I took a few days off," she said. "I'm staying at the hotel."

"I hope Charlie gave you a good deal."

"What would that be?"

"I'll go down there with you later, if you like, and make sure."

"That would be nice. Thank you."

She had a formality about her, he thought, that was touching.

"Want some coffee?"

"Sure."

He measured out coffee, turning on the percolator. The smell filled the room, along with the smell of salt and old wood.

He poured her a cup of coffee, remembering that she liked cream and sugar. He put these on the table. He wanted her to feel cared for.

"WHERE DO YOU THINK I SHOULD START?" SHE ASKED.

Larry was laying a fire. He sat back on his slippered heels as he set another piece of kindling on the pile.

"Well, you could try to get his records," he said, picking up one last piece of kindling, "but it's almost impossible to get child welfare records for someone else. Not without a court order, at least."

"That's what they told me when I called."

Outside, a tempestuous spring swirled. One moment it was all gray clouds and sleety wind; the next the sky opened and the sun ran down the mountains and shared in the glory.

"What else?" she asked.

He looked up at her. In the spring light, his face looked shaggy and old. "There's got to be a story," he said, and then explained when he saw the confusion in her face. "It's how we were trained to think. A narrative. The story of what happened. Why was Dennis on the beach that day? Didn't he see the signs? Was there an adult present? There had to be an investigation into what happened."

She nodded eagerly.

"Is there a cop here?" she asked.

"Not here in Eagle Cove. There's a constable in the next town over, Wheel Stone. He supervises three towns, spread along this coast."

"That's a lot, isn't it?"

"Depends."

"Can we talk to him?" she asked.

"Good question. I'll make some calls."

LARRY TOOK HIS PHONE OUTSIDE BECAUSE THE RECEPTION WAS better. When he returned, Amanda was still sitting in front of the fire.

"I reached that constable," he said. "He says we can come anytime. Even right now, if you want."

He liked the expression on her face then. She looked calm with satisfaction. Nature had found a course: it was forward.

CONSTABLE ROBERTS WAS IN HIS EARLY SIXTIES, WITH A THICK head of black hair threaded with silver. He sat behind a scratched wooden desk, the walls behind him covered with old-timey pictures of fishing boats. A net hung in the corner held a collection of glass fishing floats and buoys.

"Yes, I remember that case," the constable said. "You're his sister?" he asked, his eyes casting to Amanda.

"Yes," she said.

Larry spoke up. "She's trying to learn more about him."

"I don't know much about Dennis," Amanda said. "He was taken from our mother before I was born, and somehow ended up in that center."

"It was for disturbed boys, miss."

"What was wrong with him?"

"I don't know."

"Can you tell us about the incident?" Larry asked.

"Why, sure." The constable sat back. "It's been a bit. Let's see. I got a call from the woman who owns the market. Gertrude. Poor lady, she used to be more friendly. Anyhow, she said a man came running in, holding a wet shirt. He had seen the boy get swept away and gone in after him. He almost drowned, himself. The shirt washed up onshore after the boy went under."

"No remains?" Larry asked.

The constable shook his head. "When we have a drowning victim, I'd say over half the time we never recover the body. Sometimes it washes up miles away on another beach. But more often . . . it just disappears. It's a big sea."

"Why was he on the beach?" Amanda asked.

"We figured he ran away."

"'We'?" Larry asked.

The constable looked annoyed.

"The director of the center and myself. She paid me a visit afterward."

"Why would he run away?" Amanda asked.

"Boys run away sometimes, miss."

"I went to that place. Brightwood," she said.

"That's trespassing."

Larry sighed. The constable gave him a look.

"I wouldn't want you to get hurt," the constable added.

"I was hoping to learn more about him."

The constable seemed to be weighing his words. When he spoke again, it was with kindness.

"Well, I hate to put it like this, but he's gone now."

"I'd just like to talk to someone who knew him. Do you know anyone who might have known him? Maybe someone who worked there?"

The constable looked at the large clock on the wall, even though he had a watch on his wrist and a cell phone on the desk. "I'm afraid I've got to get going," he said. "Time to patrol. We've had a problem with drug runners lately. They avoid the highways, because of the state police."

"What about your report?" Larry asked.

"Confidential. You know that. Anything involving children is confidential under ORS 419B."

"But you were just talking to us," Amanda said.

"I told you what I could. I can't give you confidential reports. I'd lose my job. Your friend here knows that."

"But it's my brother."

"It wouldn't matter if you were his mother, because I'm guessing she lost her parental rights. Only the legal guardian can get police reports involving children, and that was the center, which closed years ago. I'm sorry about that, I truly am." He stood, holding his cap in his hands, and then looked abashed. "Look, I'm really sorry for your loss. It's got to come as a shock, after so many years. But down here . . . how can I put it? This happens. Every year or two, one of the towns along this stretch of coastline has a drowning. Just a few years ago, some tourists brought their little boy to the beach here in Wheel Stone. He got swept away by a sneaker wave. Never found him either. My point is, maybe sometimes you got to let the dead rest. Your brother had a hard life. No doubt about it. Maybe now it's time for you to make the most of your own."

Larry didn't look terribly impressed with this little spiel.

"Who was the man who came into the market?" he asked.

"I don't recall. I'm sorry—it's been so long."

LARRY LOOKED UPSET AFTER HE AND AMANDA LEFT THE CONSTAble's office. He kept tapping on his wheel. Amanda wondered if it was an old habit, from driving patrol.

"What do you think?" she asked, after a while.

"I think he doesn't want to talk about it," he said. "I'm not one to crap on other cops—all right, I do sometimes—but in my experience, if a cop isn't talking, there's a reason."

"I'm sorry to hear about those people. Their little boy."

"Well, he is right about that. The ocean does take people."

"How come you're helping me, Larry?"

He wanted to say something trite, like *I got nothing better to do.* And there was truth in that. But he suspected there were other reasons, and he wasn't ready to share them with Amanda. Maybe he wasn't sure of them himself.

"What's next?" she asked.

"We've got more questions now than we had before. Your brother, alone on a beach. A man who went in after him. A center no one seems to want to talk about. What the hell happened here?"

4

BRIGHTWOOD

The oldest monsters are unnamed. Unnamed monsters, Dennis learned before he even knew his own name, were the worst kind of all.

When you gave a monster a name, you had it in hand. There, that one was anger. Rage. Sexual abuse. Dennis learned the names of all these before he was four, as items the child psychiatrists crossed off on their checklists. They were looking for answers. They were looking for monsters to blame.

But the worst monster of all? That one was as cold as sleet. He climbed up the hill at night and played with your feet. He washed the tears from your face and cooed like a mother before slashing your heart to ribbons. The worst monster, Dennis knew, was like Satan from the Bible some parents read to you. He came wearing disguises, and no one knew his real name, because he had none. He pretended to be a lot of things, and the worst thing he pretended to be was love.

AWWOOOOH. THAT WAS THE FIRST SOUND, RECOGNIZED LATER AS the whistle of a morning train. It came over the hill and split the morning into two halves: before Mother left, and after.

They lived in a tiny flat. No, scratch that. That was the second home. The first had a nursery the color of butter. No. Did it? Maybe that was the third home. The homes began to blur together after a while. No. That wasn't it. The homes started as a blur, because he was never theirs, and no one really wanted him. They wanted a miracle child, an ideal. A substitute.

Dennis, the doll.

But he wasn't born to be a doll. Somehow the foster parents looked through his tender, veined chest and saw this. Instead of a terrified, beseeching child unable to voice his needs, they saw trouble. *There's something wrong with him*, said one, and a social worker who had picked him up from a home at least had the grace to say *Hell, of course there is. The child is only two and has already been through six homes.*

Scratch that. Maybe there had been only four homes before he was two.

They say inchoate memory, formed before language, is the worst of all, because it flies like bats in your bones: you cannot heal from what you cannot voice. But Dennis thought memories were like monsters. They filled the world like ghosts at dawn. There were so many, the streets were chockablock with them: You couldn't enter a new home without remembering the last. And if the memory was bad, well, there went that home too. The smell of bleach on a towel. The way the sunlight came in through a curtain. A crib. A bathtub. A face. All of them cursed by time and the ones who left him, because every time someone abandons you, it is always the first time.

HE LIKED BRIGHTWOOD AT FIRST. BRIGHTWOOD WAS A PLACE HE could understand. There were rules. No one could leave him, because this was the place the lost were left. All the boys here were throwaways. It was like being in a giant wastebasket filled with dirty tissues. You knew you were lost.

Bed. Dresser. Two shelves. Socks. A blanket. The wind came in through the window. He could press his hand against it if he liked, and no one slapped it away. No one made mouse faces at him, kissy-kissy boo-boo faces that always lied, because those ones were the worst. No one pretended to be *mentor* or *friend* or *counselor*, and mostly, no one pretended to be mom or dad.

He especially appreciated the lack of mom or dad. It was like being in a serene, open place where there wasn't a threat around every corner. No one would grab and hug and kiss him, then scowl and get angry when he didn't want to hug or kiss back. No one would pretend to know which story he liked to hear, or want to call him yet another new name—*I'm going to call you the name of a son I lost in a stillbirth*—and expect him to staple it to his chest, like he was made of latex and not flesh.

"I'm not a doll." It was what he growled when he first came to Brightwood, and that was okay. No one cared. Most of the time, they left you alone. If you were really bad—like hit another child or bit yourself bad—they put you in a locked room where you couldn't tear the rubber padding no matter how hard you tried. After a time, Dennis liked the rooms, and then finally they bored him, which maybe meant they worked after all. If they existed to harden a heart already hardened, they worked plenty well.

He could have gone on like that, growing smaller and harder by the year until he turned into one single tear that would later explode into sadness or rage, like so many of the boys of Brightwood, tumbled out into a world that didn't want them.

But then came Ralph.

RALPH TOOK THE CUSTODIAN JOB THE YEAR DENNIS WAS SIX. OTHER boys had come and gone, some to adoptive homes, but the more time you spent at Brightwood, the less likely that was to work out, and those boys boomeranged right back. One moment a boy was being shepherded out the door by hopeful adoptive parents, their hands on his little shoulders, and the next he was returned, a wilted flower, his belongings tossed helter-skelter into a suitcase.

The wide-open air hurt after a while when you are used to closed small rooms.

Besides, if you were at Brightwood, it was because you had failed at being normal. That's why they called it a home for disturbed boys. Dennis was disturbed. Otherwise he wouldn't be here.

Dennis remembered the day he met Ralph. Dennis had been in one of the isolation rooms because he had punched a hole in his bedroom wall and peed into it—it was strangely satisfying—and had spent hours locked away. The staff person who had put him there was opening the door. Dennis, a small dark cloud, walked into the narrow, dim hallway.

Ralph was down the hall, being shown the custodian closet by the director. He turned, saw Dennis, and winked at him.

That wink broke Dennis. He fretted over it for all of a day and a night, somehow miraculously keeping from destroying all the walls of his room, and finally he went back to the source of his agony.

"Why did you wink at me?" he demanded.

By then Ralph was mopping the floor. He wasn't very good at it. He stopped and squeezed the gray mop so ribbons of soapy, dirty water ran back into the bucket.

"You looked like a boy who needed a wink," he said. His voice was calm and low, and he finished by giving Dennis another wink.

Dennis felt a gust of anger. He hated it when such anger swept over him, but then he relished it, because anger was all he had in this dim lightbulb of a world.

"How would *you* know?" he sneered.

For a little boy, Dennis could make himself big. He had done it before with foster parents, and it had worked. He had been scaring people since he was two, when he realized his mother was not coming back. He started with his hands and then made his neck big. He hissed at Ralph.

But Ralph was not scared. He didn't react by shoving Dennis into the wall or pushing him into one of the small rooms. He didn't sigh or look sad. He just lifted the mop, which was still drooling gray water, and put it gently on the floor. Somehow, Ralph managed to mop the floor without ignoring Dennis, and yet at the same time did nothing to provoke him. It was an adult sleight of hand that Dennis had never before experienced.

The mop skidded right up to his feet.

It was then that Dennis noticed what small feet he had. His feet were clad in institutional sneakers, and no amount of huffing and puffing could make those feet bigger. He stared at them as if he had never seen them before, and all of a sudden, much to his surprise and that of Ralph, he burst into tears.

Ralph didn't soothe him or chide him or do much of anything else. He just rocked back on his heels like he knew what that emotion would cost him—and Dennis.

A FEW DAYS LATER, RALPH FOUND DENNIS IN HIS ROOM. DENNIS was catching and killing the black flies that clustered on the inside of the windowpane. They made a bad smell when you crushed them, but he told himself it was okay; it was what God wanted.

The custodian left the door open. Rules. No adults in rooms with a child unless others could see in. No one was in the hall. All the boys were in the front yard, kissing ass in hopes of Easter candy. Dennis told himself he didn't care about candy.

"You're quite the hard case, aren't you?" Ralph asked.

He sat down on Dennis's creaky cot. This was so out of the ordinary, Dennis was startled.

"You're not supposed to do that," Dennis squeaked, and then hated the sound of his own voice. He sounded like a baby.

"Well, you're not supposed to be killing bugs. You're making a mess of your hands."

"So?" Dennis was ready to go on the offensive. Something about this tall, kind-looking custodian scared him to his bones.

"Thought you might want to help me with something."

"What? Cleaning?" Dennis made it sound like an insult.

"Come on. I'll show you."

"You'll get in trouble."

"Probably not."

CURIOUS, HOPEFUL THAT THE CUSTODIAN WOULD DO SOMETHING bad and get fired, Dennis followed Ralph down the narrow stairs. They went through the empty kitchen and out the back door, which swung open under the weight of the custodian's hand.

The backyard was full of overgrown weeds and grass, unlike the mowed front yard, where they could hear the other children, answering in muted chorus to the rules being set down by the director for their Easter candy hunt. If they were lucky, they would each find a piece and eat it before anyone could steal it.

The forested mountains were all around them, and the ocean was close by. Dennis could smell the tang of salt. It sent a shiver of excitement through his small body that he tried to hide. He liked being outside. He wished he could be outside all the time.

"It's over here," Ralph said, leading the boy to the edge of the unkempt yard, where there was a large bush near the trees.

Dennis followed, keeping a careful distance from the man.

The custodian crouched. He lifted up a fringe of the bush. "See?"

Still keeping his distance, Dennis leaned over. There was a hole in the dirt under the bush. It was about the size of a dinner plate.

Dennis couldn't help himself.

"What is it?" he asked.

"I don't know. Too big to be for rats. What do you think?"

Dennis felt the slow, unpleasant tick of imagination. He was unused to using his imagination; it felt deeply uncomfortable, and scary. He didn't like to pretend, and he didn't like to dream. If he dared to pretend, he might think he had rights, and if he dared to dream, he might want to leave this place, and that would never happen.

No, life was safer if you just accepted.

But the custodian was looking at the hole under the bush, where it was clear something came—and something went. Something lived down that hole, and the thought filled Dennis with curiosity and the first friendly worm of excitement.

"Maybe it's a . . . creature?"

Ralph looked up as if he didn't know what asking that question meant to Dennis. Never before had he made himself vulnerable to ask such a priceless question.

"It's got to be something," the custodian said. He dropped the fringe of leaves, and the hole went away. "The director, he wants me to leave out poison. For the mice. But I'm thinking no way. What if whatever lives down that hole gets into the poison? It might die."

Dennis was staring at him. He liked it that the custodian didn't voice false concern about the boys getting into the poison. Whatever creature lived down that hole, it was the real priority. Suddenly, the dead fly stains on his hands seemed gross.

"What do you think it is?" Dennis asked.

Ralph rocked back a little on his heels. From out front came a hopeless sound. It was the near silence of thirty boys dashing for candy across a closely mowed lawn, trying to make as little noise as possible. Dennis thought their keepers wanted them silent as a form of target practice. They were shooting them in their minds.

Ralph seemed to be reading his thoughts.

"Whatever it is, imagine how quiet it must be," he said. He looked up, and pointed. "See? Your window is right there. That's why I asked you. I want you to keep an eye out. Morning and night. Let's find out what lives down this hole. Who knows? Maybe it's magic."

Dennis's little face fell. *Magic* was one of those words, like *counselor*, or *mentor*, or *friend*. Or *mom* or *dad*. *Magic* was a word grown-ups used when they wanted to lie.

But not Ralph. He stood up and stretched. He had a big belt buckle made of metal that had tarnished. His crotch was safely flat. There was nothing bad about him. Dennis could feel this. He knew it in his soul. Ralph was as safe an adult as he had ever met, because Ralph knew people lied.

"Okay," he said. "I'll watch."

Ralph smiled at him, and Dennis couldn't help it, he smiled right back.

THAT NIGHT, AND THE NEXT MORNING, AND THE DAYS AFTER THAT, Dennis began looking out his window. He studied the bush over the hole, trying to see what came out of it. But he didn't see a thing.

Ralph, to Dennis's dismay, didn't bring it up again for a whole week. By then Dennis was spitting mad. A week was forever in his world. He didn't like the pain in his heart that came from waiting.

Finally, he went to find the custodian.

"There's nothing down that hole," he said, angry.

"I was just thinking about that," Ralph said, straightening up from cleaning the first-floor bathroom. Some of the boys were shit smearers, and the walls were always a mess.

"I have a feeling that whatever it is, it must be mighty sneaky," Ralph said, carefully putting away his cleaning supplies. He carried the basket to the custodian closet and locked it, because the boys were not to be trusted around chemicals. He walked through the kitchen and out back, Dennis following him, as if he didn't have a care in the world.

Ralph crouched again, lifting the screen of bushes. The same hole appeared.

"Look there," the custodian said.

Unwillingly, Dennis crept closer.

"See that new dirt by the hole? All scratched up? Whatever it is, it's still using it."

"But I can't see it!" Dennis cried out, and punched both his legs.

Ralph didn't seem surprised. He merely glanced at the boy's legs.

"You know what we need?" Ralph asked. "A trap."

He saw the alarm on Dennis's face.

"Not a trap to hurt it, whatever it is. But a trap where we can see it," the custodian said. "Got any ideas?"

Dennis thought about it. He hated his brain. He didn't like any of the classes at Brightwood and often refused to do his classwork. The teachers thought he was stupid.

The custodian waited patiently. He began to whistle softly.

"Shut up!" Dennis growled. "I can't think."

Ralph looked amused.

"A camera," the boy finally said, then looked mad at himself. It was safer to be mad at yourself than to let others be mad at you.

But Ralph thought it was a great idea.

"That's the ticket!" he said. "We'll figure this out."

"I LOOKED AT YOUR FILE."

Ralph offered this the next time he and Dennis were together, standing outside by the bush while the custodian fiddled with an old video camera, looking confused.

The sun was in Dennis's face. He looked up, troubled.

"I was wondering why you were here."

Don't ask, Dennis wanted to say. The past was a monster ready to jump from the bushes. The past was all kinds of monsters, including the unnamed ones.

The custodian turned the camera over, as if this would make it work. "Damn thing," he muttered. "Lady at the shop said it would work."

Dennis didn't answer.

"I got it in a junk shop in a town called Seaside. You ever been out of here, since you came?"

Dennis shook his head.

"That's what I thought. Your file says you came here when you were four. Do you know how old you are now?"

Dennis nodded sagely. He was six.

"We're going to figure this out," Ralph said, noodling with the camera. "There! Wait, maybe not. Hmm. It's supposed to have a setting where you can set it to videotape, but I don't see how the batteries are going to last that long," he said, still tinkering.

Dennis crouched down, looking at the hole under the bush. He was calling it the forever hole in his mind now. He was starting to think. It was like his brain was waking up and stretching. It was like the sensation of pins and needles when your hand fell asleep from punching the walls in one of those padded rooms.

Ralph looked down at the crescent-shaped scars on the boy's arms. *Bites himself*, said his file. His first year at the center, all Dennis would say was that he was not a doll. The staff had pretended to be puzzled about this, which the custodian thought was ridiculous. Dennis had been passed from home to home like a piece of hopeful furniture that didn't work out. Who wouldn't wonder if they were real if that had happened to them?

"Ralph?" Dennis tentatively asked.

"Yeah?"

"What did my file say?"

The custodian looked very tall. The sun caught the bristly hairs growing from the top of his ears. Dennis was coming to love everything about his face. He just didn't know it yet.

"It said a bunch of lies," the custodian said.

"Like what?"

"You know. Names for disorders. Crap they have no idea about. I should know."

"How do you know?"

Ralph flung down the camera. It remained in his hand, but somehow, in his growing imagination, Dennis saw it on the ground, where it belonged.

"Why do you think I took the job here?"

Dennis shrugged. He had no idea why adults worked in a place like this and didn't care.

"I lived in a place like this, that's why."

"You lived in a center?" Dennis was agape.

"It was a hundred times worse than this. A thousand times worse.

Not because of the rules or the food. Because of what she did to us. The woman who ran the place. But what is judgment for a thing like that? Any place like this is no place for a child. Not even a child like you, or a child like me. Don't you ever forget that."

Ralph looked over Dennis to the center behind them; his face was a mask of emotions.

Dennis smiled. For the first time ever, he had been entrusted with a secret.

5

AFTER LARRY DROPPED HER OFF AT THE HOTEL FOLLOWING THEIR meeting with the constable, Amanda went for a walk. She left her hotel room and headed toward the sea. Today it heaved, like a rib cage expanding. Every day, the ocean seemed different. Some days, like today, it seemed especially alive.

She wondered where exactly on this beach her brother had died.

Tentatively, she crossed the soft white dunes to the packed sand. She leaned against a driftwood log, feeling the wind pound against her face as she took off one shoe, then the other, pouring a thin trail of white onto the gray. She slipped her shoes back on. Her ears were filled with noise, as if the ocean were telling her something.

As usual, the beach was deserted. Well, almost. Far down the shore, two beachcombers walked high above the surf, looking for shells.

Amanda walked in the other direction, toward the cliffs, hearing the sand squeak under her shoes. Little razor clam holes appeared, and clamshells dotted the shore, from where seagulls had dropped them. Larger mussel shells, glowing orange and blue, were littered among the debris. She stopped to pick one up, examining the black barnacles. It poked a hole in the heel of her thumb, and she sucked away the bead of blood.

She kept a safe distance from the ocean, worried about the sneaker waves Larry had told her about. He said you never knew when one was coming. They were like mini tsunamis. One moment the waves would seem to be striking the same pattern, and the next a sweeping wave—like a massive powerful broom made of icy water—would run far up the sand, dragging everything back with it.

The ocean was farther out right now. Low tide, she thought. The water was sucked away from the shore, pulled back with a gasp and a sigh, then rolled back up as if to inspect the sand. Out to sea were the rocks Larry had said sea lions visited. On a cloudy day, the rocks disappeared from view, but today, as the mist cleared, they popped like a lunar vision. The tops were crowned with white bird shit, but she couldn't see any sea lions. She imagined them in the waves, their dark eyes watching her.

She heard childlike laughter in her mind. *Come play*, the voices said. *Come play in the waves, Amanda.*

Had her brother ever laughed? What had he been like?

She could imagine him, running into the waves. She saw his back, framed against the sea.

All of a sudden, she felt tears in her eyes. She took a deep breath, then exhaled. She was twenty-six years old—old enough to know herself. But still she stumbled through life, feeling like an outsider, like an alien come to land. Her adoptive parents, as loving as they had been, did not understand.

Amanda felt the pull of the waves, as if there were a cord inside her. She had always known she had another family, ever since she was little. She wanted to know them. She wanted them to tell her what was wrong with her.

Surprising herself, she began to run. She ran parallel to the faraway waves, feeling their pulse pound in her ears. She ran until she was too tired to think.

SOON AFTER SHE GOT BACK TO THE HOTEL, THERE WAS A KNOCK ON her door. Amanda got up from the edge of the bed, where she was eating a granola bar and reading a research paper on polar bears.

It was Larry. Sea mist hung from his nose.

"Gertrude sent her daughter with a note."

"What did it say?"

"The note? Not much. But apparently there's someone we should visit."

He passed over the note. All it had was an address: 515 Sea Lane.

Amanda put on her parka. They walked up and down the hills until Larry stopped in front of a small cabin set deep in the trees. There were so many roads in the town of Eagle Cove that Amanda felt confused.

The door was opened by an old man—far older than Larry. A threadbare sweater hung off his shrunken frame.

"Hello there," he said. "I'm the one who made the memorial stone."

THE HANDS OF THE OLD FISHERMAN WERE AS RED AS CRABS, AND scarred with the marks of pincers and nets whirling in from the deep. He sat across from Amanda and Larry in his pristine cabin decorated with seashells. Shells were even embedded in his stone fireplace.

His wife was represented by the blue plates she had collected, which were lined up on shelves across the room.

"I volunteered for that job," he said, reaching for a pack of cigarettes. He coughed and lit one, sputtering against the cloud of smoke. As soon as he lit the cigarette, he extinguished it. "My method of quitting," he said. He ruined the cigarette with his calloused fingers, and Amanda thought about how in the city, people would sell that smoke on the street.

His eyes were lost in a maze of lines from the sea. "It happens a lot, in our work. You can't even launch by our beach here. We launch in the bay down the highway. But we come back. Beyond those rocks where the sea lions gather? Some of the best fishing around. We would stake the waves. That's code for pushing it. Getting just close enough to where the fish were without getting swept away to your death. If you get a pair of binoculars, you can see the fishing boats. They're out there."

His fingers played with the shreds of tobacco, and the smell filled the air.

"Over the years, I lost a lot. My cousin Sigrid, she died the night of the big Memorial Day storm. When we say big storm down here," he said in an aside to Amanda, "we mean big. Most of the time, the weatherman tells us when a storm is coming. But down here, in my line of work, when the weatherman screws up, it doesn't mean you're going to be late to work in traffic or get a spattering of rain on your new jacket. It means someone dies. Or a lot of someones. That Memorial Day, it was Sigrid's turn. She went down in her boat with three others. Our boat was only yards away, but I didn't see her go down. That's how hard the sea was tossing, how thick the spray. We were lucky that day. We ran for shore a few towns down. Went aground, and all was well. In the end. For me, at least."

His fingers dropped the tobacco shreds. Larry and Amanda were quiet.

"That boy should never have been on the beach."

"What do you do, if you see people ignoring the signs?" Larry asked.

"I pray" came the short, terse answer. The fisherman sighed. He looked down at the half-empty pack of cigarettes, and Amanda could see his mouth working in desire. He reached for one, then changed his mind. He stood up, stretching. Amanda saw that he had been sitting on a handmade cushion, embroidered with a fanciful starfish.

"Come on," he said. "I'll show you my workshop."

THE WORKSHOP WAS IN BACK OF THE CABIN, UNDER AN INTER-
laced canopy of pine trees dripping with vines. The sandy soil was
planted with spindly-looking tomato starts. They didn't look so good.
The sharp beach grass growing nearby was doing much better.

The fisherman pushed the door open and pulled a string. A strong
set of lights lit an immaculate workbench and a sturdy table lined with
power tools. Larry could recognize a well-ordered craftsman when he
saw one. Growing up, he had been around men like this, guys who would
snort if you picked the wrong tool. Maybe that was why he hated even
mowing the grass. He and Marjorie had hired it out.

"I started cutting gravestones after I retired from the boats. Just
couldn't do it after Sigrid." His face looked stark in the bright light.
He picked up a pair of goggles from habit. "She was special," he told
Amanda. "You know how some people are? It doesn't work to tell others,
because they didn't know them.

"These here are my tools," he said, pointing to chisels, files, and di-
amond saws. "I like to work by hand whenever I can. Makes it go slower.
I tell myself it looks better."

Amanda remembered the memorial stone, the way the tender words
were carved into the natural-looking rock. It made more sense now, what
he had carved. *Lost in the sea but not from our hearts.*

"Why did you volunteer to make the stone for Dennis?" Amanda
asked.

"Because no one from his family ever showed up, saying Hey, this
was my son or brother. No one even asked. At least not before you."
His hand fiddled with the safety goggles, and he put them back down.
"Want to hear more?"

"Yes, please," Amanda said. "What you remember of that day, if you
don't mind. What happened."

HE POURED THEM ICED TEA FROM A PITCHER, AND THEY SAT AT THE front of his cabin, on a stone patio he had cut himself. The table was as straight as a die on the leveled stone. He set down the glasses, and then moved his ashtray filled with tobacco litter and the pack of smokes next to his place.

"I used to smoke out here," he said. "Always liked it that I could hear the ocean but not see her. It used to amuse the wife how I could tell how the fishing was just from the sound of the waves."

He tapped the cigarette pack. "So. That day. We'll start there. It was spring, I remember that. Just like now. The beach would have been empty. No tourists in town. I got the call from Gertrude, at the market. She was crying. Said a boy got swept away. Her husband was still alive back then. Brett Jarvis. That man was complete and utter trash. A drunk. He died some years back. Good riddance, I say. I don't see it being good for their daughter, working in the market like that. She should be away, going to college or having an adventure, not cooped up in that market with her mother. Anyhow, I went down to help with the search, and the missus went, too, because that's how it works around here. We've all been there. What if it was one of ours? When we got down there, the constable was already interviewing that fella. I guess he went in after him. Tall, gangly guy. Mop of hair. Maybe in his thirties? He was as wet as a noodle."

"You know his name?" Larry asked.

"Nope, sorry to say. Might have seen him around, you know, at the gas station sort of thing. But never met him before."

Larry was quiet, listening.

"He was still holding that poor kid's shirt. It had his name on the back. That's how we knew the boy was from Brightwood."

"Did the boys from Brightwood usually go to the beach?"

"Hell no. They never let them out of their sight up there." He yanked a smoke from the pack, put it between his thin lips, lit it, and inhaled deeply. He coughed, realized what he was doing, and started to put it out. He stopped, took another small drag, and then gently tapped it out.

"Jobs are scarce around here, particularly in the offseason, which is nine months out of the year," he told them. "Not everyone wants to be a fisherman. Most of the kids here, they don't want to anymore. It's hard work, and the pay isn't worth dying over. It used to be sometimes one of our people would go up to Brightwood and get a job. Most didn't last more than a few weeks, maybe a few months, if they were wired that way."

Larry took a long drink of his iced tea. Amanda followed suit, and the fisherman did, too, taking a big gulp. He toyed with his cigarettes.

"What did they say about it?" Amanda asked.

He started to say something, then reconsidered and said, "I don't know, miss. I don't know how you make any place like that good for children. But some of them tried."

He looked embarrassed. He shoved the cigarette back in his mouth but didn't light it.

"I saw the isolation rooms," Amanda said.

"They would put the boys in them when they were bad. Problem is, you can't be a child without being bad, especially not in a place like that."

Amanda remembered the bedrooms, the marks from cots on the floors. The dining room.

"I met a woman once, she was the cook there," he went on. "She said they fed the boys well. Lots of potatoes and pancakes and starches like that. So they ate," he said, trying to make it better.

"That's good to know," Amanda said. She had tried to research child centers online but had found very little. Brightwood itself was a smooth stone of confidentiality.

"Anyhow, the constable interviewed that fella. Let him go. There was no reason not to. He looked awfully sick from the sea. By then we had formed search parties and were going up and down the beach. Just like we did for Sigrid, looking for remains. Never found her either." He held the cigarette in his fingers, studying it. "A week or so later, I was in the market and Gertrude said, 'Ain't it a shame that no one ever came for that boy?' Right then and there, we decided to make the stone. At least the sky could remember him."

Amanda blinked back tears.

"Why did the center close?" Larry asked.

"No idea. Some said it was money."

Larry suddenly leaned over, picked up the lighter, and lit the man's cigarette. He leaned back, savoring the ring of smoke. The fisherman took a deep drag, then another.

THAT NIGHT, AMANDA CURLED UP IN HER SANDY BED. THE SKY OUT-side was very dark. No moon. She could hear the ocean, pounding. It sounded so close, and she could imagine the sneaker waves running far up the sand in the dark, searching for her.

She turned over, closed her eyes. She felt alone, but that was nothing new. Her whole life she had felt alone, and she wondered if that would always be true.

In the deep of the night, she slept. All along the coast was pure, unadulterated darkness. In the distance, everyone could feel the waves.

Into this darkness, one man crept. He walked along the hotel's outer walls, his feet knowing the sand, feeling the rhythms of the sea. The ocean whispered to him. He stopped outside the windows of the room where Amanda Dufresne slept. He stood there for a long time, just thinking in the wind.

He had never expected it to come back. It had been twenty years—why did it have to happen now?

He didn't want to have to take action. But he would, if need be.

The past had to stay in the past.

Breathing deeply of the salty air, the man disappeared back into the dark.

6

THAT FIRST SUMMER WAS THE SUMMER OF JOY. DENNIS AND RALPH set up the video camera. It recorded for a few hours at night under the bushes, but the creature that lived there must have smelled the plastic, or sensed it, the custodian said, because the video did not show what lived down that hole.

But the waiting felt different to Dennis. The dirt scratched up by the hole was proof enough. The sun over the trees was proof enough. The world exploded with color, because he had a task now, and it was with Ralph.

Life unspooled from a golden thread and held the world upside down in its pleasure, because Dennis finally had a friend.

"I'VE GOT IT," RALPH SAID, ONE HOT DAY IN JULY. THE FOURTH HAD thankfully come and gone. Each boy had gotten one slice of watermelon and as many horrible hot dogs as he could eat. Dennis had eaten the rind of his watermelon, not knowing better. The cook had taken pictures of the kids, then got in trouble with the director, who said that wasn't allowed.

Dennis was in the backyard with Ralph, who had given Dennis a rake so he could pretend to be raking the grass if anyone came. Dennis had noticed no one seemed to care when he and the custodian hung out together.

"You know how we've been focusing on this here hole?" Ralph asked, excitement on his face. "Well, it occurred to me that maybe it's not the only one. Maybe there is more than one."

Dennis's face lit up. This idea had never occurred to him.

"You mean it has more than one way to get down there?"

"Exactly! Like two doors to a house."

Dennis mulled this over. He could picture it.

"It could have a whole house down there, with a living room," Ralph joked.

"A television!" Dennis shouted.

"A kitchen with all the appliances."

"And a—a—"

"Everything a person needs."

"A swimming pool. It's got a swimming pool."

None of the homes Dennis had ever lived in had had a swimming pool. Therefore, swimming pools were safe.

"What do you think it's doing right now?" the custodian asked.

As Dennis thought about this, he forgot about the center. He forgot about the past. All that mattered now was a mysterious hole connected to an underground world no one knew about except him and Ralph.

"Do you think it has a family down there?" Dennis asked.

"Maybe. Maybe."

There was a buzzer sound from inside. That was the school bell.

"Go. Do your schoolwork. Come back here later and we'll figure it out."

DENNIS HAD TWO HOURS OF SCHOOL EVERY DAY AFTER LUNCH. THE state had figured this was the minimum needed in such settings. It was true that most of the boys couldn't have done more even if they'd been shackled to their chairs. They fidgeted, chewing the inside of their lips and spitting blood, or staring at the teacher with such malice that she flinched. The teachers seldom lasted, until the state decided the centers didn't need real teachers. They could use anyone to teach the classes.

The current teacher, Ike Tressler, was a big man. He had a round head, like a giant cannonball. He was capable of looking back at the boys with such bitterness that even the big boys flinched. There were three classes at Brightwood. The first—the one Dennis was in—was for beginners; the second was for the middle schoolers; and the third was for the teenagers. The boys stayed at the center until they were eighteen, unless they were sent back home or to a new family. Somehow Dennis could never remember them leaving, though he always remembered the arrivals.

Dennis pretended to do the same math worksheet he had been staring at for months. No one at Brightwood bothered to monitor the boys' progress, and there was no oversight. He didn't care. He hated school.

He looked out the window, hoping Ralph wasn't starting without him.

AFTER SCHOOL, RALPH WAS WAITING FOR HIM, A HOE IN HAND.

"Figured we'd use this," he said.

"We're going to chop it in half?" Dennis asked, horrified.

"No." He demonstrated. "We'll use it to push the bushes aside. I'm afraid of poison oak. Got it once on my nether parts and couldn't sit for a week."

Dennis looked carefully at Ralph. He hoped the man wasn't being inappropriate. That was the word therapists used for people who liked to touch privates. He decided the custodian was just being friendly.

They began at the bush hiding the hole, circling around it, Ralph

using the hoe to lift up the bush and push aside weeds, Dennis following, getting down on the ground, looking for other holes behind rocks
and ferns.

"I don't see anything," the custodian called.

"Me either."

Being with Ralph gave Dennis a rare feeling. It was such a rare feeling, he had to stop and puzzle through it. It was disorienting. He had
never felt so free, or had so much fun.

Ralph looked at him with compassion.

They circled until they were in the shadow of the woods. The pine
trees filled the air with soft green and gray light.

"Are we going to get lost?" Dennis asked worriedly. He could still
see the center through the trees.

"Naw. We won't go any farther. Can you smell that?"

"Smell what?" Dennis asked. He was studying the ground. So far,
no other hole had appeared.

"The ocean. Have you ever seen it?"

"In school they showed us pictures."

"You mean you've been living here two years and you've never seen
the ocean?"

"We don't leave here."

"I'm sorry. I knew that."

"Why did you ask me then, about the sea?" Dennis asked after a
moment.

"It's beautiful. But very dangerous. It reminds me of this place. Nice
enough looking on the outside. But once you're in it? Your very heart
and soul are at risk."

Dennis was beginning to wonder why the custodian never used his
name. He decided to be brave and ask.

"Ralph?"

"Yes?"

"How come you don't call me Dennis?"

The custodian turned to him. "I remember when they put me in a center. They told me it would turn me into a good boy. But if you can make cordwood even more bent, that's what that place did to me. One week there and I was a wreck. Years later? I was hard. I was wrecked."

Dennis waited for Ralph to answer his question.

"I didn't want to use your name because your file said your foster parents called you different names. How am I to know which one you like?"

Ralph lifted another bush with his hoe. He stopped, and sighed.

"Maybe we missed it. What do you want me to call you?"

Dennis thought about it. His last foster mother had wanted to call him Brian. He had hazy memories of that mother, with her strawberry blond hair and large eyes, and how she'd said she wanted to adopt him and name him Brian because it was her father's name. He had been four at that time, and he was still four when she gave him back and the agency sent him here. He was no longer part of that family. Maybe that pretend mother would want him to cut that thread. Probably by now she had a new son, or a bunch of them, better children than he was. She could have four Brians now.

But he didn't like the name Dennis either. His birth mom had named him that. There was "boy," but the staff said that when they were mad and about to put you in a room.

That left one choice, and he couldn't bring himself to say it.

"I don't know," he said.

"Think on it."

THEY STOOD BY THE BACK DOOR. IT WAS ALMOST TIME FOR RALPH to leave for the day. Gently, he took the hoe from Dennis. He had been letting him hold it, and he knew how hard it can be to give up what you've never had.

"What do you think it's doing right now?" Ralph asked.

"Who?" Dennis asked.

"The creature."

Dennis thought about it.

"It's alone. It's making dinner."

Ralph nodded, as if this made perfect sense.

"You have a good night, son."

Dennis's eyes flew to him, and his face went blank with shock. He turned and ran away, to hide under his cot.

RALPH FOUND HIM THE NEXT MORNING, SITTING ON THE BACK step. The cook was inside, making breakfast. Sometimes she snuck boys into the kitchen and let them make pancakes with raisins for eyes.

The custodian stood above him.

"Should I apologize for what I said?"

"No," Dennis said, holding his thin elbows.

"Well, what would you like me to do then?"

"Say it again."

So Ralph said it again, and his voice was like music in the trees. It floated up to the window of the room where Dennis would sleep later, long after the custodian was gone for the day, and it caressed him there, on the glass where he had once squished live bugs. That seemed an eternity ago now.

"Son," Ralph said, and said again, and again.

Son, son, son.

7

THE *COASTAL HERALD* WAS HOUSED IN A SMALL WHITE BUILDING, the paint worn down. The town of Wheel Stone was bigger than Eagle Cove, but not by much. There was a library, currently closed, and a string of shops with lights that moved in the wind, like ships onshore.

"Can I help you?"

The man behind the counter had a long white beard over a white bib stained with ink. His teeth were nicotine yellow.

"Are you in charge here?" Larry asked.

"Publisher, editor, and reporter in one," he said.

Amanda pulled the article from her pocket, and the man put on his reading glasses and leaned over, inquisitive and smiling.

"I found this in the downtown Portland library," Amanda said. "They only had a few years of your paper. I was wondering if you have anything more—about this boy, or the place he lived."

"Ah, I recognize this." He squinted over the article. "I wrote it. See here? D.B. That's me. Dwight Bowman. Let's adjourn to my office."

HIS OFFICE WAS IN THE FRONT OF THE BUILDING, NEXT TO THE ancient printing press. The air was rich with the smell of ink, and for Larry it brought back memories of delivering papers as a boy, tossing the warm bundles from the back of his dad's van. The memory was mixed with the smell of Aqua Velva and his dad's flannel shirt. And that was history, for Larry. It faded very slowly.

"Now let's see," Dwight said, turning to the metal file cabinets lining the room. "I keep my research in here."

"What do you remember about the incident?" Larry asked.

"Not much, I'm afraid. I seem to recall visiting Eagle Cove to see that memorial. It's been some time. A lot of articles under the bridge since."

Amanda noticed one of the drawers was labeled *Storms*.

"If I have more about Dennis Owen, they will be in here." He dug deeper into a drawer. "Nope. Nothing."

"Oh," Amanda said, disappointed.

"How about Brightwood?" Larry asked.

The man dug through another drawer. "It's not the best system, I'll admit. Sometimes I'll file things under one name when they should be another."

"There's this thing called computers now," Larry said.

"Well, I know. But then you run up against the scanning problem. Years of notes, and what about all the mini cassettes I used to record interviews? I don't even think they make those recorders anymore. I keep one on hand, just in case I have to play an old tape. Maybe someday I'll find the funds to get everything transcribed, but for now, this is what I've always done. Run a story, then dump the research into one of these drawers. Here. Found it."

Dwight pulled out a folder labeled *Brightwood* in spiky writing.

He overturned the folder on his desk. A paper-clipped stack of notes, on pages torn from a reporter's notebook, fell out. And a single photograph.

He looked at the photo, then passed it to Amanda.

It showed a little boy standing next to a man, at a Fourth of July picnic. The man looked to be in his thirties but worn for his age. The boy was holding a scrap of gnawed watermelon rind and looking into the camera with an opaque expression. He had a shock of blond hair and dark blue eyes.

"Larry."

Larry looked. He would have known it in an instant.

"It's him," she said. "My brother."

"A WOMAN VISITING THE MEMORIAL GAVE ME THAT PHOTOGRAPH," Dwight said, reading from his notes. "I was going to run it, but when I visited the center, I was told I couldn't, because of privacy issues."

"Who is the man here, with Dennis?" Amanda asked.

"I think that's the fella who went in after him, but I never got a name."

"How come?" Larry asked.

"The same reason why the article was so damn short. The center couldn't talk, because of confidentiality, and the constable wouldn't talk either. None of the locals knew the boy."

"Who gave you the picture?" Larry asked.

"Let's see." He studied the notes. "She was the cook there."

"I wonder if she's still around," Amanda said, excited.

"She works at the nursing home now," Dwight said. "Don't know her personally, but she seems like good people. Let me get their address for you."

He pulled a worn copy of the coastal directory out of a drawer. "We're old-school down here," he said, looking up. "Internet goes out so often, we need to play it safe. Anyway, I print this thing, so it's only fair I put it to use." He thumbed the pages, and Amanda noticed his hands were permanently etched with ink, his yellowish nails stained gray.

"Here you go."

He passed over the nursing home's address.

SWEET SERENITY NURSING HOME, READ THE CRACKED WOODEN
sign outside the ramshackle ranch house with grooves worn into the
wheelchair ramp to the front door. Amanda followed Larry up to
the door.

They found the cook in the kitchen, sitting at a table, engrossed
in an old copy of *Southern Living* magazine. When they came in, she
quickly took off her reading glasses.

She listened, looking closely at Amanda.

"I can see it now, yes," she said.

"See what?" Amanda asked.

"You're his sister, all right."

"You knew him. Dennis?"

"Not well. But I do remember him."

"You're the first person I've found who actually knew him."

"What about Ralph? Have you found him?"

"Who is that?"

"He was the custodian. He's the one who tried to save him."

"Is this Ralph?" Amanda showed her the photograph.

"Why yes, it is. Where did you get that?"

"From Dwight Bowman at the paper."

"I forgot about taking that picture. That poor child."

"What was Ralph's last name?" Larry asked.

"Hmm. I don't recall. But don't just stand there. Sit." She signaled to
the table, which was piled with receipts and balls of yarn and everything
else that came into a kitchen because it didn't have a home.

She insisted on fetching them cups of coffee and a plate of soft gin-
ger cookies with lemon icing. She moved with the economy and delight

of a woman who had spent a lifetime in kitchens. "You came at the right time. We just finished lunch, and it's a few hours until tea. Some of the residents insist we have afternoon tea, though heaven knows why. Not one of them is British."

"I imagine they're bored," Larry said.

"They're the busiest people in town. We're always taking them on field trips to see the whales, visit local sites, you name it. Just yesterday we went to a salmon bake."

"Can you tell me more about my brother?" Amanda asked.

The cook sat and picked up her own cup, settling her bottom into her chair.

"Dennis was a sweet little boy. Well, maybe not at first. He was awfully shut down when he came to Brightwood."

"How old was he?"

"Four? The center wasn't supposed to take kids under six, but it happened. It was usually when they couldn't find another home for them. You know, because of their issues."

"What were his issues?" Amanda asked.

"I was never told. Just the cook, you know. But in the end, I think I learned more about some of those boys than anyone."

"What was he like?" Amanda sipped.

"When he first came, he was like a little animal, growling. Then Ralph came, and they got to be friends. They were always hanging out together. I'd see them out back, raking weeds, just talking. Or Dennis would be helping him with the lawn."

Larry was silent, eating his cookie.

"It wasn't creepy, if that's what you're thinking. Ralph was a nice guy. Just a little . . . odd, I think."

"Odd how?" Larry asked.

"I don't know. Like maybe he just missed out."

"Where can we find this Ralph?" Larry asked.

"No idea. I heard he moved away after it happened."

"The constable said my brother ran away," Amanda said. "Did any other boys run away from Brightwood?"

"A few," the cook said reluctantly. "It was sad."

"How did they get out?" Larry asked.

"The backwoods didn't have a fence. Too thick and brambly. Most of the kids were afraid to go back there. There were bears and even wolves. But apparently, a few weren't scared enough."

Larry thought of those thick woods.

"Were the other boys ever found?"

"I always hoped so."

"What do you mean?"

"The policy was if a kid ran away, they were taken to a more secure setting. That's what they called them. 'Settings.'"

"So you don't know if they turned back up?"

"They didn't tell me stuff like that. You know, I always hoped they'd made it to the highway, found some log truck, you know. Hitched out of town and to the city. I used to imagine them coming back, saying hello, years later. But none of the Brightwood boys ever came back."

"Dennis didn't just run away," Amanda said.

The cook blinked. Tears appeared in her eyes.

"He was a sad boy. Just a sad, sad little boy. I wanted to help. We all did. I'm sorry, miss. We did our best."

Amanda felt bad for her. It wasn't her fault.

"It's okay," she said. "You tried."

"I used to sneak boys into the kitchen, you know. They liked that. I think they liked to pretend I was their mom, or grandma. But Dennis, he never would come. I asked him a few times, but he would just look at me. I think he was afraid of love. And then . . ."

She trailed off, taking a sip of her coffee.

"Then what?" Larry asked.

"He got worse."

"Why did the center close?" Amanda asked.

"Dunno. One day there was a sign on the door. The director said it was closing. No severance pay. Nothing."

AFTER VISITING THE NURSING HOME, LARRY AND AMANDA ATE IN the fish-and-chips shop, the hot fried fish crumbling in their fingers. Amanda dipped a fry in malt vinegar. She ate to the end and dropped it in her basket.

"How are you feeling?" he asked cautiously.

Amanda looked out through the sea-speckled windows. The air in the shop smelled heavily of fish, and grease. Outside, a few bundled townspeople hurried down the street. It was spring, but still cold. Polar bear weather, Amanda thought.

"I'm not sure," she said. "I'm glad to have the picture, though."

"What did you hope to find?"

Amanda studied her ringless left hand.

"You know, when I was little, I thought I'd get married," she said. "Like my parents. They have long family trees, you know? My mother can trace her ancestry all the way back to Scotland. My father, his family was French, and they lived in New York City. His dad was a professor too. He could trace his lineage back."

Larry looked at his wedding ring. He planned to wear it to his grave.

"I think when my parents adopted me, they thought I would take on their heritage. Like a sponge. It was more like an assumption—that by adopting me, they would make me just like them. But that's not really how it works, is it? People trace their lineage for a reason, don't they?"

"Well, it could be that members of those families were adopted too."

"Touché."

She had stopped eating. She wiped her mouth with a napkin.

"I'm not saying what happened to you didn't count," Larry said, thinking he had hurt her, somehow.

"No. I understand."

But from her face, he could see that she did not agree.

8

THERE WERE MORNINGS DENNIS FORGOT ALL ABOUT THE HOLE, and days lost in the rooms, but sooner or later, it came back to him, and sometimes, deep in the night when the watchman was snoring at his desk, Dennis would creep down from his bed and stand over it, the leaves of the bush touching his legs.

Who are you? he wanted to know. *Who am I?*

Awareness came, like a rainstorm that blesses. The garden of his soul was growing. It was often weeds, but weeds are better than dry, bitter soil. He felt things now. He knew.

A TYPICAL DAY AT BRIGHTWOOD WENT LIKE THIS:

Wake-up buzzer down the hall. Feet on the floor, always cold no matter what the season. It rained a lot at the coast, and the windows always sparkled with water.

Showers. The boys showered every two days. They switched between floors. The industrial showers were on the first floor, and a staff member always lounged and watched with disinterest. In the shower, the skin of the boys was the color of cement.

The boys cleaned their pits, cleaned their groins, asked no questions. Toweled off with a square mitten of rough cloth, dropped it in the massive laundry baskets for the staff to launder in the fetid basement that no one else entered. It steamed down there on laundry days. The basement floor was cracked pavement that ran in a thousand rivulets.

Clothes on. These were picked from the shelves labeled with their names. Dennis was always a small. He never seemed to grow. It was true of all the kids at Brightwood. Hopelessness shrunk them, just as it turned them gray with despair. You could smell it on them. They did not smell like children.

Socks on, sneakers. The kids wore the same Velcro shoes. Shoes and bedding were shared because then it was easier for the staff to de- louse everything. The center was constantly fighting outbreaks of lice, ringworm, and bedbugs. The sand fleas were especially bad.

Breakfast. March into the dining room. The older boys fought with the blunted forks and bullied the younger ones. The children ate with their elbows tucked in, to protect their food. Touching was not allowed, but some of the younger kids developed swollen shins from being kicked under the table. It was so common, it was called orphanage ankle.

Quiet time/reading time. No one read. It was amazing that the hours even passed at Brightwood. Days and weeks and months and years somehow passed, and looking back, you could hardly remember what happened.

Lunch.

School five days a week—okay, more like four. Or three. Depending on how often the teacher of the day got busy, or called in sick.

Exercise. Go out on the front lawn, under the supervision of the staff. Be ordered to run and play. Most often the kids just stood there, like robots. Be told to play badminton. The net breaks and never gets fixed. On rainy days, which were often, the boys crowded into the gym, which became thick with bad smells.

Dinner. Or supper, as the cook called it. Everyone liked the cook.

She had round cheeks and poured rivers of margarine on everything. Dennis's favorite thing to eat was her corned beef and boiled potatoes, soaked in that buttery margarine.

There were too many kids at Brightwood to celebrate birthdays, the staff said, but when it was your special day—for Dennis this was in the fall—the cook snuck a cupcake or donut near your plate. The other kids were envious of even this scrap of attention.

Evening quiet time. Sometimes an activity was planned, always by the newer staff, wanting to pretend this was a nice place. They made popcorn on the stove and burned the pot for the cook to clean the next day, annoyed. They marched the kids into the dining room, where they had pushed the tables away, and everyone crowded on the floor to pretend to have fun, watching *Lady and the Tramp* or some old movie where adults danced and sang in the rain. Who ever did such a thing? After Ralph had left for the night, Dennis looked out the windows and wondered where he went.

Bedtime. The kids had their own rooms. It was to protect them from each other. There were small red lights above the doors. The staff told them these were cameras, but that was a lie. The security system at Brightwood had broken years before, and no one had gotten it fixed.

Lights out.

At night, the watchman walked the hallways, bouncing his flashlight off the walls. The kids heard it: *clunk, clunk, clunk*. Some closed their eyes and pretended it was a better sound. It could be a father, coming home from work, dropping his keys on the table, and saying, *I'm home, dear.* Or it might be that mother they all so sorely missed, even if they'd never known her. After so many years, she had come back. She was walking up the steps now.

But those were foolish ideas, in Dennis's view. He had regained his

imagination—maybe it had been there all along—and he used it for
good imagining.

In his mind, it was Ralph coming up those stairs. It was Ralph
dragging something over the walls. He was carrying a suitcase. He was
setting it down at the foot of Dennis's bed. He was saying, *Do you want
to leave now, son?* and *Will you come with me?*

And for him, Dennis always said yes.

EARLY ONE MORNING, DENNIS SNUCK OUT THE FRONT DOOR. THE
idea had come to him all of a sudden. Maybe it was the sound of the back
door opening that sent the creature into hiding. If Dennis went out the
front door, maybe the creature wouldn't be alerted.

He made his way through the woods until he was a good distance
from the bush but still within sight of the center. He could feel the waves
of sadness emanating from it.

Suddenly, he longed for the comfort of one of the isolation rooms.

He stayed in the trees. He could see the bush, and the wind-
flattened grass of the backyard. The cook moved about the kitchen,
making breakfast. The previous night's rain dripped from the trees. He
captured a drop on his hand, and licked it. It tasted like winter and ice.

He crouched, waiting.

The bush was dome shaped, and had stayed much the same. He
hadn't noticed before that the leaves were a different color than those
of the surrounding shrubs. They were reddish and drooping. It looked
like the bush had been planted there, and had not grown as part of the
natural habitat.

He stayed very still. The birds began calling, the way they do as the
sun rises. He smelled the salt wind. Inside the center, he knew, the boys
would be waking up. The staff would walk the halls, ordering them to
get dressed. Some of the kids would have snot lathered on their faces and

others would be crying, but all would be ignored. Their doors would be shut, as crisply as the lids of coffins.

The rain dripped, and the wind moved gently through the trees, and the bush stayed very still.

It was then that Dennis saw it: the tiniest of movements, from inside the bush. A single shake, like a tiny hand or paw was moving a leaf.

He froze, watching. He could feel everything all at once, all over him. The feeling shook him like a gust of wind. He wanted to yell and run and call for Ralph, who had not yet arrived for the day, or for the others. *Come look! Come see!* he would yell, and he would be a proper boy, a real boy, in that moment.

The bush parted, and it happened. It did so in the way of all true miracles, with a touch of the ordinary, even disappointment. There was not a bell from the heavens or a clap of thunder or a bolt of lightning. There was just a little boy, Dennis, age six, survivor of a lifetime of pain, crouched in the trees, watching a single bush as the reddish leaves gently parted and a wise face looked out, brown with a pink, twitching nose and fair, round eyes. Below the face was a velvety soft chest, crowned in white.

A rabbit.

"A RABBIT!" RALPH SAID.

The custodian had hidden in the woods with Dennis and seen, only briefly, the silver-brown tufted back of the bunny, before the bunny had sensed him and hopped quickly back down its hole.

"You found it." Ralph turned to his young friend with amazement. "I am so proud of you."

Dennis, for one of the few times ever, basked in the praise.

"A rabbit," Ralph said. "I never would have guessed." From his voice, it sounded like he was telling the truth. "I didn't even know they lived out here. Never seen one at the beach. Just deer and elk. Wow."

Dennis smiled, his heart full.

"So it was a rabbit all along." Ralph laughed, standing up. The sun flashed off his belt buckle. "You solved the mystery." He looked a little worried, like now Dennis had no reason to be friends with him.

"It's our rabbit," Dennis said.

"Naw, it's the world's rabbit. Are you going to name it?"

This thought had never occurred to Dennis.

"I don't know," he said. He thought of all the names the foster parents wanted to call him, before they gave him back.

"Sorry to bring that up, son."

Dennis smiled at the word.

"I'll think about it," Dennis said, but in his mind there already was a name.

Bunny, he thought. I will name her Bunny.

SPRING COILED INTO SUMMER AND SUMMER INTO FALL, AND EVERYthing was different and yet the same for Dennis, because the rabbit had appeared. Every morning, he sat in the same hidden place, and as long as the back door stayed closed, the rabbit ventured from the bush and began to nibble. As soon as the door opened, she was back like a shot down her hole.

Dennis knew now why he had never been able to spot the rabbit from his window. The long grass hid her. When a rare eagle passed overhead, Dennis frowned, and when hawks circled, he forced them away with his mind. Worried she would get hurt, he asked Ralph if there were coyotes in the brush and wolves in the mountains.

In school, he drew rabbits.

"RALPH?"

Dennis found the custodian pulling on heavy gloves in his closet.

The winter rains were upon them. There was more rain than Dennis remembered ever having seen, but maybe he just hadn't noticed before. Dennis was worried for the rabbit. What if the rain ran into her hole? Bunny might drown.

"Don't worry, that rabbit has been through a lot of seasons," Ralph told him.

Now Dennis had a new worry.

"How long do rabbits live?"

"I don't know," Ralph said. "Can you ask in school?"

"I asked Ike for a book on rabbits, and he laughed."

"I'll get you a book."

THE BOOK WAS CALLED *THE CARE AND FEEDING OF YOUR PET RABBIT*, and Ralph got it from the library in Wheel Stone, carefully peeling away the library sticker before giving it to Dennis so Dennis could keep it forever. He told Dennis that this was not stealing, but more like permanent borrowing.

Dennis took good care of the book. He hid it under his covers during the day, and when the custodian warned him in advance of a room search, Dennis wrapped the book in a plastic bag and hid it in the woods. There was no safe place inside the center.

He read every chapter, obsessively.

Chapter One: Introducing Your Rabbit. Chapter Two: What Makes a Rabbit a Rabbit? That one had drawings and all sorts of fascinating history and facts, like the difference between a hare and a rabbit (hares can run faster, for one). Chapter Three: Bringing Rabbit Home. Chapter Four: Cage Facts—Everything You Need to Be a Good Rabbit Owner. Chapter Five: Training Your Rabbit. Chapter Six: Breeding. Chapter Seven: Diet and Exercise. Chapter Eight: When Rabbit Needs the Doctor. And so on.

Now Dennis spent his quiet time reading, even finding paper to use in tracing the images in the book. He learned that his rabbit was a brush rabbit, indigenous to the Oregon Coast. *The brush rabbit is a quiet soul who rarely strays far from his den,* he read, slowly, laboriously at first. *He makes hidden paths in the brush to his feeding areas, so he can easily run back home.* Dennis's mouth moved as the words got easier with practice. *Can you tame a wild rabbit? Unfortunately for pet owners, wild rabbits cannot be domesticated. They do not take to captivity, even when captured young. Please do not take rabbits from the wild, or release your pet rabbit into the wild. Domestic rabbits are bred for captivity. Wild rabbits will not survive it.*

Dennis read names of diseases and worried about salt licks. He had nightmares where he ran away to buy a salt lick for Bunny, but when he finally found a pet store, they laughed at the name tag sewn on his shirt, and he turned his pockets inside out to find that they were filled with the eyeballs of other boys.

In the mornings, he crept outside in the cold dewy grass to be alone with the rabbit. He sat in the bushes, losing all sense of time, and it wasn't until he saw the long shadow of Ralph, letting him know that he needed to go inside or he'd get caught, that Dennis came back to himself.

When the rabbit came out, browsing along the grass, it was like the first time he lost himself. Everything was right in the world because Dennis was not there. He was caring for Bunny.

9

AMANDA WOKE UP TO A DEEP FOG. THE FOG WAS SO THICK, IT seemed to pulsate at the hotel room's windows.

She got dressed and wandered out into the bright, metallic mist. Walking in it, she felt unearthed. Her feet moved on the beach road, unseen. She lifted her hands out of the gloom. They looked like pale ghosts, attached to her frame.

Foghorns echoed up and down the coast. If she got turned around, Amanda thought, she might just walk into the sea. She could not see the ocean, or the mountains, or even five steps ahead of her.

She walked through the town, the salt-pitted street signs rising out of the mist, going past the market, which showed itself as one gloomy light, until she finally found Barker Road, and from there she climbed into the mountains. If there were birds, they were as silent as the dew on their wings.

The road, still littered with tree branches, crunched under her feet. Trees marched out of the haze before disappearing. It was an eerie feeling, like she was climbing inside a cloud.

She was warm with the exercise by the time she reached the gates to the center. The metal was slick under her hand. A breeze was picking up, moving the sparkling mist around her. The wind blew away a snatch of fog, and she could see the center rising above her.

She froze.

Looped across the front door was a string of mussel shells. She stepped closer. Someone had drilled small holes in the shells and strung them together with twine. When the breeze touched the shells, they made a clattering noise. It reminded her of the sounds prey animals make when threatened. Like the warning chattering of teeth.

Amanda turned. There didn't appear to be anyone around, but she could not tell.

She headed to the back, feeling her way past the mounds of blackberries. She turned into the neglected backyard.

More mussel shells were strung across the back door.

She looked up. There were strings of shells dangling from the windows.

THE MARKET DOOR JANGLED BEHIND HER. THE BENCH WHERE THE old-timers had coffee was empty. It was just the teen girl, behind the counter, and the sounds of her mother in the kitchen.

"I'll take a breakfast biscuit, please," Amanda said.

The girl nodded, and fetched one of the foil-wrapped sandwiches from the hot case. Amanda loved them. Inside each giant biscuit was a homemade elk sausage patty, a hard-fried egg, and a slice of Tillamook sharp cheddar cheese. Amanda tucked the biscuit into her pocket, then poured herself a cup of coffee and paid for the meal.

"I just went up to Brightwood," she said, sipping her coffee.

"In the fog?" The girl looked startled.

"Sure. Why not?"

"You shouldn't go out in the fog."

"Why's that?"

"That's when Sasquatch comes out."

Amanda couldn't tell if the girl was kidding.

"Sasquatch?"

"He lives deep in the caves in the mountains. He only comes out in the fog. People have seen him, but no one has ever caught him. Some say he's really a man, but demented. That's why people disappear in the fog."

Amanda stared.

"That's why the fishing boats don't go out either. He can swim. He has a mouthful of teeth and—"

"Aspire. Stop pulling the lady's leg."

It was Gertrude, speaking sharply from the kitchen door. Amanda could see the outline of her short, curly hair.

"Sorry," the girl said, suppressing a giggle.

"Someone put strings of shells up at Brightwood," Amanda said. "All around the doors and windows. Any idea why they would do that?"

Gertrude's face came into view. She looked shocked.

"That's an old sea tradition," she said.

"What does it mean?"

"It's to ward off evil," Aspire said, and this time her mother didn't disagree.

LARRY WAS UP EARLY, TOO, HEARING THE FOGHORNS ECHOING UP and down the coast. He opened his door to a solid wall of mist. He closed the door and decided to make coffee. He poured a cup, then opened up his old, battered laptop. The newspaperman had been right. The internet service of Eagle Cove—and the rest of the coast—was chancy. The mountains broke down signals like the storms broke down trees.

But today was a good day. Maybe the fog helped, of all things. At least it dampened the wind.

He opened up the state police website. It held the clearinghouse for information about runaway and missing kids in the state. The reports went back decades, for cases both solved and unsolved. Larry had been called for a lot of runaways in his time. Most of them turned up, safe and sound. They called from a friend's house, hungover and ashamed, or walked home from a ditch where they'd crashed the family car. But sometimes they did disappear, and years later, he might meet them in the back of his patrol car while running their name. Those cases were never good.

He opened the search function and typed. He took a drink of coffee, frowned, and typed again.

There were no runaway reports listed for Brightwood.

Larry tried expanding the search terms. Maybe they hadn't used the name of the center, he thought. He tried Eagle Cove, and then the local zip code.

There was nothing.

Finally, he went back ten years before Dennis died and began to search, laboriously, through each and every runaway child report along the coast, right up to the year the center closed.

Nehalem runaway, age twelve. That kid had been found a week later.

Seaside teen. Turned up in Portland.

His coffee was getting cold.

He tried again.

There was not a single runaway report ever filed for Brightwood.

LARRY DROVE DOWN TO PICK UP AMANDA AT NOON. BY THEN MOST of the fog was blowing away, in thick white tatters across the blacktop. Charlie was outside the hotel, washing sand from the parking lot with a hose.

"Never-ending task," Charlie said. "You know, I went to Disneyland once and found sand in my sheets?"

"It could have been the sand down there," Larry said.

"No. It was this sand. It follows you." He grinned, then went to turn off the hose. "Heard you've been asking around about Brightwood."

"You know anything?"

"Not much. Was on the search party for the boy. Just sand. And sea."

He spoke, as Larry was learning the natives did, as if the ocean was their enemy. Maybe it was. It was certainly not the picture-perfect postcard or backdrop that the rare tourist expected.

"You know, I had a girlfriend once, from the city. She settled down here. Lasted a few months. Left. Like they always do."

"You expecting me to leave too?"

"Like I said, they always do."

"Well, maybe I'll stay."

"You do that. We like having you around." He made a sudden pistol-reach gesture, and grinned, going bang-bang with his narrow fingers. "You can shoot the bad guys for us."

"That ship has long since sailed, my friend."

Charlie grinned again, but this time it looked real, and sad.

"Shame about that boy. About all the boys who lived there. Always wondered what happened to them."

Larry went to fetch Amanda. She came out of her hotel room, the bloom of youth in her cheeks. She looked very young, and Larry thought of her brother in the picture, and how they never had a chance to be together.

"Sorry I'm late," she called, smiling. Charlie tipped an imaginary cap.

THEY FOUND CONSTABLE ROBERTS AT HIS DESK, EXAMINING PAPER-work. He looked up and saw them, and a funny expression crossed his face. Then he was shaking their hands.

"We found a woman who knew Dennis," Amanda said.

The constable looked pleased. "That's nice. Around here?"

"She's the cook at the nursing home."

"Really? Have a seat." He signaled at his desk.

"We have some more questions for you," Larry said.

"Shoot. Not literally, of course."

Amanda blinked at the joke, not getting it. Larry sighed inwardly. He had heard it a thousand times.

"The cook said there were other runaways at Brightwood," Larry said. "But I couldn't find any reports."

"Hmm." The constable frowned. "I think she might have gotten that wrong. I don't recall any runaways. Not on my watch."

"She seemed quite clear about it," Larry said.

"Not that I recall." He shook his head.

"What about Dennis? Did they file a runaway report for him?"

"No need. Once they discovered he was missing, someone went after him."

"The custodian?"

The constable looked surprised. "Yes, that is correct."

"What was the custodian's last name?" Larry asked.

"I've told you I don't recall."

"But it would be in your report."

"After you left last time, I checked for the report. It's gone. I think my former secretary might have purged it. You know the law. After seven years, police records can be purged."

"Minus those for murder," Larry said.

"Are you saying the boy was murdered?"

"Are you saying your unsolved case reports were destroyed?"

"The case wasn't unsolved. The boy was swept away."

"The body was never recovered. That makes it unsolved. All you had was the eyewitness account of one man, a custodian whose last name you say you don't remember. What about that doesn't seem right to you?"

The constable was staring at Larry. The pulse in his neck became visible.

"I think we are done here," he said.

"Please," Amanda spoke up. She pulled the photograph from her pocket. She had wrapped it in plastic, to keep it safe. It was all she had of her brother. "This is my brother," she said. "I know the center wasn't your business. But it was under your jurisdiction, right?"

"Yes," the constable answered. His eyes, very dark, stayed on Larry.

"So Dennis was your responsibility."

"Yes, miss. He was."

"I just want to know what happened to him."

"I think you do know. You're just denying the truth, and your friend here isn't helping you any by chasing phantoms. It's something retired officers do, at times. They can't leave the work behind. Can they, Mr. Palmer?"

BACK OUTSIDE, THE LAST OF THE FOG HAD BLOWN AWAY, AND THE day was both bright and muted, in the distorted echo chamber of mist that Amanda was learning was the coast. In the distance, the foghorns were dying down.

Larry seemed unfazed by their encounter with the constable.

"Do you know who we haven't tried?" Larry asked, turning up his collar. "The director. The constable mentioned her before. She would know about the runaway boys. And she would have known your brother too. I don't know why I didn't think of that before."

"I didn't either."

"Let's see if the library is open. Lunch first?"

AN HOUR LATER, THEY WERE SITTING AT A TERMINAL IN THE
Wheel Stone library, which was crowded with kids listening to a story
on a threadbare carpet. The windows were moist with steam.

Larry and Amanda were looking at a screen. They had unearthed
the name of the last director of Brightwood on a listing on an old state
employee website, and from there, Larry had run a search.

"Looks like she was famous, in her own circles," Larry said.

A number of articles had appeared. All had been published over
twenty years before, in child welfare newsletters.

"Director Martha King Pioneers New Paths out of Pain," read one.

"Forging Attachments, One Boy at a Time," read another.

"Center Closing, Director Leaving for New Position."

Larry clicked on that one.

"'Martha King earned acclaim for her treatments for emotionally
disturbed children,'" Amanda read out loud. "'With the closure of the
Axis Treatment Center, King is leaving to run a facility in Oregon. She
says she's looking forward to the change.'"

Larry looked at the date. It was two years before Dennis died.

10

DENNIS WAS OUT FRONT, HELPING RALPH RAKE THE GRAVEL DRIVE-way. They were supposed to be making the place look decent for the new director. The last one had retired, and a new one was coming.

The soft summer sun made everything incandescent. In the sun, the fading scars on Dennis's arms almost disappeared. Dennis had turned seven last fall, and for the first time in his life, everything felt all right with the world.

A car appeared from down the road. They instantly knew it was the new director because the directors always drove nicer cars than anyone else.

The car pulled into the lot. The door opened, and Dennis watched as a woman uncoiled from her seat. She was tall and widely built, with a cloud of auburn hair and a crimson smile.

Martha King surveyed her new domain. She counted the narrow windows and saw, with satisfaction, the mowed front yard. Her eyes fell on the boy working. Why was he outside? She gazed at the custodian, who was staring at her with an open-mouthed look of fear and recognition.

Ralph looked down. He was choking in terror. He heard the distant sound of screaming, and it was inside him.

"I'm Martha King, the new director," she said.

Ralph swallowed. He was trying to contain himself.

She didn't recognize him, he realized.

"I'm, the, uh, custodian. Ma'am."

"What is this boy doing outside?"

"He's helping me, ma'am."

"Alone? Not as part of a group? It sounds like someone is breaking a rule here. No fraternizing, correct?"

"Yes, ma'am."

"Okay, then, back inside." She made a shooing motion with her hands. Her face was smiling, but her eyes were not. Dennis dropped the rake.

Change had come to Brightwood.

"HOW DO YOU KNOW HER, RALPH?" DENNIS ASKED.

"It's not your concern, son."

Dennis had found the man in his janitorial closet. He was hiding there. He was literally shaking.

Ralph looked over his shoulder. Martha would be watching them. She would be watching everyone, from now on. There would be no hiding from her.

"Was she at the place you talked about?" Dennis asked.

"Don't bring it up, son."

"Is she going to be mean?"

"Not in the ways you think. She has ways to be mean where everyone around her stands up and claps. That's the worst kind of meanness, son. The kind where everyone says it's for your own good."

Dennis thought of the chapter in the rabbit book where it said that if you chase a rabbit, they can die of fear. Its heart literally stops in its chest. But if provoked or for the right reasons, a rabbit will turn around and fight. It will kick, hard, with its hind feet. It will use its razor-sharp teeth.

"Did you do something bad?"

Ralph looked at the boy. Dennis was getting younger as he got older. He no longer smirked and sneered. His gaze was open and curious. His little nose even twitched. Like a rabbit's, the custodian thought helplessly. Please, God, help me save him.

"No, son," he said. "The only bad thing I ever did in this life was breathe."

THAT NIGHT, RALPH FOLDED HIMSELF INTO HIS TRUCK, HIS BODY aching from stress and worry.

He had never expected to see Martha King again.

His truck rattled as he drove down the mountain road, and he unrolled the window to catch the ocean breeze. He had told Dennis he was sent to a center when he was ten. He had not told the boy how the hot wind blew off the Arizona desert in the mining shack he had lived in with his father. He had not said that one day his father left and never returned. He found out later that the old man had gotten drunk and assaulted the local sheriff. The sheriff had said like father, like son, and taken Ralph to a place in the desert called the Axis Treatment Center.

He remembered that day, stepping out of the van that dropped him inside the barbed-wire gates. He had walked into blinding white light.

LATER, WHAT RALPH WOULD REMEMBER MOST FROM THE AXIS Treatment Center was not what happened in the treatment room—those four walls had a way of blotting out the most pernicious memories—but the lone field trip Martha had taken him and a few other boys on.

He was twelve by then, and had suffered through two years at the center. Martha said he was an intractable case. So were the other boys. The trip was educational, she said. She wanted to show them something.

They had taken a van and driven deep into the desert. Leaving the security guard by the van, Martha led the boys to the very edge of a canyon. Down below them, framed in red rocks and harsh buds of cactus, was a giant figure. It looked like a cave painting, only it had been carved into the hardpan of the desert floor.

"Do you know what that is?" Martha had asked.

The boys knew better than to answer. They waited for her to tell them.

"It's called a sleeping giant," Martha said. "There are dozens of them around here. They were carved by the first people here, maybe millions of years ago. The town was named after them. When I was a little girl, my dad used to bring me out here, to the desert. He knew where all the sleeping giants are hidden. See how this one waves at the sky?"

It was true—the female figure on the desert floor appeared to be waving at the sky.

"I always wondered, why did they make them?" Martha asked. Her voice changed ever so slightly. "All of the sleeping giants are like this. They are waving, as if asking for help."

The guard lounged in the shade of the van, drinking warm Pepsi.

"All of them alone."

Ralph had listened silently. He hated Martha with every bone in his body, and he felt as wedded to her as that stone figure cut into the desert floor.

"I wanted you to see this," she told them. "Life isn't anything without each other. We are nothing without a family. We are as lost as the sleeping giants. As lost as this woman below us."

She doesn't look lost, Ralph had thought. She looks free.

On the ride back to the center, Martha sat beside him, her long thigh bone pressing into him. He could smell her sunscreen. Martha closed her eyes and drifted off to sleep, almost on his shoulder. He had felt such an awful mixture of compassion and hate then.

THESE DAYS, RALPH LIVED IN AN ABANDONED-LOOKING TRAILER perched on top of a sandy cliff, miles from the closest town. The trailer was high above the ocean and surrounded by bent, hardy pines.

No one lived nearby. From his door, he could see the ocean.

He let himself in, seeing the day-old oatmeal dried up in the pot on the stove. He lifted the ladle, which was glued to the bottom of the pot. He set the pot in the sink and poured rusty water over it to soak. In the centers, they didn't teach you to cook or balance a budget. He had forgotten how to even tie his own shoes. They had the Velcro ones like Dennis wore. Ralph's life after his release had been one embarrassment after another.

He had finally been declared cured by Martha when he was thirteen (by then he was a mess) and sent to a nearby foster home, where the parents used the compliant graduates of the center as free labor on their irrigated farm. At sixteen, he had run away, riding the trains into the vast Midwest, where he met an old man with an apple orchard who was willing to trade him an old truck and driving lessons for a year of farm-work. Eventually, he followed the crops all the way to Oregon. He had been harvesting strawberries in the Willamette Valley when another migrant told him about the Pacific Ocean. *You have to see it, man*, he had said. So when the berry harvest ended, he had driven his battered truck to the coast. He had stopped in Wheel Stone for gas. In the gas station window, he saw a sign: CUSTODIAN NEEDED.

He had driven to Brightwood. Just seeing the building brought back memories. He didn't think he wanted the job, but he went through the motions of following the director to the custodian closet. It was when he saw Dennis being led out from isolation that he knew why life had brought him to this moment. It was to save a little boy just like him.

He poured a glass of iced tea from a cloudy jar in the fridge and sat down on the sagging couch. His walls were covered with paintings of beaches he had found in hotel dumpsters. Ralph liked to look at the paintings and then the reality. It reminded him that people often lied, and this calmed him, because it was the truth.

He drank the iced tea slowly, looking mindlessly out the open door, at the tumultuous sea.

Dennis was in danger. They all were.

11

AMANDA WAS PACKING HER CAR. SHE TOSSED IN HER BACKPACK and added a bag of goodies from the market, including a jar of Gertrude's boysenberry jam and a breakfast biscuit for the road.

Larry came to see her off. He looked sad, standing in the parking lot with sand drifting at his ankles.

"Maybe you'll hear back from her," he said.

They had found an email address for Martha King, who had retired to a resort in eastern Oregon. There were pictures of her online—she had joined a golf club and looked fit. Amanda had written her a long, heartfelt email about her brother. She had also left a voicemail on the number Larry had found. So far there had been no answer.

"She'll probably just say she can't talk," Amanda said.

"There is that."

"Thank you, Larry Palmer. You've been a friend."

"Be well, Amanda Dufresne."

THE MAN STOOD IN A SCREEN OF PINE TREES FAR UP THE DUNE, A pair of binoculars in his hand. He watched as Amanda put a bag with the Eagle Cove Market logo on it in the back seat of her car and said goodbye to the retired cop. They did not hug or touch.

She headed toward the coastal highway, and he thought of following her car through the dark trees, but it wasn't necessary.

It was over. He hoped.

On the way back down, he stopped at the memorial. He took a shell from his pocket and added it to the others strewn across the sandy soil. It was a mussel shell, and it glimmered blue-black along the softer biscuit colors of smaller shells and sand dollars. He knew that if he dug, there would be twenty years' worth of buried shells here.

THE SMELLS OF SALT AND DEAD FISH WERE VERY STRONG. MOLLY lunged upright. She was seven feet tall when standing, a massive bear cloak wrapped around muscle. Even on all fours, she was almost as tall as Amanda, who felt comfortingly small in her presence. Amanda liked feeling in place in nature.

The back of the polar bear habitat, unlike the front, was all bars and bare concrete. It made it easier to clean. Polar bears shit a lot, and their shit was very smelly.

Amanda picked up a frozen fish—the zookeepers called them bear popsicles—from the bin. "There you go," she said, tossing it through the bars. "Don't say I didn't miss you."

Molly caught the fish with her long black claws. Each claw was a deadly weapon that could rip a person or seal wide open. She held her paws delicately, and munched the frozen fish. Her large dark eyes were filled with humor.

Polar bears, Amanda told the visiting schoolchildren, were like big dogs. Very big dogs. They each had their own personality. Molly was a mischief-maker. But she was also a very sad bear. Bears had memories. You could see the past zoos in her eyes, and maybe even memories of being abandoned as a cub in the wild. A team of Arctic researchers had found Molly in an empty den and sent her to a zoo to be raised by hand.

Now fifteen years old, Molly was one of those animals who remained attached to those who knew nothing about her.

No wonder I like you so much, Amanda thought, tossing her another fish.

In the background, Arctic sounds played over a loudspeaker. Amanda always turned on the music when she first arrived. It soothed Molly.

There was a clattering of a metal door behind her.

It was her coworker Sean.

Amanda immediately stiffened. She felt around Sean like Molly must feel around others of her own kind: she didn't mix. When they put Molly in with other polar bears, she was awkward and did all the wrong things. They didn't like her, and Amanda was pretty sure Sean didn't like her either.

Which was too bad, because she liked him. Very much.

Sean had dark wavy hair, cut close. His eyes were a deep brown. He smiled at her now.

"How was your break?" he asked.

"Good," she said, too eagerly.

"You should take more."

What did that mean? Was he trying to get rid of her?

"I like it here."

"I know. Just, people deserve vacations. You're a hard worker."

"I see you have no problems taking vacation time."

Now, that was a dumb thing to say. It sounded accusatory.

But he just smiled. He had such a nice smile, with white teeth. "Damn right I don't. I deserve every minute of it, too, with all this shit shoveling. If you don't use it, you lose it."

If you don't use it, you lose it was one of those sayings Amanda had puzzled over as a child. Along with *Keep your eyes peeled*. Once her father had said that when she was eight and he was driving, and Amanda had screamed in fright. She thought he meant she should peel her eyes.

It was just one of the many things about her that were weird and unfathomable. She could do advanced-level writing but counted on her fingers. The most mundane things puzzled her. And human relationships? She felt like Larry with his nutcracker, always pulverizing her opportunities.

Amanda had learned to hide her struggles, and she did so now by returning to the task at hand, throwing fish to Molly.

"Poor girl, look at her fur," Sean said.

Molly had a habit of rubbing against the walls of her enclosure. It was stress-related behavior the zookeepers had thought would improve with a new habitat. But even with a massive icy new pool and many enrichments, Molly still rubbed in distress.

Amanda knew why, and so did Sean.

"She needs another bear," he said.

"They reject her," Amanda said, because it was true. They had tried several times with Molly, and none of them took. One introduction had even resulted in bloodshed. Polar bears learned social skills from their families, and Molly had never had one. She needed other bears, just like people needed people. It was a conundrum for Molly—and for her.

Amanda finished throwing the fish. When she turned around, Sean was gone. She felt bad, like she had missed an opportunity.

The zoo opened for the day, and the air filled with the hot sugary smell of frying elephant ears and the scent of buttery popcorn. Children appeared in great noisy numbers, like flocks of birds. Amanda put on her bright red zoo uniform jacket to go out and speak to them.

"Molly wouldn't survive in the wild," she told a school group. "She needs to live here."

Their teacher spoke in the singsong voice of tired women everywhere. "How lucky she is! Isn't she lucky?"

"No," Amanda replied. "No one is lucky to live in a cage. Even if it's nice."

The teacher faltered.

"But it's the best we can do," Amanda said.

The teacher led her charges away.

"Why did you say that?" Sean appeared at her side. There was only curiosity in his face, nothing more. But Amanda was afraid to answer.

"HOW WAS YOUR TRIP?"

Amanda sat across from her mom at her dining room table. Lines of worry traced her mother's face, and there was new silver in her hair.

"It was okay," Amanda said, and told her a little about her visit to Eagle Cove.

She saw the emotions cross her mother's face. Her mother didn't want Amanda to know she was threatened by Amanda's search. She wanted her to think all was well.

"This man, Larry, he's nice?"

"Yeah, he's cool."

"Well, it's good to be careful."

"Of course, Mom."

Her mother reached for her hand.

"We just want the best for you. For you to be happy."

"I know."

Amanda couldn't help but think she had been a disappointment to her parents. They were both college professors, at Reed. They listened to NPR and talked about things Amanda often didn't understand, or didn't want to understand. But still, they had stuck by her, from her first days as a colicky, impossible-to-soothe infant. She loved them deeply.

She and her mother clutched hands, warmed by the touch. When they let go, Amanda felt better.

She picked up her coffee.

"Mom?"

"Yes?"

"If you had found out about Dennis, would you have taken him?"

Amanda saw her mother's face freeze, and in that moment, she knew. Her mother scrambled for what to say.

"We would have looked into it, for sure."

"I know you only wanted one child," Amanda said.

"Yes," her mother said, relieved.

Amanda knew she wasn't being fair. Dennis probably had a slew of problems by the time he was sent to Brightwood. Her parents weren't required to take in another child, especially one with issues. And yet she had wanted her mother to immediately say *Of course* and *That's your brother just the same as if I birthed him, too, just like I always told you over the years. I always told you that I loved you as much as a biological child. I wouldn't leave your brother out in the cold.*

Amanda looked around the kitchen she had known forever. The same antique teacups hanging from hooks under the cupboards. The same counter her father had installed. The same wobbly flowerpot she had made in grade school, holding yet another generation of begonia.

"Amanda, honey?"

"Yes, Mom?"

"You know I love you. I can't describe how much I do."

"I know, Mom."

"What do you need?"

What I cannot have, Amanda thought.

AMANDA LIVED IN A TINY STUDIO APARTMENT NEAR THE ZOO. SHE had moved out when she was twenty-two. She had been afraid to move out, and yet desperately eager to be independent. It was the numbers that scared her—rent and utilities. Due dates and calendars.

Her first years on the job, she called her mother from work every day. She got a fifteen-minute break in the morning, and one in the afternoon. Lunch was easy to figure out—that was an hour. You left at noon and came back at one. But fifteen minutes was hard. She would call her mother and ask, full of shame, "Mom? I just got my break. It's 10:11. That's what the clock says. When do I go back?" And she'd hear the catch in her mother's voice as she would say, "At 10:26, dear." Eventually, Amanda learned how to set her phone timer, and no longer needed to make those calls. But she still remembered the catch in her mother's voice, and everything it implied.

It had only been in the last year that she got the apartment lease in her name. Before that, she gave her parents the rent and they paid it for her. She remembered the look of puzzlement in the banker's eyes when she set up the automatic payments, because Amanda didn't understand that ninety-nine was one short of a hundred. Things like that had always been so hard for her. So hard.

Despite batteries of tests, no one had ever figured out what was wrong with her. Autism had been ruled out, as well as various learning disabilities. Besides a bad case of dyscalculia, she had no diagnosis, and no help.

She had learned to survive with a number of tricks. When paying cash, she always used a large bill, to cover any extra. She filled her gas tank because she didn't understand halves and quarters. She avoided travel. The trips to the beach had been a big step for her.

She sat on the edge of her bed and surveyed her domain. She kept her apartment spotless. Her desk was covered with stacks of research about Molly. Amanda was very good at research. Just like she was good at driving, or anything else she learned through experience.

She thought of Sean. She liked to fantasize that he liked her back. She thought about what it would be like to have him here, with her, right now. He would not be smirking at how confused she got when actors made jokes on television. He would not be rolling his eyes when she counted change. He would be nice to her. That was her greatest hope: a man who would love her as she was.

12

"WHAT ARE YOU DOING?"

Dennis startled. Martha King was standing above him. She had snuck up on him while he crouched in the bushes, waiting for the rabbit to appear.

It had been almost two weeks since Martha had arrived, and so far nothing bad had happened. If anything, things were better. Martha had told the staff to take notes about the boys, not just when they were naughty but also when they said please and thank you. She told them to stop using the isolation rooms so much, and to write down when they did. She even gave the cook permission to have birthday parties for the boys, and then sat in the corner and scribbled while they sang. An air of prosperity and professionalism settled over the place. Martha was in charge.

"Looking for something?" she asked.

"No, ma'am. Just sitting in the bushes."

"An odd pastime for a little boy. How old are you?"

"Seven, ma'am."

"What's your name?"

"Dennis."

"Dennis what?"

For a moment, Dennis couldn't remember his last name. He could smell pine resin, and for some reason, the rubber of her shoes. She wore hospital shoes.

"Dennis Owen, ma'am."

"How old were you when you came here, Dennis?"

"Four."

"Tell me again why you are in the woods?"

"A bird, ma'am. I like to look at birds."

Her face showed her distaste for his lie.

"You're the one I saw with the custodian," she said.

He was too smart to lie about that.

"Yes, ma'am."

"Hmm. Has he ever tried anything, you know, inappropriate?"

"No, ma'am."

"You know what happens to boys who lie, don't you?"

"They go in the isolation rooms."

"Is that what they teach you here?"

"I guess so." He was getting tired of the questioning. The rabbit would have been scared away by now. He stood, awkwardly. Martha leaned over to pick a tiny pine needle from his shoulder.

"Go inside now."

THE NEXT MORNING, SEVERAL LARGE BOXES ARRIVED IN THE MAIL from Arizona. Martha King chose an empty room at the end of the treatment ward. It was soundproof and secure, with a locking metal door. The walls were bare concrete, but she dressed up the room with thick rugs, unrolled with the help of Ike Tressler, who was settling down under her leadership. She held trainings and instructed the staff on her ways. They were there to help the boys, she said. Not punish them.

She set a plastic bucket chair in the room, for her to sit on. On one of the soft rugs, she arranged piles of pillows, sheets, and a rolled-up rug. Then she sat back and looked over the room, satisfied.

In her office, she reviewed the files of the boys at Brightwood. There were thirty boys at the center, with room for more. She was thinking about expanding the upper floor.

She made a list. The names of the boys who had been here the longest and were the most troubled—with diagnoses like reactive attachment disorder and oppositional defiant disorder—were at the top.

Among these names was Dennis Owen.

She would start with a group of eight, she decided. They would get the most intensive treatment, but all the boys of Brightwood would eventually benefit from her methods.

Dennis would be first.

There was a knock at her door, which was open.

It was the cook. The cook smiled at her. She liked having another woman in charge. So far, the two got along. Martha never looked down on her staff. In fact, she made them feel crucial.

"The dining room is ready for your inspection, ma'am."

Martha had asked the cook to make the dining room more like a real dining room, and not an institutional one. It was important that the boys be prepared to leave for real families, she had said. The cook had rearranged the tables and even added centerpieces, with fake flowers in vases.

"I can't wait to see," Martha said, and got up to take a look.

DENNIS WOKE TO THE SMELL OF BACON AND EGGS. BACON WAS A rare treat at Brightwood, and he jumped right out of bed. He could hear other boys waking, up and down the hall.

"Knock knock."

It was Ike Tressler, at his door. The man looked uncomfortable in his new dress shirt, worn at the instruction of Martha.

"She wants you," he said.

DENNIS WAS LED DOWN THE TREATMENT WARD. AT FIRST HE thought he was being taken to isolation, and wondered why, but Ike kept walking until he came to the end of the hall.

Ralph was in his custodian closet, getting ready for the day. He saw Dennis, and his expression changed. There was a look of sorrow on his face that Dennis could not understand.

Martha was waiting outside her new treatment room.

"Come, Dennis," she said.

Ralph watched as Dennis was led inside the room and Martha closed the door behind them.

Inside the room, Martha sat in her chair and signaled for Dennis to sit on a rug. She read over his file. But she was not really reading. She was studying him, and preparing.

"Do you know why you are here, Dennis?"

"No. I'm missing breakfast."

"You can have breakfast later."

Martha always did the treatments on an empty stomach. Sometimes the children got sick.

"There won't be any left," he said.

"Well, then, next time."

Dennis frowned, angry. She watched his anger carefully.

"You sound like a spoiled child," she said.

"Spoiled?" He lived in an institution. How spoiled could he be?

"A respectful child doesn't talk back to their elders."

"I want bacon and eggs."

"Well, you won't have any today."

Dennis could feel his temper boiling up. But if he had a tantrum, he definitely wouldn't get breakfast. He quelled himself.

"I want—"

"In this room, you will learn to respect and obey adults."

"If you hurt me, I'm going to re—"

"This is legitimate therapy, Dennis. There will be no child protective services reports, because I am doing what I was hired to do."

He looked at her out of the side of his eyes. A new fear began in him. It was the fear of an inmate who has learned he can be legally executed.

"Now let's get started."

"With what?" His mouth was dry.

"Holding time," she said, and smiled.

HOW DO YOU DESCRIBE HOLDING TIME? A WOMAN GIVEN THE treatment as a child in a center in Evergreen, Colorado, wrote many years after her experience:

> For the therapist, the goal is to break down the child. Nowadays we call this coercive restraint therapy, and some would describe it as more akin to torture than anything related to genuine attachment. But since the 1980s, hundreds to thousands of foster children have been given holding time in centers across the United States. The exact number is unknown because no one has bothered to keep track. At the Evergreen Clinic, I was wrapped tightly inside layers of sheets until I begged for release. On some days I was tickled until I wet myself, or had my stomach pressed until I cried. These techniques are supposed to reduce the child to an infantile state. It is only then, holding time therapists believe, that the child can begin again. The goal is to cause complete psychological collapse.

After months of hold time therapy, I was deemed cured. In truth, I had been destroyed. I have not been the same since.

THAT NIGHT, DENNIS CRAWLED INTO BED, FEELING HOLLOWED OUT with pain. He looked out the dark window. Martha King had reached down inside him and plucked out a part of him, from his very soul. He didn't think he would ever get it back.

He closed his eyes and thought of the rabbit, of her beating heart. He imagined her curling up with her paddle feet up close to her belly to sleep. She protected her soft belly in the way he could not.

"CAN I HELP YOU?"

Constable Roberts, fresh from his fortieth birthday party, was in his office, hanging a fishing net in the corner. He had been constable for several years but had yet to get around to decorating the place. His wife had suggested the net. Privately he thought it would look stupid, but marital harmony was more important than decor.

Ralph stood in the doorway, uncomfortable.

"Wanted to see if I might speak with you, sir."

"Why, of course. Have a seat."

Ralph sat down nervously.

Constable Roberts sat down across from him. He folded his hands in his lap and smiled.

"I'm worried, sir, about the boys."

"What boys?" The constable looked confused.

"At Brightwood, sir."

"Right." The constable had little interaction with the center.

"It's the new director, sir."

"I didn't know they had one, but go on."

"It's what she does to boys."

"And what is that?" Constable Roberts asked.

The man across the desk seemed sincere, but if there was one thing Constable Roberts had learned in life, it was that sometimes those who felt right were wrong. The very best of us could be wrong.

"She calls it holding time, sir."

"Holding time?"

"It's scary, sir."

"All right, then. Tell me more."

"She wraps kids inside sheets and rugs. She says it's to make them feel like they are in the womb again. So they can start over."

That didn't sound so terrible to Constable Roberts, but he kept his opinion to himself. He wasn't the one being wrapped in a sheet, after all.

"She keeps them wrapped up tight, sir, sometimes for hours. She does it until you are begging and pleading."

The constable looked calmly at Ralph.

"How do you know this?"

"I was in her—place—in Arizona."

"What was it called?"

"Axis Treatment Center, sir."

Constable Roberts wrote a note on the pad on his desk.

"You mean you worked there?"

"No, I, uh—"

Constable Roberts looked up.

"You were a resident there."

"I was just a boy."

"Does she know this?"

"No, sir. She doesn't remember me, sir. It's been a long time. I look different now."

"I'm sure you do. What do you want me to do about this?"

"I want you to stop her, sir. Stop the holding time."

"Is this a therapy other people know about?"

"Yes, sir."

"Social workers and the like?"

"Yes, sir, but they don't know what it does to you. They just think she's doing the right thing. She says she's helping kids. But she's not, sir."

"I'm not sure what I can do."

"Just take a look, sir."

"All right."

"Don't tell her I was the one who came here, sir."

"I won't."

DRIVING UP THE MOUNTAIN, CONSTABLE ROBERTS REFLECTED ON how not once, in all his years driving patrol and eventually being elected constable, had he ever been called to Brightwood. The grounds looked nice enough, he thought as he reached the gate and was buzzed in.

"I'm here for the director," he told the bald man at the door.

"Hold on."

The smell coming from inside was distinctive, a mixture of rich cooking, sweaty socks, and bleach. It wasn't necessarily bad, but it was compelling.

"I'm Martha King."

He took in a tall, well-built woman with auburn hair and a measured smile. She looked exactly like a director should, he thought. Capable and kind.

"Constable Roberts."

"How can I help you?"

"I got an anonymous report," he said. "Someone concerned about the children here."

"Well, that's not good. Please, do come in."

THE BOYS WERE LINING UP IN THE HALL FOR LUNCH, AND THE CON-stable took in their silent faces. Martha gave him a tour. He saw the bed-rooms, the dining room, the classrooms, and, finally, the treatment ward.

He was surprised by the isolation rooms.

"I don't like these," Martha said, with a look of distaste. "My understanding is the last director relied almost exclusively on them for discipline."

"And you?"

"I'm interested in helping these boys."

"How do you do that?"

"With therapy."

He stopped at the final room.

"This is our attachment therapy room," she said.

"Holding time?"

"You know of it?" She looked surprised.

"I did a little reading, before I came here," he said. "You have a reputation."

"I've treated hundreds of children, and with lasting results."

Constable Roberts thought that if there had been a problem with her methods, there would be police reports by now. But when he had run her name through the system, there had been nothing.

"The boys—do they like this holding time?"

"What makes you think they wouldn't?"

"Might explain the call I got."

"All breakthroughs involve struggle, Constable. But none of the boys are ever harmed. I promise you that."

He could think of nothing else to ask.

"Is there anything else I can do for you?" she asked.

"I'd like to speak to one of the children," he said.

HE WAITED ON THE PORCH, AND SOON ENOUGH, MARTHA BROUGHT
a boy to him. He was small, and had narrow shoulders, which drooped
down like wilted petals.

"This is Dennis."

Constable Roberts walked Dennis over to a bench. He had a boy
this age. His son and this boy were nothing alike. His son had perpetually grimy hands and wiggled when he walked. Dennis looked like he
was carved out of concrete.

"Dennis, I understand you live here."

The boy stared straight ahead. It was like he had turned his brain off.

"I'd like to ask you a few questions."

The boy looked like he wasn't going to answer.

"Does anyone hit you here?"

Dennis shook his head.

"How about restrict your food or water?"

A pause, and another shake.

"This new director, she does a kind of therapy called holding time.
Have you had holding time?"

Dennis hesitated, then nodded.

"What is it like, son?"

The boy didn't answer. He folded his mouth into a tight line.

"If there is something happening here, you can tell me."

"Like what?" Dennis finally spoke.

"Like abuse."

Dennis's face showed his confusion. How was he to know what was
abuse and what was not?

"What do you think of this place?"

The boy turned to stare at the constable.

"The cook is nice," he finally said.

On the way back to town, the constable thought about what he would write in his report. The problem was he had nothing to report, and he wanted to do a good job. He decided he would call down to where Martha had had her last center. Maybe they had a sheriff or someone he could talk to.

MARTHA HELD A STAFF MEETING THE NIGHT AFTER THE CONSTABLE visited. She asked the cook to make treats, knowing it would please her, and set an empty jar on the table so the other staff could give her a tip. The staff of Brightwood were not used to feeling appreciated: they stood around the dining room, eating the cook's homemade donuts, and drinking the hot coffee she had brewed.

"Now," Martha began. "I understand change is hard. Maybe some of you have questions about my methods."

The staff looked confused. Ralph stood in the back. There was nothing on his face. At one time, Martha had made it so he could hide nothing from her. But years on the road had fixed that.

"Did something happen?" Ike said. He was already Martha's biggest defender.

"Everything is fine," she said, and smiled.

"I saw the constable's car yesterday," one of the staff ventured.

"He paid us a visit. I don't mind. We have nothing to hide, do we? My concern is whether any of you have concerns. I want you to feel you can come to me. To talk."

No one spoke. The night watchman yawned. The cook looked flustered, from a long day on her feet and the unfamiliar evening coffee.

Martha seemed disappointed. She and the staff made small talk after that, and she noted a few problems—there was too much bleach in the laundry; it made everything smell—and they all went home. The treatment room door was locked, the room empty. The isolation floor was empty, and the boys upstairs could have been invisible, as far as their silence went. The cook washed the dishes and left for her place outside Wheel Stone. Martha drove her nice car down the road. She had rented a place up the coast, in a newer development. She missed the desert. She had lost a lot, she thought. She'd had to leave her hometown and strike out to a new place, forfeiting friends, familiarity, and a climate she loved. Now she was all alone, in a cold and wet place where the sky never stopped raining. It was a terrible loss.

It made her, she thought, understand the boys.

13

LARRY MISSED AMANDA, MORE THAN HE'D EXPECTED TO. IT WAS A sharp pang that reminded him of the hollow loss of his wife. Marjorie was gone, but Amanda was still alive, which meant maybe she would come back.

He returned to his world, which seemed even more limited than before. He walked up and down the beach. He browsed the market.

"He wasn't the only one, you know," Aspire said.

"The only what?" he asked, puzzled. He had been examining cans of beans and thinking about a dish his wife used to make, with white beans cooked with ham and pineapple. She called it Hawaiian Toot-Toot.

"The only boy who died."

"What do you mean?" Larry turned to her.

Her mother had appeared behind the door.

"Aspire," Gertrude said. "I need help with the dishes. Go on now."

"Hold up," Larry said. "What did you mean?"

Her mother sighed. "I told her not to tell tall tales."

"I'm not telling tales, Ma. Dad wrote—"

"Your father." The mother stopped her, shaking her head angrily. She looked away, and Larry saw a pain she tried to keep hidden from her daughter. She didn't want to bad-mouth a dead man, no matter how much he deserved it.

"Go on now," she told Aspire. "Just go on."

Aspire removed her apron, smiling.

"Come on," she told Larry, who had put down the beans. "I want to show you something."

ASPIRE OPENED THE SHED BEHIND THE MARKET, AND BACKED OUT an old beater car Larry had never seen before. He looked at it skeptically.

"We can take my car," he told her.

"No. I want to take this."

Larry got in uncertainly. He didn't like letting others drive.

"This was my dad's car," Aspire told him. "My mom hates to drive."

"Where are we going?" Larry asked, looking at the rusted floor with trepidation.

"Just down to the cliffs."

Aspire drove carefully down the old beach road, which petered out into hardpan covered in sand. Down the beach, ocean waves slammed into the side of the cliff and shot spray up forty feet.

She stopped in the shadows of the cliffs.

"The tide won't reach up here," she said, opening the glove box. Larry saw a stack of mildewed papers, a leather eyeglass case, and a pair of old binoculars. Aspire reached for a small notebook on top.

Larry strained his head trying to see the top of the cliffs. The waves hitting the rock face sounded like shattering glass.

"This is what I wanted you to see."

The girl held out the notebook.

Larry took it. The pages were stained with seawater, and tiny grains of sand had stuck to the paper. The notes inside were written in an indifferent scrawl.

Went to the constable. He doesn't believe me. No one does.

He turned the page. There was a drawing of a sea monster.

"That's not it. The next page."

I know what I saw. I am not lying. I did not imagine it.

The picture on the page was of a manlike creature, made long with shadow, carrying what looked like a body over his shoulder, through the woods.

Underneath, in all capital letters, was written: SASQUATCH.

"SASQUATCH?" LARRY SAID.

"Well, not that, exactly. My dad liked all the old stories. Sasquatch. The Basket Woman. That's this witch who roams the woods and puts children in her basket. Or the giant sturgeon who lives at the Bonneville dam and eats people. But just because he liked the old stories doesn't mean he didn't see something."

Larry looked again at the drawing. Her dad had been a good artist, if one with a shaky hand. The figure in the woods had a sense of foreboding to it.

"Why didn't you say anything about this before?"

"My mom says not to stir the pot. It was one thing to direct you to the guy who cut the memorial stone. She said this would have given that woman false ideas. We would be scaring her over nothing."

Larry was inclined to agree with her mom. The drawing was probably the result of a fevered imagination. From what the old fisherman had said, her dad had been a drunk too.

"Are you the one who hung the shells?"

"No."

He handed the notebook back. Aspire took it like it was precious and put it back in the glove box. The car smelled funny to Larry, like wet bones.

"I want to go see the cliffs," Aspire said, opening her car door. "Come on."

Larry followed her reluctantly, the wind buffeting them.

They walked, passing the large rocks, until they got closer to where the waves met the mountain. It was low tide, and the sand was pitted with dozens of tide pools. The pools were filled with sea stars glowing with orange and purple. Sea urchins, oozing water, opened their tentacled mouths as Larry and Aspire passed.

"This is close enough," Aspire said, though the ocean was still a distance away. There was a jumble of massive rocks along the side of the cliff, and Larry could see bleached driftwood caught high on the cliff face, which was red and wet and crumbling.

It was oddly quiet here, as if the wind had captured a pocket next to the stone walls of the cliff.

"My dad used to come here," Aspire said. "Sometimes elk fall, and he would find their bodies, hung up on the rocks. He cut up their antlers and sold them as dog chews in the city. My dad spent a lot of time outside."

"What happened to him?" Larry asked.

She pointed, far above them, to where the rocky point of the mountain jutted over the sea.

"He came here and jumped. They never found his body either."

"I'm sorry," Larry said.

"I used to come down here and talk to him. But he never answered."

"It must have been hard on your mother," Larry said.

Aspire kicked at a strand of seaweed coiled on the beach. A little crab raced out from under it and dived into a tide pool.

"I think she was relieved, honestly."

Larry had no reply to that.

"We had better go," she said. "The tide is coming in."

They turned around. The wind plastered their jackets against their backs.

Aspire cast a careful look at the waves behind them, as if to make sure they weren't catching up. She and Larry climbed the final rocks to the car. It started with a sputter.

Aspire carefully backed the car up, then turned around.

"I wish I didn't live here. Sometimes I think that. But then I'd have to leave my dad there, in the sea. I'd have to leave my mom and the market."

"You could always come home for visits."

"Yeah. But it isn't the same then, is it?"

"No," Larry said. "It is not."

BACK IN HIS CABIN, LARRY PACED IN A CIRCLE BY THE FIREPLACE, restless. Finally, he pulled out his copy of the local telephone directory. He found the number for the nursing home. The cook answered—the front desk was on break.

"Yes?"

Larry gave a little preamble he'd rehearsed. He was learning to add in the niceties people expected, instead of just barking into the phone.

The woman sounded amused.

"How can I help you?"

"You said boys ran away. The constable denies it ever happened," Larry said. "Who did the center call, when a child went missing?"

"The social workers."

"You didn't call the police?"

"The policy was if anything happened with one of the boys, the director was supposed to call their caseworker."

"By director you mean Martha King?"

She sounded surprised. "Yeah. Her. I haven't heard her name in ages. I wonder how she's doing. Nice lady."

"She wasn't there that long. Maybe three, four years before they closed?"

"That sounds about right. They closed not long after Dennis died. Honestly, I think it hurt her, but she didn't mention it."

"She gave the boys some kind of treatment, right?"

"Yeah. I didn't know much about it. It seemed to help some of them."

"But not Dennis?"

"No. Not Dennis."

14

"YOU'RE FIGHTING IT," MARTHA TOLD DENNIS.

Hours had passed, and Dennis was a snot-nosed mess. Martha felt frustrated. Dennis was one of the hardest boys she had ever tried to crack. She had been using the rug, which was for her worst cases. But even when Dennis was finally reduced to begging and pleading, she could see in his eyes that it was not real.

Like now.

She held a baby bottle in one hand. This was one of her techniques. The child needed to accept the bottle—accept the feeding. Once they suckled, their eyes soft and warm, she knew they would be open to accepting a new mother and father. She could send them confidently on to a new foster or adoptive home, but always with a warning to the parents: If the child became oppositional or defiant again, the parents could return them for more holding time.

The boys knew this. They, too, were warned.

Dennis lay, collapsed, across her lap, his shirt soaking wet from sweat and saliva. He let her put the nipple past his wet lips. She watched as the bottle dripped milk into his slack mouth. He looked up at her, and she could see herself in his eyes. She was tired from hours of struggle. Holding time was exhausting.

He spit the nipple out.

She yanked the bottle away, furious. She took a deep breath.

It wasn't good to get angry. She stopped the treatment, but she could see the victory in his eyes. He believed he had won.

"We'll try again tomorrow," she said. It wasn't his fault he was disordered and incapable of love.

He looked up at her, the thoughts stirring in his eyes.

"I will not give up on you," she said.

MARTHA KING BELIEVED IN HOLDING TIME. SHE HAD STUDIED AT the clinics in Colorado, under the approval of the state medical board. The method had been lauded by Nobel Laureate Nikolaas Tinbergen and praised on mainstream news programs such as the *Today* show.

Her favorite book, always on her shelf, the pages dog-eared, was *Holding Time* by a child psychiatrist named Martha G. Welch. "Rejection begins as the child tries to escape your embrace, your gaze, or your words," Welch wrote. "The child may spit, kick, writhe, butt, scream, turn purple with rage—or his sad crying may break your heart."

Martha King believed that the foundation of all disorders was rage. Break through the rage and you achieved order. "If you use holding time regularly," Welch wrote, "chances are you won't have much need for punishment."

Welch believed that holding time cured everything from autism to hyperactivity. For believers, holding time was the magic cure-all for the nearly half million kids in foster care growing more troubled by the year. And in no place was the cure more needed than in places like Brightwood, which were overrun with gross immorality and dishonest, deceitful boys.

Martha King was especially eager to try the cure on the increasing number of homosexual boys sent to the center.

WINTER CAME, AND A VAN APPEARED IN THE PARKING LOT. THE boys gathered on the porch to watch.

The weather was raw, and the air was filled with the sound of seagulls blown in from the storms. The seagulls landed on the roof of Brightwood and covered it with bird shit.

"Boys, welcome our new residents," Martha called. She was bundled into a warm jacket, her teased hair coiling in the wind.

The new boys left the transport van. The social worker at the front, who looked exhausted, handed over their files with a cold hand. Staff unloaded their belongings from the back. A few of the boys had suitcases, but most used garbage bags.

Dennis stood at the end of the porch, near Ralph.

The boys were to replace those who had recently left for new homes, most likely for good, Martha had said. Some of those boys were part of the group Dennis was in. His own treatment, she said, was not going well.

There was a waiting list, now, for Brightwood. Not just for foster kids, but for children adopted overseas and domestically whose parents were disappointed with their behavior.

As Dennis watched, the last boy jumped off the van. He was small and slender, with glowing skin and buzz-cut hair. He had an earring in one ear, and a ready smile that faltered when he looked up with wonder at the tall gray building above him, and the row of watching gulls.

THE NEW BOY SAT NEXT TO DENNIS AT LUNCH. THE COOK HAD made grilled cheese sandwiches and tomato soup. It used to be one of Dennis's favorite meals, but he had mostly lost his sense of taste. All he tasted anymore was the rug.

"Hey," the new boy said.

Dennis didn't reply. He watched soup run off his spoon.

"My name is Reggie. What's yours?"

"Dennis," he said.

"How old are you?"

Dennis had to think about it. Months of holding time had polished his mind clean. He couldn't even remember his last birthday. Had the cook celebrated it? He didn't think so.

"Eight," he said.

"I'm twelve."

There was silence.

"How long have you been here?"

Dennis didn't answer.

A staff member watching the boys scribbled notes about their behavior. He had been instructed to keep an eye on these two.

DENNIS WAITED NEAR THE FRONT DOOR. MARTHA HAD MADE IT harder to see the rabbit—the staff was always watching the boys now—but recently he had discovered he could slip out during shift change.

When no one was looking, he darted out the open door, dashed into the trees, and found his new hiding spot. He crouched down, relieved.

There was a crackling of brush.

Dennis whirled around to see Reggie behind him.

"What are you doing?" Dennis hissed.

"I followed you," Reggie said. He looked proud of himself. "What are you doing?"

"Shut up!"

"Why?" Reggie crouched next to him.

"You'll scare her away!"

"Scare who?"

Dennis was angry. He didn't want to talk. He wanted Reggie to leave. But more than that, he wanted him to shut up.

"It's—a creature," he muttered.

"Really? Where?"

Begrudgingly, Dennis pointed.

"You have to be quiet," he said.

Reggie obliged. He sat down comfortably next to Dennis and leaned against his shoulder. Dennis looked down at the intruding flesh but did not move away. It actually felt nice.

The two boys sat in the woods. It was very quiet. The air was oddly warm for winter, a gentle breeze stirring in the trees. The woods were spicy with the smells of pine and fir, and the licorice scent of ferns. The birds began to chirp. A woodpecker beat against a distant tree.

Under the red bush, there was a small shaking. Dennis held his breath.

The rabbit came out of her burrow. Her little nose was wet with dew.

"Oh, *look*," Reggie whispered.

The rabbit hopped a few feet, and began to eat. Her little mouth chewed the grasses, and it was just like Dennis was being fed, down in his soul. All the pained, emptied places Martha had created were being refilled. Just looking at the rabbit filled him up.

Reggie's entire body relaxed. Dennis felt his warm shoulder, and the lean of his head. A single hand lay against the worn gray of his pants.

"I call her Bunny," Dennis whispered.

The rabbit looked up. Her eyes were very dark, like black discs of light. She resumed nibbling.

Reggie reached for his hand. Dennis put it back. The boy leaned against him some more, hungry for human comfort. They sat like that, watching the rabbit eat.

"We should go back," Dennis whispered.

Rising slowly, they backed out of the trees, leaving Bunny filling her belly on the fresh, sweet grass. Leaning over, the two boys ran back to the center. They ran across the lawn, to the front porch, and darted in the door.

Martha was standing there.

Dennis felt his stomach drop.

But it wasn't Dennis she was looking at.

It was Reggie.

"Just in time for your treatment," she said.

15

THE NEXT MORNING, LARRY CALLED A CHILD PROTECTIVE SERVICES worker he knew from his police days. Patty had driven a Harley—Larry remembered that. She had pulled up on calls with a teddy bear tied to her back seat. The children liked the motorcycle. It made Patty relatable. But the bear was the clincher.

Often the first responder on the scene, Larry had called Patty many times. He had called from drug houses where the walls were covered with pornography. He had called from outside closets where children had been tied up and muzzled. He had called, once, because a four-year-old girl had a telltale rash around her mouth. The rash turned out to be a venereal disease, and the one who had given it to her, her father.

Patty happened to be up the road in Seaside, visiting a sick uncle. She and Larry met at a bar there, not far from the promenade, where tourist shops were just opening for the season. Seaside was nothing like Eagle Cove. You could wade in Seaside, under the right conditions. Those were not today. The wind buffeted the wide windows of the bar.

"It looks like a hot toddy day," Patty said, tossing her leather jacket over the back of a chair. The bar was dark and homey.

"Make that two," Larry told the barkeep, who wandered away.

The drinks soon arrived, with a heady aroma of whiskey and lemon.

"My, that's strong," Patty said, taking a slug. "Just what I need."

"Surprised to find you down here."

"Well, I wanted to check on my uncle. And scope out the coast in case I want to move here like you did. I'm almost at retirement. The way things are going, I figure I better get out now."

"I hear ya," Larry said.

They drank, feeling the whiskey settle into their bones. Sand peppered the windows. Larry looked over the tossing sea. Some things didn't change. They had a lifeguard tower here, though, for when the sea was sedate. That was never going to happen where he lived.

"So," she said. "Tell me how I can help."

Larry told her about the lack of reports for the boys who'd run away from Brightwood.

"That sounds about right. The agency keeps everything inside."

"What do you mean by that?"

"A kid gets raped in a center? File an internal report. Someone runs away? Another internal report."

"Rapes and runaways should be reported to the police."

"And often they are. But let's talk about what happens when they are. The child's name and information is protected by confidentiality laws. That means the police can't put their name on the news or put the report into the online databases or even use their name with witnesses. In some cases, they can't even tell their parents. Their hands are literally tied in an investigation."

"Okay. So what happens then?"

"What do you think? Nothing happens. I worked a case where this little girl turned up dead in a ditch. Turned out she had gone missing from her foster home. The worker had called the police in the town she went missing in. The next town over? Never even heard of her. How could she have possibly been found under those circumstances? Months had passed, Larry. Months."

She took another slug of her drink. The low lights of the bar glittered in her long hair.

"So the cook might be telling the truth."

"I'd say it's likely. If boys ran away, the director probably called their caseworkers. Did the caseworkers call anyone? Maybe. Maybe not. How will you ever know?"

"But there would be internal reports."

"Good luck getting them."

"What about someone like you, on the inside?"

"You'd need a name for me to search. But how would you know their names, with the laws keeping them secret? This is why we have an estimated twenty thousand children missing from the foster care system, and no one has the faintest idea where they are."

Larry put down his drink. The alcohol was making him feel muzzy. He rarely drank anymore and decided he didn't like it.

"The unmissing," he said.

She turned to stare at him.

"Yes. Exactly."

She finished the last of her toddy and signaled for another.

"You want another?"

Larry looked at his unfinished drink. "No. You can finish mine, if you like. I don't have germs."

"Funny, I always took you for a drinker."

"Must be my charming personality."

Larry was liking this moment, despite the subject matter. He felt more like himself but a newer, more rested version. He had thought it was gone forever.

"You thinking about going back into business?" she asked, as if reading his mind.

"I'm retired."

"You could always become a private investigator. Lots of retired cops do that."

"I'm old."

"Well, who isn't?" She let out a laugh that reminded him of Marjorie. She drank her second toddy, her cheeks flushed.

"You still ride a Harley?"

"Yeah, but I was thinking if I move down here, it seems like a recipe for death. All these winds and wet roads."

"So there's no way to learn more about runaways from Brightwood?"

"I didn't say that. Let me do some digging."

AMANDA WAS STANDING BY A VIEWING WINDOW OUTSIDE THE PO-lar bear habitat. From here, visitors could look through the smeary glass—the staff tried to keep it clean, but kids were always touching it—into an underground den. The den had been made of concrete, painted white to imitate snow.

Molly knew it was not snow. When real snow came, Molly raced and ran like a frantic child. Visitors thought it was cute, but Amanda could see the desperation in the bear. In the real snow, Molly was looking for her mother. She tunneled under it, searching for the secret dens bears made.

She watched Molly now. It was a rainy spring day, and a few visitors walked under big umbrellas. The zoo had regulars—lost souls like her. Amanda watched them drift past.

Molly was looking at her.

The giant bear had crawled down into the den. She was crouched inside, looking out at her keeper, her massive paws nearly touching the glass. Amanda felt a wave of emotion, and most of it was shame. She often felt complicit in some great wrong, only it was the wrong of life.

"I'm sorry," she said, lightly, to the bear. She was wearing her bright red zoo jacket, and she knew Molly recognized her. Sean said Molly stared at every blond woman when Amanda was not around, searching for her. But it was like being offered a plastic apple when you're hungry, Amanda thought. Molly was hungry in her soul.

"How is she?" Sean asked, stepping beside her. He had been cleaning the walkway and held a broom and dustpan in his hand.

"She knows the white concrete is not snow," Amanda said.

That was a stupid thing to say, and she immediately worried Sean would say something sarcastic. A lot of guys his age would. It was what passed for intimacy for them. But Sean was never sarcastic. He never made fun of her.

"Are there any studies about polar bears and color?" he asked.

"Not that I've seen," Amanda said. "I think if Molly lived in gray concrete, it would be the same to her. We paint it white for us."

The bear was staring intently at Amanda. Molly completely ignored Sean. That was progress, at least—earlier in her life, Molly had attacked male humans. No one knew why.

"I wish it was colder for her," Amanda said.

Sean pointed into the artificial den.

"What kind of den is that?" he asked.

"What do you mean?"

"I read that polar bears have different kinds of dens. There are sleeping dens. Then there are the maternity dens."

Amanda turned to stare at him. He was right. They hadn't thought of that when constructing the fake den. No wonder Molly seemed to have such mixed feelings about it. Especially the viewing glass. The den the zoo had made was the size of a maternity den. Mother polar bears dug those deep, and didn't break open the snow entrance until their babies were several months old. They lived in darkness until then. Snowy, warm, feral darkness.

"Wasn't she found in a maternity den?" Sean asked.

"Yes," Amanda said slowly. She was thinking of the stacks of research back at her apartment. She wasn't good at math, but she was doing her own addition.

"Do you mind if I run home for a minute?" she asked.

AMANDA DIDN'T BOTHER TO TAKE OFF HER RAIN JACKET. SHE WENT immediately to her desk, and the neat and orderly piles of research on top.

In one stack were reports from Molly's previous zookeepers and her medical records. In the next stack were research articles about polar bears, many of them unpublished and from obscure sources. The third stack held information about the area where Molly had been found and the polar bears specific to that region.

Amanda went digging through the last stack, with wet hands. She pulled out a sheet titled Anger Bay Research Station. It contained the names of the staff working the station where Molly was found.

Searching through the second stack, Amanda found an account of the rescue in *National Geographic*. She had read this before, but she read it now with new eyes, thinking of the den. The team at the station had found Molly abandoned in a maternity den. It was a cold April, they said. A week later, they had found the carcass of her mother on the ice. It had been partially consumed by other bears.

Amanda dug out an unpublished paper on the Anger Bay polar bears. Polar bears were distinctive by region. They mated and gave birth at different times, depending on their genetics. The polar bears of Anger Bay typically gave birth a little later than most, in February.

She used her fingers to count. Molly had been two months old when she was found.

Taking a deep breath, Amanda combed through the papers, finding more articles about the rescuers. She began checking their names against the staff list, marking them off as she went.

There was one name left. One man had not talked to reporters.

She sat down abruptly, rain flecking to the floor—she would wipe it up later—and opened her computer and began to search for his name.

LARRY WAS JUST SITTING DOWN FOR SUPPER—HE HAD MADE Hawaiian Toot-Toot and was looking forward to tasting it—when Amanda called.

He picked up the phone eagerly.

"How is the coast?" she asked.

"There's an ocean. And sand."

The joke seemed to go over her head.

"You called earlier? I was working."

He told her about the drawings by Aspire's dad, and his talk with Patty.

"What do you think it all means, Larry?"

"The constable would say we're chasing shadows."

"No. We're learning about Dennis. And Brightwood."

She was very literal, he thought.

"I think I'm going to come back down," she said. "I have something else to do down there too."

They hung up. Larry took a bite of his Toot-Toot. It wasn't very good.

"It's just not the same without you," he told the urn on the mantel.

16

DENNIS AWOKE IN THE MIDDLE OF THE NIGHT. IT WAS THE HOUR OF dreams. He made his way down the hall on silent feet. He could hear the night watchman downstairs, snoring at his desk.

The second-floor bathroom was dark and empty. He peed, looking out the window at the trees.

There was a sound. He turned, his eyes adjusting. A boy was sitting in the corner. It was Reggie. He had his back against the wall, his head in his hands.

Dennis went and sat next to him. The floor was very cold.

Reggie flinched and moved away.

"Are you okay?"

Reggie turned his face to the wall.

"She said I'm sick," Reggie whispered.

"She tells me the same thing. She tells me I have to accept the bottle. I'm never going to accept it."

Reggie shook his head.

"She said it's unnatural."

Dennis was confused.

"They must have told. My foster parents."

"Told what?"

"There was this time . . . I drew pictures. You know."

Dennis didn't know.

"It was . . . two boys."

"Oh."

Dennis was vaguely aware there were boys at Brightwood who liked other boys. He never really thought about it. They left him alone, which was all that mattered. As long as they didn't mess with him or the rabbit, he didn't care.

"My foster dad was very angry. He made me pray. Then he sent me here."

"Did Martha put you in the rug?"

"She tickled me, all over. She pressed her face against mine and told me I hated myself. She said that I think of boys because of what my mother did to me. But I don't hate women. I miss my real mom."

"I don't."

Dennis felt his bottom get cold on the bathroom floor.

"You need to give in," he told Reggie. "The quicker you give in, the sooner she'll let you leave."

"How do you give in?"

"I don't know. I've tried."

The two boys sat against the cool wall. Eventually, the clouds blew away from the moon, and it was revealed, perfect in its entirety.

"We should go," Dennis said. "If they catch us, they'll put it in our notes. The more times you are bad, the more treatment she says you need. The longer the holding time, and the longer you have to stay here."

He stood, and put out a hand for the older boy, lifting Reggie to his feet. They didn't speak again for the longest time.

DENNIS HAD STOPPED TALKING TO RALPH. WHEN THE CUSTODIAN passed in the hallway, Dennis walked by, his eyes straight ahead.

When Dennis dreamed, it was of sleet. The world was full of ice. He was a soft puppet, made of rags and tears. Martha held him, cajoled him, tormented him, and still Dennis could not give her what she wanted, even when he desired it himself. There was a small hard rock in him that said no. Fight back.

So he fought back.

Martha called in Ike Tressler, and he pinned Dennis to the floor, so much it hurt. But not even the dragon breath of Ike moved him.

"You might be a failed case," Martha said. "I have never had a failure."

There had been boys at Axis who took years to cure, she remembered. That was okay. She had the boys until they were eighteen. She would not send a boy on to a foster or adoptive home until he was cured.

Dennis was led from the room, vomit down his shirt. One night he had to be carried, his clothes soaked with drool and sweat. The custodian found him later, tucked into his cot. When his caseworker visited, she talked briefly to Dennis, who refused to speak. She spoke to Martha, who said, "He is very disordered."

Nights swirled past, in color. The whole world was dead.

One night, Ralph passed Dennis a note.

Watch out your window.

The next morning, Dennis stood at his window. Ralph was standing by the bush, holding a rake. Gently, while Dennis watched, the custodian cleared back the long grass above where the rabbit traveled. He did it in just one spot, visible only from above.

"I ALREADY WENT UP THERE," CONSTABLE ROBERTS TOLD RALPH, who had just appeared in his office.

"I know, sir. But . . . he's getting worse."

"Who?"

"Dennis, sir. The boy you spoke to."

"How do you know I talked to him?"

"I was watching."

The constable looked at him. The coastal towns were full of men like Ralph, wanderers who finally blew up against the lip of a rock and stayed there.

"If I go speak to him, will he tell me he's being abused?"

"Probably not," Ralph admitted. "He doesn't trust anyone. That's the thing with holding time, sir. You stop knowing what's real. You stop trusting anyone. Even yourself."

"I called down to where she was before," Constable Roberts said. "The sheriff there told me she was a pillar of the community."

"You mean the sheriff in Sleeping Giant?"

"Yes. Did you know him too?"

"He's not a nice man, sir."

Constable Roberts sat back. Maybe Ralph just had an axe to grind with Martha King, and anyone else from Sleeping Giant.

"It's not right, what she's doing, sir."

"I'll go back."

THE CENTER LOOKED DIFFERENT. THERE WERE FLOWERS ON THE dining room tables. The isolation rooms were empty, and the boy seemed quieter. A group was exercising on the lawn, under the guidance of a staff member. Yet Constable Roberts was troubled. He couldn't even say why. There was something in the boys' faces that pushed him ever so slightly sideways.

Martha King looked irritated this time. She had just come from the treatment room, where she was finishing with Reggie. The boy, slack-jawed, had been carried to bed by Ike Tressler, who had a hand up his shirt, on his warm back.

"Yes?"

"Just checking in," he said.

"I'm under the supervision of the state," Martha said. "There is no need for you to be checking in."

"I took a shine to that boy you introduced me to. It occurred to me we get a lot of offseason fishermen in our towns. We could connect the boys with mentors. Kinda like our own big brother program. The men could show them the boats. Take them whale watching."

She smiled at him, but her eyes said no.

"The boys here are severely emotionally disturbed, Constable. If they were capable of going on unsupervised outings, they wouldn't be here. I do appreciate your concern, though."

"I'd like to see your therapy room again."

"I truly do not see the problem."

She walked him to the room. He noticed the door had a lock. He knelt by the pile of damp sheets and touched them.

"These smell like urine."

"Boys have accidents, Constable."

"I think the law says you are required to give them access to a toilet."

"I do, sir."

"Then why are they pissing themselves in here?"

He stood, smelling the tang of vomit too.

"It's not uncommon during regression therapy that the child reverts to an infant-like state," she said. "In fact, we encourage it. We want them to start over again. There is a lot of research to back my position."

In truth, there was not, but she believed there was, and now so did he.

"You want them to feel like babies?"

"Yes, sir. Most of these boys, if not all, have experienced profound trauma. Many times before they can even remember. We take them back, get them to discharge all the rage. The maladaptive behaviors fall away. No more defenses. They are as open as—the wide blue sky."

"Hmm." He was gazing at a spot on her jacket. It looked like puke. She looked down, saw it, and wiped it hastily with a handkerchief pulled from her pocket.

"I want to see that boy again. The one I talked to last time. Dennis."

"I truly hope that will conclude your business here, as I need to get back to work."

THEY WERE IN HIS ROOM. DENNIS WAS LOOKING OUT THE WINDOW. Constable Roberts stepped closer. He could not figure out what the boy was looking at. Finally, he saw it. There was a small rabbit crouched in the grass below.

"Dennis," he began.

The boy had a hollow place at the base of his skull. The constable looked at this as he talked.

"I won't lie to you, son. I know Martha King is respected in her field. But you look sad. Is it the holding time?"

Dennis turned to him. His eyes were empty. But storms threatened, deep inside.

"She told me I need to break," Dennis said.

That's what it's really about, Constable Roberts thought. He thought of prisoners of war. He knew exactly what Martha King was doing to these kids. She was breaking them down.

"Can't you just comply?" he asked.

Dennis looked away.

"I don't know how, sir."

AFTER LEAVING THE CENTER, CONSTABLE ROBERTS DROVE INTO THE town of Eagle Cove. He had never spent much time there—he had no

reason to. Once or twice he had gone to talk to Gertrude about her husband, but talking to that woman was like talking to a brick wall—in her
eyes, all he saw was the dreams she'd had of her husband, not the truth
of the man. So he had stopped doing that, after watching the way Brett
smirked from the shadows, like he had pulled a fast one on the constable,
getting drunk and making trouble and having his missus defend him.

Still, the constable dropped in now. Brett was nowhere in sight.
Gertrude had pulled her curly hair back into thick pigtails and put on
pink lip gloss. She looked young—and worried, like he was there to ask
about her husband.

She relaxed after he bought a sandwich and a drink. He tore into
the sandwich, hungry, looking at the walls. On the bench, an old man
cleared his throat. The constable waited for the blizzard of words, but
they didn't come. He walked outside, looking over the beach. It was
fine weather, and through the trees, on the mountain behind him, lived
a troubled boy, as neatly disappeared from the world as the card in a
magician's trick.

In the distance was the hotel. The constable walked over, admiring
the work Charlie was doing on the place. It wasn't well done, but at least
it was work. The man had filled planters with potting soil and spindly
roses that were already dying. The constable contemplated telling him
what kind of plants grew well in the coastal mists but then decided not
to. No one likes a know-it-all.

"Hello, Constable," Charlie said from his front office.

The two had met recently when Charlie had bought the abandoned
hotel. Like so many coastal refugees, Charlie had come with big dreams,
soon chastened by sand. He had arrived holding a newspaper ad, in his
case for the vacant hotel, where sand had piled up in the corners of the
rooms. Charlie had swept it out and kept grinning, and he still kept
grinning, even though the customers he had hoped for had yet to come.

"What can I do for ya?" Charlie asked, tinkering behind his counter.

"I was wondering, you ever have any contact with that center?"

"What center?"

"Is there more than one? Brightwood, up in the woods."

Charlie looked up at him, frowning. Then he returned to the tape machine he was trying to fix. "Naw, why would I?"

"Dunno. Thought maybe you'd know something."

"Nope. Wouldn't know anything about it."

The constable drummed his fingers on the counter. The hotel owner looked up, irritated, and he stopped. Charlie grinned.

"You let me know if you ever hear anything, all right?"

"Well, sure, but what am I looking for?"

"Dunno yet. Guess I want to make sure those boys are okay."

"Well, why wouldn't they be? Kids today are spoiled," Charlie said. "Some of them need a place like that. Do them good."

Constable Roberts didn't agree, but he didn't say anything. The man probably knew nothing about the center. Like most of us, he thought. Out of sight, out of mind. He watched Charlie tinker for a moment—the man seemed to have no idea what he was doing—and left.

Outside, he stopped at the rosebush. Yes, it was dying.

DRIVING OUT OF TOWN, THE CONSTABLE REMEMBERED A CASE HE'D had years before. He had gotten a call about a bad smell coming from a trailer out in the woods. Arriving, he had found a disinterested father, drinking beer on the couch. The living room was filled with dirty children's toys. The constable had stepped into the backyard, which was overrun with weeds and thigh-high brush. He had caught the smell then, with a windblown slap.

In the middle of the yard was an old well. He had leaned over and—

The constable didn't like to think of it. He had arrested the man, who had blinked blearily. It had been a full week. That's what bothered the constable then and now. A whole week, and the man had never even noticed his child was gone.

That's what Dennis made him think about.

The child had tried climbing out, you see. He had been trying when he died.

17

"I'D LIKE TO TAKE MORE TIME OFF," AMANDA TOLD HER BOSS.

He was a tall, gentle man who drove a Volvo covered with old punk rock stickers. He was currently wearing a threadbare shirt that said *Alice Donut,* and when he invited her into his office, he offered her a gumball from the machine in the corner.

Like most zoo people, he was a misfit, and so Amanda felt she fit in—as much as she ever did anywhere.

"Well, you've certainly earned it," he said, opening up her employee file on his computer screen.

"Can I get a few weeks? It's not summer yet."

Summer was their busiest time. No one left in summer.

"Sure. Right now?"

"I already talked to Sean. He said he could cover."

"Is there a problem here? If there is, we want to work it out." He looked positively distressed at the idea there might be a problem.

"No problem here."

"You know Molly like no other. You are important to Molly, and to us. I hope you know that."

His words warmed Amanda. For most of her life, praise had been scant, and criticism plenty.

"I'm trying to figure out how to help her."

"Any ideas you get, bring them to me."

"When can I leave?"

"Sooner the better, before summer season. Do you want me to ask why, or let well enough alone?"

That was a really nice way to put it, Amanda thought.

"It's personal."

"If you need any support or assistance, we're here for you."

"I feel bad leaving Molly."

"I used to feel that way, in my first job. I worked with primates in a filthy zoo in France. Now, *that* was a hard job."

Amanda pulled out her phone. She started using her finger to count weeks in the calendar app. Her boss watched her for a moment. He turned to his computer, printed out a form, then signed it. He circled a date at the bottom.

"Call me by this date."

"Okay. Thank you."

"Send us videos of you. Molly might like that."

"That's a great idea," Amanda said.

THE NEXT MORNING, AMANDA WAS BACK DOWN AT THE COAST, her backpack at her feet, checking in at the hotel. The parking lot was lined with empty planters, she noticed, and the vacancy sign was always on.

"I gave you the same room," Charlie said.

"Am I the only one here again?" Amanda asked.

"Not this time. Got a couple, traveling down the coast. He's a photographer. They're from Portland too. Maybe you can talk to them." He said it like everyone from the city knew each other.

She wondered if she had packed enough. She decided if everything got dirty, she could go to the laundromat in Wheel Stone. Maybe she could watch someone else use the machines first.

"Want to use the same bank card?" he asked.

"How much will it be?"

"Don't you worry. I'm giving you the discount. Don't want that old man down here, chewing me out. Might have to shoot me."

"Larry wouldn't shoot anyone. I don't think he even has a gun anymore."

"You look like your brother, you know."

Amanda was shocked. "How do you know what Dennis looked like?"

He looked abashed. "Sorry, I was cleaning your room last time—went in to collect the dirty towels, like I told you—when I saw the picture on the desk. I know you're trying to learn about your brother, and that boy looked just like you."

He said this like he wanted her to be impressed with how smart he was to figure it out.

"Did you have this hotel when my brother died?" she asked.

"Sure enough. Bought it a few years before that, with help from a friend."

"You didn't see Dennis . . . that day?"

"Nope. Too far down the beach, and hidden by the dunes. They change shape, you know. The dunes."

"How so?" Amanda looked out the window.

"Sometimes, like now, they're low. Then you look out your window the next morning, and they've grown. Some years, they're hard to climb. Others, you can practically walk to the beach without lifting your legs."

He had dark brown eyes and a narrow, sun-speckled skull. She was curious about him.

"Have you lived here all this time?"

"Got a room behind the office. Do all my own repairs."

"Are you ever lonely?"

"Why should I be?" He grinned. "I got my hotel. I like to watch the ocean. It's surprising what you see, if you look long enough."

"What do you see?"

"All sorts of things, miss."

He stopped smiling. He was looking intently at her.

Amanda took her room key.

"Enjoy your stay."

LARRY MADE FRENCH TOAST, WITH THE THICKLY CUT HOME-CURED bacon Gertrude sold at the market. It was peppery and delicious. Amanda demolished hers but didn't eat the end pieces. Larry had noticed she didn't finish the ends of anything. Her plates were always littered with corners and triangles.

"That was delicious," she said. "Thank you."

"Now," he said, picking up his notepad. "I thought we could make a list. What do we know and what do we need to learn?"

"Ralph's last name," she said.

"Good idea. He would know about the runaways too."

He wrote, *Find Ralph.*

"Dennis might have had friends. Maybe we can find another boy who was at the center?" Amanda asked.

"That might be hard," he said. "Because of the laws."

He wrote it anyway. *Friends.*

"What about other people who worked there? Not just the cook."

Other staff, he wrote.

He thought of Martha King. "You ever hear from that director?"

"No. Nothing."

He wrote, *Martha King.*

They finished their coffee, and Larry tidied up, with her help. He watched as she loaded his dishwasher, slowly, as if afraid to mess it up.

THE PUBLISHER OF THE *COASTAL HERALD* WAS BEHIND HIS COUNTER, laying out the next edition on a white drafting table. Larry stopped to watch, fascinated. Dwight Bowman was doing it old-school, with grids for the articles. Each one was set carefully into place.

"Mr. Palmer," he said, without looking up.

"You remember my name," Larry said.

"Looked you up, after you left. You earned a few medals in your time."

"Really?" Amanda turned to look at him.

Larry changed the subject.

"We were wondering if you keep old telephone directories. Like from twenty years ago."

"Sure. They help in a pinch when you're writing obits—you can look back and find old neighbors to interview."

"Can we get the ones for a few years before Dennis Owen died?"

"Give me a sec." He meticulously lined up a column called Recipes from the Shore and then wiped his hands on a grayed towel. "Be right back."

In a few minutes, he returned carrying a small stack.

"Mind if I ask who you're looking for?"

"That custodian who went in after Dennis," Larry said, dividing the stack between him and Amanda. "The cook said his name was Ralph. We figured there can only have been so many Ralphs who lived down here back then."

"You'd be surprised."

"Got a place for us to look at these?"

"Wish you would have asked before. You can use the reading room. It's where they came from."

AMANDA AND LARRY SAT AT A LONG WOODEN TABLE SMEARED WITH dust. The shelves of the cold room were lined with old telephone directories, law books, ancient copies of *The Associated Press Stylebook*, and stacks of coastal tide tables.

Larry thumbed past ads for fishing guides and a crab shack up the road, and a man selling homemade razor clam shovels. He found the residential listings and began to read, amused. Whoever wrote the listings—maybe Dwight himself, bored—had added whatever the locals desired, whether it was their title, age, or occupation. One woman had listed herself as "homemaker extraordinaire."

Amanda read next to him, turning the pages.

"Here's a Ralph," Larry said. "Hold on. His occupation is student. Never mind."

He kept thumbing. Amanda read silently.

"Here's one. Ralph Higgins," she said.

She spun the directory around, showing him. There was an address listed, but no phone number. Larry checked his cell service and looked the place up. The map led to a remote-looking cliff off the highway.

"Want to go see?" he asked.

DWIGHT WAS STILL LAYING OUT HIS NEWSPAPER. HE FIDDLED WITH an edge. There was a large blank space, Larry noticed, on the front page.

"Hey, hold on," Dwight said, calling to Amanda. "I was wondering, since you're trying to learn more about your brother, maybe I could write a story about it? Like, 'Woman Looking for Information on Long-Lost Brother.' Might be a nice little human-interest story, and people could come out of the woodwork for you."

"Looks like you're saving a spot for it," Larry said, pointing.

"I was going to put a wire story there. Slow news week, and I'm tired of writing about storms. When I saw you two walking in, I thought, Hey, there's a story there."

Amanda looked at Larry.

"What do you think?" she asked.

"Let's talk about it."

"Let me know as soon as you can," Dwight said. "I go to press tonight."

THE OLD TRAILER AT THE TOP OF THE CLIFF HAD BEEN ABANDONED years before. The roof was starting to fall in, and the furniture inside had been soaked with sea mist. A heavy, almost physical smell of mold hung in the air.

"He must have left when the cook said," Larry said as they inspected the place. He used a stick to pick up a mildewed shirt.

Amanda noted the couch, with ticking stolen by birds, and a nail on the wall where a painting had hung. That painting, of a serene tropical beach, was now on the floor, bleached with time.

"He didn't take anything," she said.

"This is what we call a skedaddle, in my business," Larry said. He opened a desk drawer. It was empty. "Looks like he took his personal effects, though."

Amanda went through drawers too. Any papers left had long since disintegrated or been chewed by mice. She picked up a Bible, then dropped it when she saw it was full of beetles. Larry smiled at her. A lot of people would have shrieked, but Amanda seemed remarkably unflappable.

"At least we have his last name," she said.

"That we do."

Larry stepped outside and held his phone up to check the service. Then he called the local post office and asked if there was any forwarding address. Far too long had passed, as he had guessed.

He hesitated, then pulled up a contact.

"Hey. Larry Palmer here. Yeah. Doing all right. You? Okay. I was hoping you could run a name for me. Ralph Higgins. Someplace in his fifties now. Lived on the Oregon Coast. I got an old address, for a trailer."

Amanda stepped next to him, looking over the sea.

Larry listened. "Thanks," he said. "Yeah. I'll be in touch."

"That was a former colleague of mine," he said to Amanda after hanging up.

"Did they find anything?"

"Nope. This was Ralph's last known address. No death listing either."

"What does that mean?"

"He could have died in the woods someplace. Or got buried in a pauper's grave. It happens. There's a lot of unidentified dead in this country. It's also possible he went off the grid, or is homeless. My friend is going to keep checking to see if he turns up. I'll do some research too."

The waves smashed below them. Amanda breathed deeply.

"What do you think about the article idea, Larry?"

"It's up to you. I don't think it will hurt. It might even help, like he says. Flush out people who knew Dennis, or the center. But it's up to you whether you want your business out there like that."

"Would you be in it with me?"

"Ugh. I hate myself in pictures. I look like a gnome."

LATE THAT NIGHT, A MAN STOOD ON A STREET IN WHEEL STONE. HE was wearing a heavy jacket and a hat pulled down over his face, but no one would have seen him anyway. It was raining, and it was dark, and the fog was back, threatening beyond the rim of sea.

He was reading a fresh copy of the paper under a weak streetlight.

"Portland Woman Looking for Information on Long-Lost Brother."

He read, knots forming in his stomach. "Amanda Dufresne came to the coast to say goodbye to her brother, Dennis Owen. But questions about his life have brought her back, in the hopes someone will remember the boy. Dennis Owen lived at the Brightwood center . . ."

There was a picture of Amanda, taken hastily outside the newspaper office. She was standing against the dirty white wall, her blond hair blowing in the wind. She looked very pretty, he thought. She had her hands bunched in her pockets. Larry was standing nearby, looking like a grizzled little bear.

"Anyone who knew Dennis, or has information about the center, is asked to contact Amanda. You can reach her by email at . . ."

He crushed the wet paper in his hand, then smoothed it out. He rolled it into a tube, and shoved the tube into the nearest trash can. Behind steamed windows, the town of Wheel Stone slept. He walked quickly up the street. A hot coal of anger burned inside him.

18

"WHAT DO YOU WANT FROM ME?" DENNIS SCREAMED FROM INSIDE the rug. The sharp, spiky wool fibers were embedded deep in his lungs. They felt like shards of glass. He had been fighting for hours. Bit by bit, layer by layer, Martha was excavating him, finding terror where none had existed before.

His shirt was soaked in sweat. More sweat ran into his eyes. His skin radiated the caramelized smell of fear. His eyes were dilated, and his breath was ragged. Martha King had rolled him tightly inside the rug, and then taped it shut. His shoulders were bruised. He could barely move his fingers. In the pure darkness, he was sure he was being buried alive.

He thought he was dying. He *was* dying. The last resistance inside him melted into pure sorrow, pure terror. He felt the fear puddle at his feet. Everything in his mind was swept away except one last broken desire.

"Save me," he whispered.

"I will save you," Martha said, leaning down.

"Yes, please. Please! Just tell me what to do!"

He no longer sounded like the boy she had met nearly a year before. Martha rejoiced inside to hear this brand-new voice. It was the voice of a little boy starting anew. From here, she could help him.

"Please!" Dennis cried from inside the rug.

"You need to tell me your secret," Martha said, leaning close to the air tunnel she had left in the rug. The smell of her breath traveled to the sweaty, panicked boy. It reassured him. He breathed it in, desperate.

"My secret?" The sweat ran into his eyes in the dark.

"I know you have one. Every child who fights the holding time has a secret, and they keep it close, as a barrier against change. Once you tell me your secret, you will start to heal."

Dennis cried. He knew she was right. He would tell her everything, and start over.

"The rabbit," he wept.

"The rabbit?" Martha remembered the day in the bushes. So that was what the boy kept sneaking out to see. A rabbit.

Instinct told her that could not be all.

"What else, Dennis? Tell me what else you have been hiding."

"Ralph," he sobbed. "I love Ralph."

He felt her hands then, on the rug around him, unrolling him. The fresh air came as a shock to his wet body and compressed lungs. Dennis took a deep breath, and almost fainted. Martha King lifted him into her arms. The flesh that had once repelled him now felt welcoming. He even liked her smell. She rocked him. Dennis melted into her arms, and when she offered him the bottle, this time he accepted it. She looked into his eyes as he fed, pleased by what she saw: pure emptiness.

She could fill this vessel. New parents could fill it too. There would be no more fighting, no more resistance. Once she got rid of all his false loves, Dennis could begin again.

"A rabbit," she said, shaking her head.

She leaned forward, her voice caressing him.

"Where is this rabbit, Dennis?"

DENNIS SAT AT A TABLE, EATING. HE HELD THE FORK LIKE A ROBOT. Reggie sat next to him. There was a hole in his ear where his earring had been. Martha had made him flush it down the toilet. Afterward, Ike Tressler had taken him to the gymnasium to practice wrestling.

Martha came into the dining room and walked among the tables. She was pleased to see the quiet faces. She stopped to touch the cheek of one little boy, who simpered at her. She smiled at the staff member in the corner taking notes.

Martha came up behind Dennis and Reggie. They could hear her rubber-soled shoes on the floor. Dennis stared straight ahead. She put her hand on his shoulder.

"You are doing so well," she said. "Maybe soon you will be ready for a new family."

"I DON'T WANT A NEW FAMILY," DENNIS SAID TO RALPH.

The custodian had found him sitting on the back steps. The cook had left the door open to air out the kitchen from a particularly redolent pot of corned beef and cabbage she was cooking. The custodian stood behind Dennis. For the moment, he thought, they were safe. Martha was in the holding time room with another boy.

Ralph spoke quietly.

"You have to go, if she decides to send you away."

Dennis stared at the bush, as if he wished the rabbit would materialize right then and there. But he knew she would not.

"Can you talk to her?" Dennis asked.

"I don't think that will do any good."

Dennis put his head in his arms. "I don't want to leave you."

"It's for the best if you leave. Maybe you'll get a good family. Maybe they'll understand you."

All Dennis heard was maybe, maybe. More likely he would be sent

to strangers who would want what he could not give, and he would be
away from Ralph and the rabbit, and he would never see them again for
the rest of his life. As much as he hated holding time, he didn't want to
go to a new home. He wanted what he could not have: to be left alone
with Ralph, the way it had been before. That was as good as his life had
ever been.

"They won't like me. I bite myself."

Dennis showed him the fresh marks on his arms.

"I'll never love new parents," Dennis said. "It's too late."

"Don't say that," the custodian said, but he knew the boy was telling
the truth. The only kind of family for a kid like Dennis was one with
a great deal of understanding, and Ralph didn't think homes like that
existed. When Martha said she wanted to find Dennis a new home, it
would probably be like the one Ralph had been sent to. A place with
someone looking for free labor or for kids to abuse. There were foster
families out there that made Martha look like a treat.

"I hate her," Dennis said. "She thinks she took everything from me,
but I still have my hate."

In the shadows of the hall behind them, Martha King listened quietly. She turned and left, swiftly. The cook, clanging pots and pans in
her kitchen, did not see her go.

"DIG THERE."

Dennis woke from sleep, hearing the words outside. He jumped out
of his bed and ran to the window. Below him, in the hazy first light of
an early spring morning, was Martha.

Next to her was Ike Tressler. He was holding a shovel.

Hurrying into his shoes, Dennis ran down the stairs and out the
open back door. Martha smiled to see him coming.

"What are you doing?" Dennis whispered.

"Shears," she said, and Ike set down the shovel and picked up a pair of shears. Martha had told him they needed to get rid of a rabbit living behind the kitchen. Rabbits were vectors of disease, she had said. They carried ticks. Ike didn't know if this was true, but he didn't care either.

"Cut down that shrub," she said.

"No," Dennis whispered.

Ike began to cut down the bush. He started at the branches, which fell away. Dennis felt rooted to his spot. Martha kept smiling at him.

The pruning left a splintery, awful-looking trunk. Now the hole underneath was open to the world.

"That's where the rabbit lives," Martha said.

"I'll do anything you want," Dennis begged.

"It's time to give up things that do not serve you, Dennis."

"I won't look at her anymore, ma'am—"

"When you are free from this unhealthy attachment, you will be free to love new parents."

"You don't need to hurt her. *Please.*"

"You are still holding on."

Ike began digging. Sandy soil erupted from the hole. It was cold with spring, and the soil rang against the shovel.

"Ralph!" Dennis suddenly screamed. He looked around, panicked. "Ralph! Ralph!"

"You'll have to give up your unhealthy attachment to him, as well," Martha said.

"Keep digging," she ordered Ike, who had stopped, confused.

As Ike resumed digging, Dennis ran up to him and tried to pull the shovel out of his hands. Martha made a signal, and a staff member who had come outside held the boy. He wrapped his strong arms around Dennis. The boy kicked and screamed and twisted.

"Should I take him inside, ma'am?"

"He needs to watch. This is part of letting go."

Above them, a circle of eyes appeared. The boys had been awakened by the screaming, and watched out their windows.

Ike reached the den. It wasn't deep. He knelt down, peering into the hole.

"I see it!" he called out, excited.

Dennis fought against the arms holding him.

Ike reached inside the hole. He recoiled, yelling.

"The motherfucker bit me!" He grabbed his shovel and went after the rabbit, digging ruthlessly at her, then using it to whack down inside the growing muddy pit. Dennis struggled, screaming over and over again.

"Got it," Ike said, hauling a limp, muddy body from the den. The dead rabbit looked very small.

Dennis broke away and ran to her.

Martha watched. Now Dennis could leave his false attachments behind and find real love within a family, at the knee of a strict but loving father, just as she had.

Dennis had never expected to hold the rabbit. She was as light as air. Tears were running down his cheeks. He felt them drip onto his arms. Ike began to refill the hole. The staff member who had been holding Dennis looked ashamed.

Dennis wanted to run into the woods with Bunny and find a bush that would bring her back to life. But he knew there was no such thing. There was just a dead rabbit in his arms, and Martha, smiling at him.

From out front, there was the sound of tires on the gravel.

"Ralph," Martha said.

The custodian came running. He took in the scene in one glance.

"Clean up this mess," Martha told him.

DENNIS HAD TAKEN TO TWISTING SHEETS INTO ROPES. HE WRAPPED things around his neck: string he found in the kitchen, phone wires he tore from the wall.

Ralph ran to the boy, cutting the wire that was cutting into his throat.

Dennis looked up, his eyes blank.

"It's okay, son," the custodian whispered.

"No, it's not," Martha said.

"Do you need more holding time, Dennis?" she asked.

Martha was puzzled to see the lack of reaction. She wondered if killing the rabbit had been taking it too far, then decided it had been necessary, and this behavior was the last line of defensiveness in the boy. She would push through, to the cure.

Ralph watched helplessly. He held the cut wires in his hand.

"Suicide attempts," Martha said, "are a sign you need more holding time, Dennis. It is apparent you are not ready for a new home. But it's okay. I can keep you as long as we need."

Dennis did not reply. His eyes looked like a dead cow's.

"Put him in an isolation room," Martha told Ralph, then walked away. She was worried. Some of the boys at Axis had become suicidal too. She didn't understand why.

19

THE MORNING THE PAPER CAME OUT, AMANDA WAS OUTSIDE THE
Mystic Sea Aquarium. It was in an old building on the promenade in
Seaside. The clapboard was peeling, and through the front windows,
Amanda could see tanks of seals. Visitors were throwing them pieces
of fish out of tiny paper cups.

Inside, Amanda found a smiling woman behind a turnstile and a
foggy window lined with postcards and bags of marbles. The smell was
very strong and reminded her of the penguin habitat at the zoo.

"Five dollars," the woman said.

"I'm here to see Pete Ashoona," Amanda said.

"I'll call him." The woman turned to a phone beside her. "May I ask
who is here to see him?"

"Amanda Dufresne. I work at the Oregon Zoo. With Molly, the
polar bear."

The woman soon hung up.

"He says to go inside. He'll be right down."

The dark interior was lined with tanks filled with fish. In the middle
of the room there was an exploration tank for children, with sea anemo-
nes and starfish. Another open tank housed a giant octopus. He was
tucked under a red rock with bubbling seawater, looking out malevolently.

"You came to see me?"

Amanda turned to find a large man wearing a faded denim vest over a plaid shirt. He had long gray hair and a broad, sun-stained face. He wore a faded red bandanna knotted around his neck.

"Amanda," she introduced herself. "I work with Molly."

"Long time since I heard that name."

"I was hoping you could help me."

"How so?"

"I'd like to hear what happened."

"Weren't there enough articles?"

"Yes," Amanda said, pausing. "I have a few questions."

"Such as?"

"We know now that polar bear mothers rarely abandon their young," Amanda said. "It only happens when the cub is sick. Molly was not sick."

He didn't answer.

"Plus, Molly was only two months old when she was found. Her mother would not have broken her den for another month, at least. Maybe something happened that got her mother spooked. But I don't see her just leaving her like that."

"Let's go for a walk," he said.

They left the aquarium for the wet, windy beach. The ocean at Seaside was much calmer and flatter than at Eagle Cove but, Amanda imagined, just as cold. The town was bigger than Eagle Cove, but only a few people were out on the sand.

"What made you look for me?" he asked.

"You were the only one who didn't talk to the press."

"You're smart."

"Not really," Amanda said.

"I never wanted to talk about it. We all make mistakes, right? Those men were my friends. Friends stick up for each other. They didn't mean to do anything wrong. I believe that to this day. But they ended up heroes, with funded research positions, and I ended up here, working at a coastal aquarium, writing research reports no one sees."

"Was it like they said?" Amanda asked.

"No, it was not."

"I want to help Molly," Amanda said.

"You think knowing what happened will help her?"

"Yes, I do." She stopped and looked at him. The wind picked up her hair. "Maybe it will give me an insight."

They resumed walking. The town began to fade behind them. Ahead of them was only sand, and then the mountains, jutting into the sea. On the other side of the rugged range was Eagle Cove. This entire land, Amanda thought, could not be tamed.

"Another thing doesn't make sense," Amanda said.

"What's that?"

"The reports said the mother was found dead on the ice. But female polar bears don't den on the ice."

"She could have gone there."

"But why would she? Wouldn't she have returned to her den?"

He kept putting his hands in his pockets as he walked beside her.

"When I got the position at the research station," he said, "I was elated. First Native at the station. I had big dreams. Turned out they wanted an errand boy. My job was transporting them—I have a pilot's license—and picking up their dirty laundry. Literally. You have never met a filthier bunch of men in your life."

"I guess they weren't your friends, after all."

"Maybe not. Maybe not."

A FEW HOURS LATER, AMANDA WAS LEAVING THE AQUARIUM WITH a small stuffed seal in one hand. Pete had given it to her.

They stood by the octopus tank to say goodbye. The octopus, seeing the man he knew, swam out. Pete tinkled the water in greeting.

"Why do you stay here?" Amanda asked.

"Probably the same reason you are at the zoo. You start caring for the animals. Did you know, years ago, some guy broke in here and 'rescued' a captive giant lobster? He ran with the poor fellow to the ocean, fell, and killed him. That lobster would have never survived in the wild. This octopus? Maybe he would. Maybe not. I don't know, and I like living in the unknowingness. It is a comforting place to be. I have a feeling—no, I am certain—that you like the unknowingness too. You are okay not knowing it all."

"I have to be," Amanda said, tinkling the water. The octopus glared at the intrusion.

"He's like your bear. He knows when the people will not return."

"Thank you for helping me."

"I think you're closer to your answer now."

"I am. The question is, can I do it?"

"Good luck, Amanda." He smiled and held out his hand.

She took it. "See you around, Pete."

"WHERE WERE YOU?" LARRY ASKED. HE WAS OUTSIDE THE HOTEL, looking worried.

"I had an errand," Amanda said.

She was aware she sounded terse and softened her reply with a smile.

"We got a lead from that newspaper article," Larry said.

Amanda checked her phone.

"Nobody down here emails anyone. There's a man in the market who wants to talk to us."

THE MAN WAS SITTING ON THE BENCH RESERVED FOR LOCALS, AND Gertrude—her face now visible—was staring from behind her kitchen door. Her daughter just looked intrigued.

The man was wearing what appeared to be three jackets, one on top of the other. Larry could smell him from the door. Larry knew this hot, fecal smell from the streets. It was the smell of a man who had not bathed for weeks and, quite possibly, had a drug or alcohol problem on top of it.

There was dandruff on his once-shaved scalp. His blue eyes were embedded in pouches, and his mean little mouth looked collapsed.

"Ike Tressler," he said.

"You wanted to talk to us?" Larry asked.

"Take him outside," Gertrude said.

THEY STOOD UNDER SOME TREES NEAR THE MARKET. LARRY OF-fered to get the man a cup of coffee, but all he wanted was a bottle of Mad Dog, which Larry wasn't inclined to provide. Ike sat down on a log. He didn't look tired but rather too restless to stand. He had big shoulders and ropy hands.

"I saw the article," he told Amanda. "I knew your brother, at the center. Other boys too. One I remember—Reggie. He was a nice boy. I haven't been the same since the place closed. Tried to get other work, but no one wants me."

Larry looked at him skeptically. He knew men like this. He would ramble on until Larry and Amanda gave him what he wanted, which Larry suspected was more than fortified wine.

"What are you looking for?" Larry asked.

"I don't know. Just wanted to talk. That's what the paper said, right? You're looking for information."

"Right," Amanda said, moving closer. She sat a distance from Ike, on another log. The wind whispered through the trees. Across the dunes, she could see the ocean. It was quieter today. Mist blew in great clouds, and the sun flashed off the water.

"What can you tell me about my brother?" she asked.

"He was okay. I mean, a bit of a brat, to be honest. Wouldn't do his schoolwork, never smiled at anyone. Had to put him in the isolation rooms a lot, at first, to teach him. He never did learn, I guess. He tried to kill himself. You probably knew that."

Amanda looked confused.

"I mean, not just at the end. Before then. I think Martha got tired of the boys here. They weren't like other boys, she told me once. The ones she had before. The ones here were always fighting back." He gave a chuckle, then coughed, spitting into the dirt. Larry looked away. He remained standing, his hands at his sides, a skeptical look on his face.

"Anyway, I was the teacher there, for a time. Then Martha put me in charge of other things. I liked it there. Like I said, I never found other work after that. The fishing boat captains, they didn't like me. Can't say I liked them either."

There was a noise behind them. It was Gertrude, who had left the market. Her legs looked very thin under her flowered dress. She was wearing heavy brogans with a pair of men's socks that were falling down.

"Those are Brett's socks" was the first thing Ike said.

Gertrude looked uncomfortable being outside.

"You knew Brett?" Larry asked.

"We used to drink together at the bar in Wheel Stone. Before they eighty-sixed me and him together. Hey, would you get me some wine, Gertrude? A bottle of Mad Dog. I got money." He reached into one of his filthy jackets, the one closest to his undershirt, and pulled out a handful of dirty bills. Larry noticed they had blood on them. Ike smiled at him. "I hunt for my supper."

"How do you make money?" Larry asked.

"Here and there. Odd jobs. Sometimes I chop firewood. Or I do what Brett used to do and collect the fallen antlers in the woods, saw 'em up, and sell them for a dollar a chunk at the farmer's market in Wheel Stone. You can make forty dollars or more off a single rack."

He held the bills out to Gertrude. She took them, silently, a look of distaste on her face.

"Why did you come out here?" Amanda asked the woman softly. The sun flashed again, and flocks of tiny sandpipers raced across the sand. Suddenly, everything felt too much for her. There was too much going on, and yet nothing much was happening. It was confusing to her. She felt like her mind was tracking a million things at once.

"I remember this fellow, from back in the day," Gertrude said in her husky voice. She used the toe of her brogan to touch the dirty man's leg. "It's true, what he says. He knew my husband. They'd go rousing, sometimes. Asshole, is what he is. And maybe more, from what my husband told me, over the years. Right, Ike?"

He stared at her, his mouth trembling. Then he reached for his bills, trying to grab them back out of her hands. She held them tight. "I'll wash these when I'm done," she called over her shoulder as she walked away. "I'll have your wine coming right up, Ike."

"What was that about?" Amanda asked as they watched her back retreat into the market, the door swinging behind her.

"Yeah, what was that about?" Larry asked, turning to the man.

"Nothing," he said sullenly. He yawned, showing the remains of his teeth. Then he sunk into his three jackets and waited for his wine.

Amanda tried to count the sandpipers on the beach—she was always practicing with numbers—but they were too far away.

"Why did my brother try to kill himself?"

"I think he succeeded."

"I know. How come?"

He shrugged. "They were just kids. Do you think you could spare a few dollars, for the information?"

"I knew it," Larry said.

THAT EVENING, PATTY MET LARRY AND AMANDA IN A SEASIDE restaurant. She was wearing her leather jacket paired with a sparkly purple scarf, and she gave Amanda one of the warmest smiles Amanda had ever seen.

"Larry told me about you," she said.

Amanda took her seat, looking up at the chalkboard menu. She hated chalkboard menus—they dripped all over with curlicues and drawings, confusing the words. Amanda liked her words in a straight line.

"I'm sorry about your brother," Patty said. "We don't talk enough about sibling bonds in our culture. We expect to outlive our parents. It's our brothers and sisters we hope to keep for life."

"Yes," Amanda said. She was glad someone understood.

"Were you in foster care too?" Patty asked.

"I was adopted at birth."

The waitress appeared.

"I'm having the seafood special," Larry said.

"Me too," said Patty.

"I'll have—the ham sandwich," Amanda said, picking something at random and then feeling foolish.

"Coming right up," the waitress said.

"A ham sandwich is a funny thing to order in a seafood place," Larry said.

"Maybe she feels like having a ham sandwich," Patty said, smiling at Amanda. "Men," she whispered. "Always wanting to criticize."

"I found your runaway reports," Patty added, passing a manila envelope across the table to Larry.

"Hey," he said, surprised and pleased. He opened the envelope to see three reports, each stamped *Confidential*.

"If anyone asks, they didn't come from me," Patty said.

Larry passed each one to Amanda after he read it. The reports were short, only a page long each. Each had a name, and a brief description of the boy. All three boys were said to have run away in the middle of the night. Amanda had seen missing pet reports with more information.

Steven Spirit, age thirteen, read the first.

Joey Madrone, age nine.

Angel Lopez, age eleven.

The waitress returned with a pot of coffee and filled their cups.

"How did you find these?" Larry asked Patty.

"A social worker I know. She had kids at the center. These are the internal reports."

"What does this mean?" Amanda asked, pointing to an abbreviation.

Patty leaned over. Amanda could smell the leather of her jacket.

"UTL. Unable to locate," she said. "That means—"

"I know. They couldn't find him."

"About this number at the bottom—" Larry began.

Their food arrived. Amanda regretted ordering the ham sandwich. It looked plain next to the plates of salmon swimming in some sort of herb sauce, with banks of rice alongside.

Amanda lifted the top piece of bread, checking what was inside. She did this quickly, feeling it was impolite. She took a cautious bite.

"I was just going to mention that," Patty said. "I didn't recognize the area code, so I looked up the number. It's for the sheriff in Sleeping Giant, Arizona."

"They called *Arizona?*" Larry asked.

"That's the town where Martha King worked before," Amanda said.

"That's right," Patty said approvingly. "The caseworker said the director told her she had notified law enforcement. That's the number the caseworker was given."

"Let me guess, the caseworker never heard from this sheriff," Larry said.

"Actually, she did. He told her not to worry, he was taking care of it. She filed her reports and moved on. It's all she could do."

Amanda was looking at the dates the boys had run away. She counted on her fingers against her leg, under the table where Larry and Patty wouldn't see.

"Any of these boys ever turn up?" Larry asked, eating his salmon.

"Not that I could find," Patty said.

"I'll look too."

Amanda stopped eating her sandwich. She was still hungry, but if she tried to finish it, she would feel compelled to leave a corner of it behind, and this might draw Larry's attention, which she didn't feel she could handle at the moment. She decided to take the rest back to the hotel and finish it there.

"Where did you go to school, Amanda?" Patty asked.

"Cleveland in Portland."

"Go Warriors." Patty smiled. "No college?"

Amanda turned away. She was not going to say she had graduated with a modified diploma. You can't attend a university with one of those.

"Larry told me you work at the zoo. You're the lead keeper for the polar bear. That's a pretty big achievement for your age."

"Thank you." She had a feeling the woman was testing her. She resented it. She was slow, not stupid.

"The worker who gave me these reports, she remembered your brother."

"Really?" Amanda looked up.

"She told me about a custodian who worked there. Said he wanted to adopt him."

20

RALPH STOPPED THE SOCIAL WORKER OUTSIDE. HE HAD BEEN WAIT-
ing weeks for her to come. The social workers were supposed to visit
their charges once a month—twelve times a year—but Ralph knew with
weather and illness and turnover, it was more like three or four times a
year. Sometimes even less.

"Ma'am," he said.

"Yes?" The woman looked tired. She carried a stack of files, and her
eyes were red from the road.

"Are you the caseworker for Dennis Owen?"

"Dennis?" She checked the files in her hand. "Yes, I am."

"That's what I thought."

She looked ready to move on.

"He's a good boy, ma'am."

"I'll take your word for it. The last time I came, he wouldn't speak
to me."

"You know how it is. The boys stop trusting the system."

"I can't change that."

"I want to talk to you about him."

She took in his battered boots, his dirty jeans. The stubble on his
unshaved chin and the veins in his eyes.

"And you are?"

"I'm the custodian here. But I know the boys, ma'am. Dennis needs help."

"He's in the right place for it, then."

"She— He needs a different kind of help, ma'am."

"Martha King knows what she's doing."

There was a small edge of annoyance in her voice.

"I know that I'm just the custodian here, ma'am. But maybe . . . maybe you could look into what Martha is doing here. The treatment."

The annoyance in her face turned to disbelief.

Ralph stopped. He knew talking to her wouldn't do any good. He had tried talking to his caseworkers as a boy too. They did nothing.

She turned away.

"I want to adopt him," he said.

"You'd like to what?"

"Adopt Dennis. Please."

RALPH SPENT A LOT OF TIME FIXING UP THE TRAILER. HE SCRUBBED the peeling countertops in the kitchen. He hid the worst of the exposed wires. Finally, he sat on the edge of the stained tub and wept.

He went outside when he heard her car.

The social worker had given him a thick stack of home-study forms. He had filled these out to the best of his ability. They hadn't been very good at teaching at Axis, just like they weren't at Brightwood. He had written down his income, and answered the questions about his personal life, even his sex habits—he had none; Martha had ruined that for him. He puzzled over the question about what his parents had done for a living. Ralph didn't want to write down that his dad had gone to prison, so he left that section blank. He left the financial history blank too.

There was one sheet for past addresses. He tried to remember all the places he had lived before coming to Brightwood. He wrote down a few, but when he saw their names, like Camp 12 Berry Plant and Seneca Farms Green Beans Camp, he felt bad.

"Thank you for coming," he told the social worker as she got out of her car.

She looked from the decaying trailer to the unfenced cliffs and unruly ocean below.

"This way," he said, showing her into the trailer. "This will be his room." He'd bought a new bed and a used dresser from the junk shop in Seaside. He had put a stuffed animal on the dresser. Ralph had never had a stuffed animal, and he thought the boy would like one.

She reached for the light switch, and he stopped her.

"Not that one, ma'am. This one."

She turned on the lamp he pointed at, and then looked back at the exposed wires barely concealed by the dresser.

In the living room, she peered around, smiling at the ocean paintings as if she got the joke.

"Dennis can do his homework here," he said, hopeful.

"Where will he go to school?"

"Um, there's got to be a school close by, right?"

"It's all the way in Seaside. The bus doesn't come this far."

"I'd drive him, ma'am."

"You'll be at work when he gets out. Do you have plans for after-school care?"

"I'll get a different job."

She walked through the trailer, making marks on her checklist.

Safe wiring? *No.*

Clean water? She turned on a tap. Rusty water poured out. *Unknown.*

Egress in case of fire? She tried a window. *No.*

Septic system? She walked outside. The trailer appeared to drain into an illegal brown field. *Sanitation does not meet legal requirements.*

Child-safe environment? She looked toward the ocean, where the boy could simply run to the cliffs and fall right over. *No.*

Can adoptive parent meet the therapeutic requirements of the child? In his file, Martha had written that Dennis was not ready for a regular family. He needed more treatment.

No, she wrote.

She tore off the pink copy under the sheet for Ralph, then handed it to him. Her eyes were kind.

"I'm sorry," she said.

HE FOLLOWED HER TO HER CAR.

The wind from the ocean lifted her hair as she opened the car door. He held the forms out to her, like an offering.

"We have to have standards," she said.

Ralph didn't know whether to laugh or scream at that. Instead, he let the papers go. The ocean wind took them and blew them into the woods.

IT WAS VERY LATE, AND MARTHA WAS LOCKING THE FRONT DOOR behind her. Her head was swimming with tiredness. She was looking forward to a hot bath and the soft bed in her house up the coast.

When she was younger, she could pull twelve-hour days. She had run off pure excitement, the full-steam-ahead feeling of knowing she was at the cutting edge of a brand-new treatment destined to save lives. She had felt satisfaction, as if she were fixing some great wrong that had been done.

Now such long days exhausted her. Her knees hurt, just from kneel-ing beside boy after boy. Maybe she needed to put down more rugs. But she knew it wasn't just that. It was the mind ache of so many children. Their distressed cries filled her ears, and sometimes she had a hard time keeping their names straight.

She made it to her car, then turned around. This was not her car. It was the night watchman's car. It looked nothing like her car.

Funny. How tired she was. The boys were strong. Maybe it was the salt air, or all the good food. They fought. You wouldn't think they would be so strong, but they were. They were like wire.

Shaking her head at herself, swinging it wildly in the cold night air to wake herself up, she found the right car. She drove slowly down the dark mountain road, the car's headlights piercing the darkness.

All the way home, she kept thinking she had forgotten something.

IN THE STILL OF THE NIGHT, A BOY NAMED STEVEN LAY WRAPPED in a rug. He had been left there, in the soundproof room. Martha had said she was going for a break and would be back—maybe by then he would be willing to let go of the sickness inside him.

He had long since wet himself. The cold, wet rug was wrapped very tightly around him. Martha had taped it shut with long pieces of strong tape. Sometimes, when he was most resistant, she taped the ends shut too. Then all was darkness. Like in the womb, Martha said. But for Steven, thirteen years old and diagnosed with reactive attachment disorder as well as homosexuality, the howling darkness was more like being trapped inside a narrow pipe. He could not wiggle free. He struggled to breathe. It had been hours, he thought. His ribs hurt. His lungs ached.

Weakly, he began to fight back again, inside the thick wool.

The hours passed. Back in her rental home, Martha slept like a child, with her hands folded between her soft thighs. It was funny, she was thinking in her sleep, how she didn't even like the top sheet tucked in. Martha King hated to be restrained. She hated the feeling of anyone on top of her. Which was odd, she thought as she spiraled deeper into sleep; the part of therapy she liked the most was when she lay on top of the boys and pressed, to let them know adults were always in charge.

Steven breathed shallowly. The air inside him had grown very warm. Stars danced in his eyes. Little by little, he felt his body grow cold. It started with his feet, narrow and bony in the rug. His hands, trapped next to his sides, went next. The coldness crept up until it encased his heart. He struggled harder, then, as if he knew what was coming. In his fevered coldness, shot through with silver and pain and darkness, he was trying mightily to escape a monster, and the monster was coming for him. His heart expanded in terror. He could not run. He could not hide. He was darting through the woods. He was stuffed under a culvert, and, dear God, he was being buried alive. The dirt was falling on him. He was everything and nothing all at once.

His heart, unable to bear the strain, stopped. His final breath, a tiny little squeak, escaped.

At that very moment, warm in her own bed in her nice home, Martha awoke with a start.

She was suddenly quite sure of what she had forgotten.

21

"NO SIGN OF THOSE RUNAWAYS," LARRY SAID, LOOKING UP FROM HIS computer. He was sitting at his kitchen table after supper the following day, while Amanda rested in front of the fire. She looked tired. She opened one eye.

"I looked too," she said.

"Ditto Ralph Higgins. My friend in the bureau hasn't found any sign of him."

Amanda was drowsing, thinking of bears, ice, and dens. She wished her brother had known a safe place. He wouldn't have gone in the ocean then.

"What do you think happened to them, Larry?"

"The boys? They could have gotten lost in the woods. It happens."

It sounded like he didn't believe it.

"Or?" She was staring into the flames.

"What Patty told me, about the unmissing, got me thinking. Someone could kidnap or murder kids from foster care and no one would be the wiser."

"Why would they do that?"

"Lots of reasons," Larry said, thinking of them.

Larry looked at the list they had made. It had grown, with scribbled notes in the margins. He saw the note *Friends*.

"That guy, Ike Tressler, outside the store. He mentioned a kid named Reggie."

"You're right. He did." Amanda sat up now, awake. The image of her brother in a warm bear den disappeared.

"Reggie is usually short for Reginald, and that's not the most common name. Maybe Patty can run it for us, in her system. How many boys named Reginald could there have been at Brightwood at the same time as Dennis?"

"Good idea. She can try plain old Reggie too."

He picked up his phone, made the call. From her place in front of the fire, Amanda watched him. She was growing fond of Larry. It made her feel guilty because while she loved her parents intensely, she didn't feel at ease with them like she did with Larry. They had always been her helpers. She had always felt they wanted her to be different.

It started to rain, hard. Amanda realized she should get back to the hotel before it got worse. She got up, stretching.

"Reggie Dupree," Larry said, hanging up and writing down the name. "He was there with Dennis."

"Can you find out where he is now?" Amanda asked, zipping up her parka. Larry looked out at the rain. "You're going out in that?"

"It's only going to get worse. Gertrude said another storm was coming in."

"You walking?" he asked, looking at his computer.

"Yeah. My car is at the hotel."

"Want a lift?"

"No, I'll be fine. I like walking."

"All right," he said, looking up Reggie's current address.

She left, the door swinging behind her.

AMANDA WALKED BACK TO THE HOTEL, HER SHOES SQUISHING IN the rain. She was glad she had packed another pair. She would dry these out by the baseboard heater in her room. It smelled like an electrical fire when she turned it on.

She was glad she'd left Larry's when she had. A strong wind was picking up, rattling the windows on the empty cabins and shaking the power lines. It reminded her of the storm her first day here. She could hear the whining power of the wind. It whistled as it came off the ocean, blasting up the dune road.

She strode down the steep hill, taking care on the wet pavement, and turned down the beach road. The howling wind blew the rain against her face. She sunk her head deeper into the hood of her jacket. Her face was so wet, she could barely see. She opened her mouth, tasted the rain. It tasted like salt, and life.

There was someone behind her.

She felt it suddenly, with a strange fever that rushed through her body—she whirled around, aware he was there.

The man was buried in a thick jacket. His hood was pulled all the way up, and he had wrapped something—a dark, wet bandanna, maybe—around his face to hide his features. Rain dripped off his arms. In one hand, Amanda took in with a shudder, he held a dark metal object that glinted under the rain.

A knife.

Amanda turned and ran. She felt the road under her feet and the slash of rain against her face, was conscious of her lungs burning in the salt air with her panicked intake of breath. She could feel him behind her, running, too, trying to catch her.

She knew if she went into the woods, all would be lost—she could feel intuitively that this man knew the woods. If she stayed on the road, he would catch her too. He would kill her and dispose of her body in the waves or over a cliff or in the woods. There were a dozen places to dispose of someone here. Wasn't that what she and Larry had just been talking about?

Amanda was glad for her strong legs, for her healthy heart and young lungs conditioned by hard work shoveling shit and working with the polar bear. She sprinted hard, then took a sudden sharp turn across the road and began barreling over the wet dunes, directly toward the sea. She could feel him pause behind her, and then follow.

They were going to play chicken.

THE MAN CHASED AMANDA. HE HAD THOUGHT HE COULD SURPRISE her—he had been right behind her, knife at the ready, when she had sensed him and turned around. She had an awareness, he thought, learned from working with the great bear.

Now she was running, flat out over the low dunes, stumbling and then righting herself. She found the packed sand and charged toward the sea. For a moment, he was flummoxed. Was she trying to kill herself, as her brother had done? She wouldn't be able to see the waves in the dark. She might plunge right in.

No, he realized. She was daring him to follow her, and take the risk.

He did. He chased after her, across the damp sand. The sound of the waves ahead of them was very loud, crashing in the dark. He could sense them more than see the ocean, a glimmer of liquid that spoke a volume deeper than time. Amanda angled down toward the surf and then ran beside it, the waves high above her, crashing into the sand. At any moment, a wave might sweep over them and take them into the sea.

He ran behind her. She was daring him, and daring the sea. His lungs ached. He was not in the same shape he had been twenty years before, when Martha King first called him from Brightwood in the deep of the night, and he remembered picking up the phone, saying, "Yes?"

For you, I will always say yes.

The shape ahead of him was growing distant. Amanda was getting away. He could not see in the dark and was afraid of the sneaker waves. The sound of the ocean was distracting him. A huge wave suddenly crashed over the sand, flooding his boots, and he found himself running away from the sea as much as following her.

Ahead, in the slashing rain, her back disappeared, and only the ocean was left, roaring at him and sending fingers of doom searching for him.

AMANDA MADE IT TO THE HOTEL, PANTING AND SOAKING WET. HER shoes were like clumps of sand. Rivulets ran from them as she ran across the parking lot to her room and, with shaking hands, unlocked her door.

She slammed it shut behind her, trembling.

She looked out the window. She saw nothing, besides rain blowing across the nearly empty lot. The only cars parked were hers and Charlie's truck. The front office was dark, all the lights off. She peered farther into town. Everything looked dark.

She scrambled for her phone, wet in her pocket. The service was out. The hotel phone was out too. She didn't want to chance going outside for help. The man could be there, waiting with his knife. Shaking, she dragged a chair under the doorknob. She had seen it done on television. Then she went and sat on the floor, against the bed. She held the phone in her hand, praying for service.

Morning did not come for a very long time.

"MORNING, MISS."

It was Charlie, outside her door. "Lost power last night. You okay?"

Amanda peered outside. The day seemed unnaturally bright. She checked her phone. It was back on. She shut the door without answering and called Larry.

"Larry, I'm scared," she said.

22

MARTHA WENT RUNNING FROM HER CAR. SHE WAS FUMBLING THE keys in her panic. The building rose above her. The night watchman had gotten up for his rounds, then fallen back to sleep at his desk, snoring with his chin on his chest. There was a circle of damp on his blue shirt.

She let herself in quietly, fear coursing through her. She made her way quickly down the treatment ward. Halfway there, she saw she had put on old sneakers. *You know why*, a voice whispered to her.

"Please, God, make it not true," she whispered to herself, stealing down the dark hall, with its closed, empty isolation rooms. "Please. I will give you anything if he is okay. Please, God," she prayed like a child.

She unlocked the therapy room door, slammed on the lights. A single bulb in a wire cage illuminated the room.

The rug was still rolled up on the floor. It was clear from the shape what was inside it.

Please, God, let him still be alive.

Martha King fell to her knees. She put her hands on the cold, rough fabric of the rug. For some reason, for the first time, she noticed the sticker on the underside. It said *Waterproof weave*. She had ordered this rug because it looked tough. Her mind was full of jumbled maudlin thoughts.

She tugged at the ends of the tape and peeled him open, as if he were a rotting grape. He had thin hair for a child. His eyes were closed. There was a purple rim around his mouth, and a glaze of vomit.

She knew exactly what the medical examiner would say.

Death by asphyxiation. Death by terror.

Murder.

There was a small chance they might say it was an accident. But not if the authorities went digging into the Axis Treatment Center, and what had happened there. It would be the end of her career, the end to her life, and, more important, the end to a groundbreaking therapeutic method.

Martha touched the dead boy. Gently, she pulled him out of the rug, and she held him in her lap—she was still wearing her overcoat—and rocked him against her ample chest. She held him with tenderness and with love, because in her mind, it was all just a mistake. A big, terrible, awful, never-to-be-repeated mistake. The poor boy had been left alone.

He still deserved therapy. He still needed holding time.

Martha held him, rocking him, weeping a little, and eventually her tears ceased, and she started to think of what she needed to do, to protect herself and her future patients.

LATER, WHILE THE NIGHT WATCHMAN STILL SNORED AT HIS DESK, a lone figure stole from the back of the center. He wore a hat, and a thick coat with the collar turned up. Over his shoulder he had slung a form wrapped in a sheet. In the other hand he held a shovel.

The figure slipped into the woods. He carried the shape into the mountains, the pale moon a sliver that turned the lichen-covered trees to ice. Eventually, he figured he was far enough away. He began to dig under a tree, noticing how easily the sandy soil loosened and fell away.

When the grave was deep enough, he pushed the body in. There was no prayer. The dead are dead; only the living have hope.

BRETT JARVIS WAS HAVING A BAD NIGHT.

He had been kicked out of the bar in Wheel Stone and had somehow driven back to the beach at Eagle Cove, though he couldn't remember doing so. When he came to, he was sitting on a log on the beach, listening to the ocean howl in the dark. He was dressed warmly, in an oilcloth jacket and worn boots, but all he felt was the rush of cold blood inside his heart.

He looked at the bottle in his hand. It was empty.

He tossed it away.

Getting up, he stumbled down the beach.

HOURS LATER—HE HAD NO IDEA HOW MANY—BRETT FOUND HIMself deep in the woods. He wasn't lost, though. Brett Jarvis had grown up in the woods; his dad had been a hunting guide, and Brett knew the mountains like the back of his hand. He didn't even need a compass. He could orient himself by the direction of the salt wind.

The trees were dark around him.

I've been in a blackout, he thought. Oh well. He had been in worse ones. Once, four days had passed and he'd woken up in Astoria, vomiting on the boardwalk near a bull sea lion who had been watching him with curious interest.

Chuckling to himself, sick with fear at what he had become, Brett tasted the salt wind and righted himself toward the sea. If he kept walking—or crawling, if need be—he'd eventually reach the ocean. Then he could figure out exactly where he was, and head home. He didn't want to spend the night in the woods. It was cold, and wet, and the sand fleas were bad this year.

BRETT WAS CRAWLING, LABORIOUSLY, OVER A ROTTED LOG WHEN he heard the noise.

Brett knew all about forest noises at night. There were the calls of owls, and the soft rumple of voles under the soil. Deer and elk moved in the brush, mountain lions chirped, and the rare wolves howled. There was the distant sound of the ocean, and the feeling of the underground streams, rushing under the rocky mountains into the sea.

Even utterly trashed, Brett Jarvis knew the difference between a forest sound and a human one.

This was a human sound.

Someone was in the brush, a dozen or so yards ahead of him.

He slowed, peering intently into the dark trees. Suddenly, he realized he wasn't far from Brightwood. That place gave him the creeps. When he was a child, his mother's favorite threat was that she'd give Brett away. She never did, but he had lived in fear he might wind up in a place like Brightwood, where boys never got to go hunting or fishing or even just sit on a piece of driftwood.

Ahead of him, illuminated in the pale moonlight, there was a creature walking through the woods. The forest shadows made it seem ten feet tall. The creature was carrying what looked like a body wrapped in a shroud. At the end of its long arm was a shovel.

Brett stopped, frozen.

The creature did not see him. It kept moving, through the woods, carrying the body.

CONSTABLE ROBERTS LOOKED ACROSS HIS DESK. BRETT JARVIS, smelling like a rat had died inside his mouth and been left to rot there for a few weeks, was nearly collapsed across his desk. His eyes were bright red from burst blood vessels.

"You gotta do something," Brett muttered.

"Sasquatch doesn't exist, Brett."

"Yeah, but I saw him."

Constable Roberts wasn't going to argue with a drunk.

"Okay. You saw Sasquatch."

"He's stealing boys from that place."

"Brightwood?"

"Yeah. He had a shovel. He was going to bury him."

Since when does Sasquatch bury his victims? Constable Roberts wanted to ask the man. But he knew better.

"I've had no reports of any missing kids from Brightwood."

"It just happened. Last night."

"Fine. I'll call them. Do you want me to call your wife?"

"Naw. That bitch doesn't want me."

"Can't say I blame her," the constable said.

"You're a fucked-up asshole, Constable Roberts. Think you're so high-and-mighty—"

"All right. I think we're done here. Now, you want to sleep it off in my cell? Or do you want me to take you to the hospital? You look like you need a dry-out, Brett."

"Fuck you and the horse you rode in on."

Constable Roberts felt bad. Brett Jarvis was a loser and a fuckup, but everyone hoped he would get sober, because on the rare occasions he did, he was a tender and sensitive man. It was that man, Constable Roberts suspected, that Gertrude still hoped would return. He couldn't blame her. It was a blessing they didn't have kids, because Brett would make a lousy father.

"Yeah. Fuck you," Brett reiterated as he stumbled out into a misty cold day.

The constable followed him.

"At least let me give you a ride home," the constable said. He didn't want Brett behind the wheel of his car. He also didn't feel like wrestling the man down. Brett could be a scrapper. The constable had ended up bruised more than once in their encounters.

"Naw," Brett said, crawling into the back seat of his car. "I'll just take a nap here."

"Give me your keys, Brett."

The man handed them over.

"I'll give them back later," the constable said. "When you feel a bit better."

"Fuck you," Brett said again, in case he had forgotten to say it before.

23

CONSTABLE ROBERTS THOUGHT OF THAT LONG-AGO ENCOUNTER now, as he sat across from Amanda in her hotel room. It had taken over an hour for him to arrive, because of fallen trees from the storm.

Amanda sat on the bed, her blue eyes like steel, her hair at her shoulders. Larry stood next to her, looking like a pissed-off bulldog.

"What did he look like?" the constable asked.

Outside, Charlie was picking up branches that had blown into the parking lot, and Aspire was standing down the street with Gertrude, talking about what had happened to Amanda. By now, everyone knew—and Larry wasn't even sure how.

"I couldn't see his face," Amanda said.

She held her own face in her hands, as if she were going to cry. But when she looked up, her eyes were dry. Amanda had cried a lot as a child. The years of feeling like an outcast, forever standing outside special-education classrooms while the kids who attended regular classes passed her by, had made her tearless. And tough.

"It's all right," Constable Roberts said soothingly. "You say you had left Larry's cabin. Who knew you were there?"

Amanda thought carefully.

"I guess anyone could have seen me walking there. I went down the beach road and then up the hill. I came back the same way."

The constable thought of the woods. The cemetery. There were a dozen places for someone to hide and watch.

"I'll get right on it. Though I'm not sure where to start. Do you feel safe here?"

"Charlie told me he can put another dead bolt on the door."

"I'd feel better if you stayed with me," Larry said. "Unless you want to go back home. It's okay if you do."

"I thought we were going to Portland, to find Reggie."

The constable wondered whom they were talking about. He was sure it had to do with Brightwood, but he didn't want to ask.

"We are, if you're up to it. I can drive."

"What about my car?"

"We'll leave it here. Later, if you decide you want to stay in the city, I can drive you back to pick it up."

"Okay," Amanda said.

The constable rose. He could see the fear on the young woman's face. He felt bad for her.

"You said this fellow had a knife. What kind of knife? Did you see it?"

"What do you mean?" Amanda asked.

"Well, there are different kinds of knives. Look at pictures of them and get back to me if any of them look familiar."

AMANDA SLEPT DEEPLY, ONE HAND PRESSED AGAINST HER CHEEK, the side of her head against the cold car window. Larry felt strangely peaceful. When he was a cop, he always had a destination. He was always going someplace, helping someone. Being someone.

Since Marjorie died, he had been no one. It wasn't just her death that he was grieving, he realized. He had been Marjorie's husband and a police officer. Now he was neither.

Well, he was Amanda's friend now.

As they reached the passes—there was snow on the distant mountains—Amanda stirred, and awakened. She tried her phone. No service. She yawned, stretched, and then rummaged through her bag.

"Looking for something?" Larry asked.

"Just this," she said, pulling out a bottle of water and taking a sip. The color was back in her cheeks, and there was a red mark from where she had been resting against the glass. "I was going to check pictures of knives on my phone."

"You could tell me what it looks like."

"Long, curved. Like the tip went up."

She remembered the glittering knife in the dark. The rain had made a shroud of the man, and outlined the knife.

"It had a hook on the top, like this." She drew in the air.

"Sounds like a hunting knife with a gut hook."

"A gut hook." Amanda sounded sick.

"It's okay. I'm here with you now," Larry said, and he could have been back at work, driving a victim to the hospital, or talking to a young, distressed witness in the back seat, letting them unravel their life.

THERE WAS A SMALL DARK SCAR ON REGGIE'S EAR, WHERE AN EAR-ring hole had once been. His partner, a much older, heavyset man with silvering hair, stood at the window of their downtown apartment. He turned, concerned.

"Of course I remember Brightwood," Reggie said. "And your brother. And everything else." His voice faltered.

Larry and Amanda were sitting in antique chairs upholstered in damask. The apartment was a riot of chintz and color. Outside, the streets of Portland pulsated. Amanda appeared to have recovered from her ordeal, but she still looked tired.

"We're sorry to bother you," Amanda said.

"It's okay. I got Jerry here. Right, Jer?"

His partner smiled, but his eyes looked worried.

"Right."

"You were a cop?" Reggie asked Larry.

"Yes."

"Knew a couple of gay cops, years ago. Seemed like there were more of them, for a while."

"We had a program. The chief then was a woman."

"They used to come in and have coffee at Roxy's. That was when Jerry had his antique shop."

"Couldn't afford the lease anymore," Jerry said.

"When did you two meet?" Amanda asked.

"When I came to Portland," Reggie said. "Boy, was I a mess. Jerry met me after I got off the Greyhound. Eighteen years old and dumped from the system like a bag of rotten potatoes. Not a dime to my name. The prognosis, as they say, was not good."

His voice was soft, husky. There were fine lines around his eyes.

"What can you tell us about Dennis?" Amanda asked.

"I wish it was better news. I do. That place destroyed us."

"You were there until it closed?"

"I barely even remember the final months." A pained expression came to his face. "After that place, I got sent from home to home, ended up in a lockdown facility. If it wasn't for Jerry here, I'd be on the streets. Selling myself."

"We look out for each other," Jerry said.

Larry glanced up at the much older man.

"We were friends for a long time," Jerry said, knowing that look. "I hired Reggie in the shop. He lived in the little room above it."

"It took me forever to talk him into a single kiss," Reggie added, smiling.

As Reggie's smile faded, Jerry looked back out the window, waiting. The air was heavy.

"Brightwood," Reggie said.

He looked at Amanda.

"Your brother deserved better. We all did."

"What happened?"

"What didn't happen? In my case, it was conversion therapy."

Amanda looked confused.

"For homosexuality," he said.

"I thought holding time was for attachment issues."

"According to Martha King, it was for everything. I wouldn't be surprised if she claimed it cured the common cold. She's a true believer. They still use holding time, you know. In the centers. They just call it by different names now. Rage reduction therapy. Compression therapy. Rebirthing therapy."

"I didn't know that," Amanda said, troubled.

"Forty years. That's how long Martha King was in business. She danced away into retirement. Not once did anyone stop to ask the kids, is this right for you?"

"She won't talk to us," Larry said.

"Of course she won't. She doesn't like questions. There's a group of us. Survivors of holding time. There aren't a lot of us alive and functioning. The suicide rate was off the charts. Many ended up in prison or murdered. Of course, people like Martha would say we were destined for that anyhow. She would say we were lucky to get any help at all."

He touched the scar on his ear.

"There are even some kids who believed in it," Jerry said.

"It's true," Reggie agreed. "I've talked to a few who are convinced Martha saved their lives. They have to believe that, you know."

"How come?" Larry asked.

"Because they never left that room. You've heard of Stockholm syndrome? Some say it doesn't exist. But I know there is a way it does. When you're in that much terror, the person who finally releases you becomes the only one who can save you. Even if they were the one who put you there in the first place."

"We were told some of the boys ran away," Amanda said.

"I never believed that," Reggie said.

"Why not?"

"I remember that first boy they said ran away. Steven. They said he had run away in the middle of the night. But I didn't see him at dinner. I think something else happened to him."

Larry sat straight up.

"What do you think happened to him?" he asked.

Jerry turned from the window, his face a mask of pain.

Reggie looked at his hands.

The air grew even heavier.

"There was a man there. Ike Tressler. Martha had him help. He would come in and hold us down. And afterward . . ."

There was a long silence.

Larry looked at Amanda. She understood too.

"I'm sorry," Amanda said.

"It wasn't Dennis, if you're wondering. It was me. Me and others they knew were gay. He said he was teaching us a lesson."

"We met him," Larry said.

"He's still around?" Reggie looked stricken. "I was hoping he was dead."

"He's alive."

Reggie's reaction to the news was painful to watch. They could see the walls and floor fall away from him, and then he was falling, falling to where his partner was the only one who could catch him.

"Jer—"

"I got you," the older man said. "We should stop this conversation."

JERRY RODE DOWN THE WHEEZING ELEVATOR WITH THEM. THEY had left Reggie upstairs, in the small bedroom.

"Will he be okay?" Amanda asked.

"Doesn't have much choice," Jerry said.

"I'm glad he found you."

"That woman, she just fucked those kids up. Distorted every idea they ever had of love and trust. What Ike Tressler did to him was just the cherry on top."

They stepped outside into a noisy, bright downtown day. People rushed by, bags beating time at their hips. A street prophet stood across the road and yelled, and a homeless woman shook her cup at Amanda as she passed.

On the sidewalk, Jerry shook their hands, saying he would call them if Reggie had any more information. He left them standing in the sun.

Larry looked ill at ease.

"I have something to do," he told Amanda. "Can you keep yourself occupied for a few hours?"

"Sure. I have an errand close by," she said.

He turned abruptly and wandered off. Amanda thought she had never seen anyone look more lonely.

LARRY STOOD AT THE CEMETERY GATES.

Blessed are the pure in heart, read the inscription above him. A statue of the Virgin Mary stood to the side, her hands outstretched. Someone had left a pacifier in her palm.

He held a clutch of flowers he had picked up from a roadside stand. It felt inadequate for what he was about to do. He had walked here across the lawns of the main cemetery, shadowed with trees. This part of the cemetery was very empty, and very quiet.

Taking a deep breath, he walked through the baby cemetery gate. The graves here were impossibly small. Toys had been piled on some, soaked with recent rains. Larry remembered the face of his wife as she looked up from the toilet, blood splashed on her thighs.

Trembling, he found the graves.

Palmer, said the stone. There were four tiny graves, one for each of the children they had lost. None had taken a breath. None had lived. All had been stillborn or lost before.

Once, as the end of her life drew near, Marjorie, blinded from pain, had turned to him and asked if he remembered. To his eternal shame and regret, he had pretended he didn't know what she was talking about. It had been so long since she'd brought them up. For decades, she had come here alone. His wife, who developed such social anxiety she could barely leave the house, would still come here, her only outing in the final years of her life.

Not once had he come with her. Not once had he honored her request. He had put it off until she stopped asking. Once he had even yelled at her. *I don't want to go there! Will you just let it go?*

Larry knelt, putting the paltry flowers on one of the graves. He hadn't thought to buy four bouquets, and now he wondered if he should divide the flowers, so each lost child could have their own. He was pretty sure they didn't care now. The one who cared, whom he should have shepherded, was in an urn on his mantel back home. She was the one watching, thinking, Too late, Larry Palmer.

You are too late.

WHILE LARRY WAS VISITING THE DEAD, AMANDA WAS AT THE Oregon Historical Society. While what Amanda wanted to know wasn't specifically about the state, the researchers there had been an invaluable help in locating obscure information about Molly.

"There you are," one of them said, waving, as Amanda entered. "I got that tooth you ordered."

He pulled a polar bear tooth in a glass case from beneath his desk. The tooth was yellowed, with scratch marks on the surface.

This was the tooth from Molly's mother. Amanda had located it in an obscure museum catalog, after Pete had told her about it.

"I wonder why they took it," the historical society researcher said.

They both leaned over the handsome tooth, gleaming like ivory in its case.

"As a talisman," she said, glancing up. "A lot of researchers approach their subject like a hunter with a big gun, ready to take a prize. They think if they say it's for knowledge, it makes it all right."

"It's the attitude that counts," the researcher said, smiling at her. He had wispy blond hair by his large ears, and pale blue drooping eyes.

"Is the tooth on loan?" she asked.

"I don't think they really care," he said. "It's not considered to be of any value. It's been tampered with, as you can see. Someone took filings, once. Probably trying to figure out her age."

"That's good to know," Amanda said. "Because I'd like to do the same."

"Tamper with it?"

"Yes. I'm going to ask someone to do some tests. Nothing that will harm it, though. Would that be okay?"

"It's all yours. But first, fill out this form."

LARRY WAS AT THE COURTHOUSE, LEANING AGAINST THE COUNTER, talking to some of the sheriffs. He straightened when Amanda arrived, and made stiff introductions. The officers stood a little taller in her company.

"This way," Larry said, hustling her down the hall. "You don't want to date cops," he said. "Trust me, I should know."

"You were one," she said.

"Exactly. Here, the records room."

He ushered Amanda in, hovering over her protectively while she took a chair in front of a computer. Then he pulled up another chair and showed her how to run names through the various court records systems, including the federal database.

It wasn't hard, Amanda soon learned.

"I already checked for Ike Tressler," he said. "Now you run him."

"Okay," she said. She felt the comforting weight of the tooth in her bag. "Nothing," she said after a few moments.

"Right. Which doesn't mean he hasn't done anything. He just never got caught."

"We should ask the constable about him," she said.

"Agreed. But first, let's run Ralph. Maybe there's something my friend at the bureau missed."

Amanda typed in the name, searching for court records. Nothing came up for Oregon, but there was a match in the federal database.

A Ralph Higgins swam up on the screen. Amanda enlarged the photo.

"Not the right guy," she said. "Too old."

"But the same name," Larry said, peering close, so close she could see the pores on his nose. "Check it out."

"Ralph Higgins Sr.," she said. "You think he was his father?"

"Possibly."

Ralph Higgins Sr. had been arrested, tried, and convicted for assaulting a public safety officer many decades before. It had happened in a place called Sleeping Giant, Arizona.

"Feel like an airplane ride?" Larry asked.

Amanda had been thinking how she should go see her parents, tell them all that had happened. But she didn't want to do that. This was the first time she had ever done anything without their guidance or help. It was also the first time, besides when she was at work, that she felt like herself.

"I'd like that very much," she said.

24

IF MARTHA KING WAS TIRED OF SEEING THE CONSTABLE, THIS TIME she didn't show it. She looked fresh-faced, as if she had been out taking a walk on the beach. She smiled at the constable and then shook her head, bewildered, at his account.

"The man who reported it is a bit of a local reprobate," he said.

"Well, that explains that, doesn't it?"

"I'm sorry to have bothered you, ma'am."

"It's fine." She smiled.

"The next one is ready, ma'am."

The constable turned to see a man in her doorway. It was the same bald guy who had answered the door the first time the constable had visited the center. The odd feeling came over him again.

"Constable Roberts," he said, rising with one hand outstretched.

"Ike Tressler," the man said, reluctantly shaking it.

THE CONSTABLE WALKED DOWN THE BEACH AFTERWARD, WHICH he rarely did. He had grown up at the coast and could tell you, you sure got used to it. He imagined the city landscape was the same for city kids.

He saw the roof of the hotel behind the ever-shifting dunes. In the front office, he stomped the sand from his shoes, which was a futile gesture. Charlie looked up from where he was reading a car magazine.

"You back about that center?" Charlie asked.

"Yeah. How'd you know that?"

"Why else? Seemed like you had a bee in your bonnet before."

The constable smiled at the quaint expression. The man was a mishmash of ineptitude, hard work, and a cheerfulness that approached bonhomie.

"Heard a rumor," the constable said.

"What about?"

"Maybe someone saw a boy in the woods." The constable didn't want to explain more.

"I don't go in the woods much myself. Not into hunting."

"You like fishing?"

"Some. Don't do it much."

"What *do* you do for fun, Charlie?" he asked.

"Run this hotel. It's a full-time job."

"No offense, but you're not exactly swimming with customers yet."

"They'll come."

"You ever worry they might not?"

"Damn, Constable. Way to cheer a feller up. I make enough to get by."

"The people who work at the center, you ever see them?"

"Nope."

"What about a big bald fellow? Name of Ike Tressler."

"Didn't I just say I never see them?"

"All right." The constable put his hands in his pockets.

"Hey, Constable, when you're out and about, maybe think of suggesting this place to people? Like maybe if you go to one of them police officer conferences in the city. You could pass around some brochures."

"You got brochures?"

"Naw, but I could make some."

"Sure. Why not," Constable Roberts said, though he had no intention of recommending the hotel. The city cops he had met would have no interest in staying in a place like this. They stayed in the resorts up the coast.

BACK IN HIS OFFICE, CONSTABLE ROBERTS RAN IKE TRESSLER. HE was not in the local directory, or in any of the yearbooks the constable kept on his shelves. Finally, he called the department of motor vehicles and got his address. It was listed as way up the Nehalem River, in the woods. In his adjoining office, which functioned as the local records storage room, Constable Roberts pulled the land deed.

Ike Tressler had bought his place almost a decade before, with cash. He had written down Brightwood as his place of employment. He had no past, and no history the constable could uncover.

Curious, the constable drove to Ike's place. He found a small cabin, solidly built. The sun reflected on the nearby bubbling river, which was rich with salmon. The sky was complacent overhead, and the constable knew the woods were full of deer and elk. It was a sportsman's paradise.

The chimney was cold, and there was no vehicle out front. Ike was apparently still at work. The constable tried to peek inside through the curtains. He caught a glimpse of a kitchen counter. He walked around back and found a small shed, for dressing game. An out-of-season turkey was hanging in it. The constable frowned.

"EVENING, CONSTABLE," THE BARTENDER AT THE WHEEL STONE Tavern said.

Constable Roberts wasn't fond of the tavern. It was the scene of too many brawls between drunken fishermen, and he never got called on most of them. The bartender had been raised on the fishing boats, where the only law was that of the captain. It didn't even occur to him to call the police. The same was true of many of the locals.

It was just as well, the constable thought, sitting on a stool. Otherwise he'd have to arrest most of the men in the town, instead of just seeing their bruised faces the next day, and hearing the stories.

"I'll have the Tillamook chili cheese dog," the constable said, knowing he—and his wife—would regret it later that evening.

"Coming right up. Drink? Or can you, on shift?" There was an edge to the man's voice.

"Pepsi, please, if you got it."

"Course we got it."

The constable looked around the bar as he drank his soda. There was the mandatory bank of pinball machines in the corner, and the newer addition, the bane of every adult protective services worker in the state: video poker games. A few widows in town had become so addicted to these games, they lost every penny they and their husbands had ever earned. Constable Roberts had been called after one of them—a Mrs. Simmons, who later had to be sent to an assisted living facility in the city—had been evicted after a foreclosure. She hadn't paid her utilities for months, and her fridge was empty.

He remembered her paltry belongings in the street. The world could be a sad place.

The chili dog arrived. The bartender stood there for a moment, like he knew damn well the constable was there to ask him questions. Constable Roberts picked up his knife and fork—those dogs were tasty but messy—and began to eat. The bartender left to tend to two tourists down the bar. They were drunk after a day spent crabbing in the local bay and starting to get obnoxious. Constable Roberts was suddenly glad the bartender rarely called him.

"So?" The bartender was back. He had kicked out the asshole tourists.

"Just enjoying my meal. And wanting to ask you about this fellow," Constable Roberts said. He handed over the driver's license photo of Ike Tressler he had printed out. He felt a little foolish, because he had no reason to suspect the man of anything. He just had a bad feeling about him.

"Yeah, I know him. Comes in here drinking sometimes."

"Alone?"

"Mostly. Sometimes he's with that fucker Brett Jarvis. But Brett drinks with anyone who will buy him a pint."

"His wife has a whole cooler at his disposal."

"I heard she puts a lock on it at night. Otherwise her husband would put her out of business."

"I don't recall seeing this fellow around, myself."

"Well, why would you? You see everyone who lives on the coast?"

"No," the constable said, finishing his hot dog. He weighed his words. "He ever talk about work?"

"Naw. Just sits there and complains about the fishing boats and how he would never work on one."

"Why's that?" The constable held back a burp.

"Probably just lazy. Why you asking about Ike?"

"Dunno. Curious about him."

"Yeah, right. You're curious about nothing, Constable."

Constable Roberts wanted to ask why the bartender had a beef with him, then decided he didn't care. Some men were automatically opposed to the law, except when it suited them. He was sure the bartender was more than fine with any law he handed down himself.

"Okay," the constable said, pushing away the empty dish in front of him.

The bartender looked like he felt a little bad. "Sorry. Makes you seem like you think you're too good for us, you know."

"What does?"

"That you so rarely come in."

I got a wife and kids, the constable wanted to say, but he knew most of the men there could say the same. He wasn't out to shame anyone. "Don't want to get in your business," he said, finishing his Pepsi. He could already feel the chili dog doing a number on his insides. "Besides, if I see a crime, I got to do something, right?"

The bartender laughed and picked up the dish, wiping underneath it.

"Yeah, you're right about that. But that fellow, he seems harmless enough. Just a big asshole. Got plenty of those down here, thinking since they know one end of a gun from another, they're the man. Never once seen him with a woman, you know. Just sits here, alone, mostly, complaining about the cost of a pint until it's time for him to go home, wherever that is."

"Never talks about work?"

"Never."

"Talks to Brett sometimes?"

"Yeah, but who doesn't, when that man gets in your face? Wish someone would buy him a toothbrush."

"It ain't his teeth; it's inside him," the constable said, paying for his meal. The bartender didn't argue. No one in Wheel Stone offered comps—it would be the end of them, and the constable preferred it that way.

"Come again," the bartender said.

IT WAS LATE, AND IKE WAS TIRED.

"You go on," Martha told him. It had been a long day, starting with the visit from the constable, and then more boys than they had ever treated in one day before. It seemed Martha wanted to treat more and more kids over time. She was getting harder with them, too, but maybe that was for the best. She knew best.

"You sure?" he asked.

"I'm sure." She looked sweaty and disheveled, with a fresh bite mark on her forearm where one of the boys, panicked at going once again into the rug, had bit her. She had been a little tough on that boy, Ike thought. And he was no stranger to toughness.

"I'll finish up here," she said, smiling at him. She had applied lipstick that morning, before the constable came, but it had long since worn off, into a faded rim around her mouth. It made her look strangely hostile.

"Okay. Don't work too hard, ma'am."

"I've just got this one more boy," she said. The boy in question was already in the room behind her, waiting.

Dennis and the other boys were in the dining room. One of the newer staff members was trying to teach them card games. It wasn't going so well. Dennis let the cards flutter from his hands, like they were poison or something. It irked Ike, but he wasn't on shift anymore. Let the evening staff handle it.

He left, crossing the parking lot, feeling ill at ease. Most of the cars were gone for the day, including the cook's. The night watchman would be on his way in. It was later than Ike had thought, and Martha was still there. He turned to look at the dark building, feeling troubled.

He climbed into his creaking truck. It had room for whatever he wanted it to hold. Hunting gear. Once, a dressed elk. He liked being in the woods, on his days off. He had never learned hunting as a boy, but he was learning it now.

25

LARRY HAD NEVER WANTED TO BE A DETECTIVE. DETECTIVES showed up after the worst had happened. As an officer, Larry sometimes got to be the person who prevented the bad thing from happening at all.

But then, times and the bureau had changed. It had never been perfect—not by a long shot. They had cops every bit as racist as the ones today. What they didn't have, Larry felt, was the sort of bristling defensive anger that ran, hot as an electrical current, through the newest generation of police officers. In his days, brutality was a given. But there were still a lot of men like him, cops who took satisfaction from a normal workday or night, and the call of sirens was not a call to arms.

Now here he was, playing detective with Amanda, leaving a hot rental car agency outside a small southern Arizona airport, traveling across the desert. Every few miles, they passed a white jug of water, sweating in the heat.

"What are those for?" Amanda asked.

"In case we break down. So we don't die of thirst."

She looked out her window after that, at the mirage of red hills in the distance and the strips of white and brown sand, like a dappled hide on the coat of a great animal bucking the earth.

THEIR FIRST STOP WAS AT THE OLD AXIS TREATMENT CENTER, abandoned in the desert just as Brightwood had been at the coast. The sand had blown up along the concrete walls.

"This place closed when she left too," Larry said.

There wasn't much of an exercise yard—it was too hot here—but instead, there were narrow domed walkways between the buildings, which had windows with white metal bars, the paint now peeling. There was a droning silence, like insects were buzzing far away.

Larry noted the curling razor wire on the top of the walls. The gates were closed with a thick padlock. An empty guard station stood near the entrance.

Amanda looked into the dry desert hills. "Larry?"

"Yes?"

"Why do people make places like these? I mean, why not just have decent foster homes? Pay people enough to take care of kids and help them with their issues?"

"If only it was that easy."

"Maybe it is, and we just pretend it's hard."

Larry looked at the road into town. The sun was relentless.

"Let's go find the sheriff," he said.

"NAME OF DUNCAN," THE SHERIFF INTRODUCED HIMSELF, WITH A big smile. He stuck out a giant paw for Amanda to shake, and she felt immediately comforted in his presence. He reminded her of Molly, right down to his bright, dark eyes.

"Axis?" he asked, signaling for them to sit. Instead of chairs, he had a white leather couch, with the head of a bighorn sheep above it. The air-conditioning was blasting. He swiveled in his chair, like a big child.

"Do you know why it closed?" Amanda asked.

"Recommendation of the last director. Wasn't cost-effective.

Nowadays the state sends the kids to that place near Cibola. They can fit a couple hundred kids there."

"You mean director Martha King?" Amanda asked.

"Yup. I remember Martha. Nice lady."

Larry cocked his head. "You were the sheriff back then?"

The man looked a bit young for that, Amanda thought.

"Oh no, my goodness. I was in high school."

"Who was the sheriff back then? Can we talk to him?" Amanda asked.

"Would be hard to. He's dead now."

Amanda looked out the window at the desert. The sheriff station abutted a small jail outside of town. It felt very lonely.

"Where you all from?" he asked.

"Oregon," Amanda said.

"Makes sense. You better put on some sunscreen, or you'll be a cinder before the day is out. Your cheeks are bright pink."

Amanda felt them. They were hot to the touch.

"We're curious about this court case we found," Larry said. "Involving a man who assaulted the previous sheriff here."

"Anyone who assaulted Walter King surely paid his dues. That man was old-school."

"Walter King?" Larry asked. "Was he any relation to Martha King?"

"Of course! She was his daughter. I mean, still is. Last I saw her, she was down for his funeral, years back. Haven't seen her since."

Things, Larry thought, were starting to add up.

"Is there any way to find out if a boy went to Axis?" Amanda asked.

The man shook his head. "Those records are long gone, miss."

"What about runaway reports from there?" Larry asked.

"I can't answer that." His dark eyes had grown cold.

"Why not? Wouldn't those reports be filed here? Same with the ones Martha King called down here for Brightwood, the center she ran in Oregon?"

The sheriff said nothing. His eyes fell on the buttons of Larry's dress shirt. They were cheap and plastic. He studied them for a long time, and Larry could tell he was doing the internal guessing game of any officer. Should he share? Why bother? It could only create trouble for him.

"I'll take a look. Get back to you."

The man no longer reminded Amanda of Molly.

"I'm sure you will," Larry said.

"WHAT DO YOU THINK?" AMANDA ASKED, LEAVING THE COOL OF THE sheriff's office for the blast of desert heat.

"I think no one likes a scandal," Larry said.

THEY WERE ON THE OUTSKIRTS OF TOWN, HEADING TO THEIR cheap hotel. Across the road was a sea of sand broken up only by creosote bushes, and in the far distance, the hazy red mountains.

Amanda pointed to a sign at a dirt road turnoff.

"What's that?" she asked.

Larry slowed.

"'Sleeping Giant Intaglio Protection Area,'" he read.

"I've never heard of it before," she said. "Can we go see?"

He peered at the cyclone fence in the distance. It wasn't far. He turned the rental car down the dirt road.

AT THE CHAIN-LINK FENCE, AMANDA GOT OUT OF THE CAR. SHE looked through the fence at the massive figure on the desert floor.

"It looks like a giant man," she said.

"How can you tell it's a man?" Larry asked, peering through the fence. It was very hot, and little sand cyclones stirred in the wind.

"Oh. I see."

Amanda giggled. It was a rare giggle, and he was glad to hear it.

He read the plaque nearby. "This says they're called intaglios. They were made by people who lived here long ago, but no one knows exactly why."

Amanda felt very small standing above the sleeping giant.

"Can we go now?" Larry asked. He could feel the bald spot on his head burning in the sun. Neither of them had thought to bring a hat.

As they left, Amanda turned back to look at the giant figure spread-eagled on the desert floor, his hands open as if beckoning allies from the sky.

"Oh," she said, realizing it then. "This is one of the sleeping giants, Larry. The ones the town is named after."

THAT NIGHT, AMANDA GOT AN ICE CREAM CONE AND WALKED THE streets of Sleeping Giant. It was like a swath of irrigated strip mall in the desert. Larry stayed back at their hotel, with hot towels wrapped around his sore knees.

She stopped in front of a tourist shop with Mojave dolls in the window. She finished her cone, carefully wiping her fingers on the napkin, then stowing it in her pocket to throw away later.

A burst of friendly cold air greeted her as she entered the store.

"Can I help you?"

The woman inside looked like a local, with leathery skin and bleached hair cut into shingles.

"I'm curious about the intaglios."

"Here we call them sleeping giants."

"Do you have any books on them?"

The owner led Amanda past a necklace display dripping green turquoise to an alcove in the back lined with expensive illustrated books.

"Here's one. A local historian wrote it."

Amanda peeked at the price. It was above the limit she had for spending. When she went food shopping, she used the calculator app on her phone.

"I'm sorry, I can't afford that."

"The author lives in town. He loves to talk."

"We have to leave in the morning."

Something occurred to Amanda as she looked into the woman's face.

"Did you grow up here?" she asked.

"Yes, I did, as a matter of fact."

"Did you ever know anyone named Martha King?"

The woman looked slightly peeved, like Amanda was asking after a local celebrity and had passed over better ones.

"Of course I knew Martha. Her daddy too."

The woman set the book back on the shelf.

"She ran a center my brother went to."

"You mean Axis?"

"No, it was in Oregon."

"What do you want with Martha?"

"It's a long story," Amanda said.

"Listen, I'm closing here. Want to grab a beer? There's a nice pub down the road. We can sit outside, feel the desert breeze."

AT THE PUB, AMANDA MET THE BARTENDER, WHO ALSO REMEM-bered Martha—she had done a lot for the town, he said—and a skinny, sad-looking man who said he remembered the center; and a woman who said, knowingly, she had known the sheriff. Amanda tried to get these people to talk, but the bartender seemed too busy, and the man and woman were knee-deep in beer. But plenty of others wanted to share, and Amanda's table on the deck became a hive of activity, with people pulling up chairs, welcoming the breeze on their sweat-dampened foreheads.

Night fell like a hammer. There was no sound of the ocean but one of profound neglect. Nature was silencing here.

"There he is," the lady from the shop said, waving wildly as a man approached their table. "The historian I told you about. I was hoping he would come."

HE WAS A SMALL, DEEPLY TANNED MAN IN A SHORT-SLEEVE SHIRT with roached hair bleached white by the sun.

"So," he said, taking a seat after being introduced. "You're asking around about Martha King, and the sleeping giants."

"I am." Amanda smiled.

"Is there a connection?"

"I guess they both come from here," she said.

The bartender came over, taking the historian's order for a beer. The lady from the shop was inside by the jukebox, dancing with a friend.

"What do you do?" the historian asked Amanda, curious.

"I'm a zookeeper," she said.

"Really? Which animal?"

"Polar bears."

"We have animal figures, too, in the desert. We've identified ancient species of mountain lions, insects, and what might be a prehistoric bear."

"Are all the figures empty inside?"

"That's interesting. Martha asked about that too. She came to me wanting to know more about the sleeping giants. I've been studying them a long time. The only one that does. It's funny, what people stop seeing in their own backyard."

He took a long drink.

"Want one?" he asked.

"I have a hard enough time thinking straight when I'm sober," Amanda said.

"At least you're honest about it," he said, putting down the beer.

"How come they're called sleeping giants?"

"Well, they are giant."

"But the one I saw didn't look like it was sleeping."

"Exactly. They all have their eyes open and are waving at the sky."

"Why are they called *sleeping* giants, then?"

"Funny. You keep asking the same questions Martha did. The myth is that if the sleeping giants are awakened, they will take revenge on all of us."

"What for?"

"Those crimes, my friend, are no longer remembered."

He shook his head, drinking his beer.

"Beer thoughts," he said, smiling.

Amanda didn't think so.

"What was Martha like?" she asked.

"She wasn't herself, that day she came to talk to me," he said. "She was always so professional. She cared a lot for those boys. She'd do them favors, help them out in life. But that time, she was upset. It was right before the center closed and she left town. Funny to think you and I are here, talking, over what, twenty years later? Having a similar discussion. Only you don't look afraid."

"She did?"

"She did."

He stopped and drank.

"At least have some water," he said. "You're making me feel alone."

Amanda waved for the bartender. He soon returned with a glass of ice water. She took a sip.

"Martha asked me why the sleeping giants are empty inside. Those were her exact words. She said it bothered her, all of them being so empty inside."

"What did you tell her?"

"I said I didn't know."

"Did she ask anything else?"

"Not that I remember. Next thing I knew, she had taken a job in Oregon."

Amanda put down her water.

"Are there any social workers in town?"

A THOUSAND MILES AWAY, MARTHA KING SET DOWN THE PHONE. She had recognized the sounds of a desert bar at night, the jukebox in the background. It had been Mitch, the bartender at the pub in Sleeping Giant. The last time she had seen him was at her daddy's funeral. She had come and gone in a day.

"There's a young lady in town," he said. "She's at a table right now, talking to the historian."

"Thank you," Martha said, hanging up.

She looked out her window into the night. The Oregon desert was always cold, even when it was hot. The sun was higher here, and the moon didn't look right in the sky.

She had been exiled before. She would not be exiled again.

She picked up the phone.

It needed to end, now.

26

RALPH STOOD OVER THE GRAVE OF THE RABBIT.

He had buried her in the woods, thinking Dennis would want
to visit her once he got better. But that was wishful thinking. Dennis
spent almost all his time in isolation now, when he wasn't in treatment.
Martha had come in speaking against the cells and then ended up using
them even more, for the boys like Dennis.

The rabbit would be bones by now.

Ralph had run out of ideas.

"I DON'T KNOW WHAT TO DO," HE TOLD DENNIS.

He had waited until the isolation ward was empty, and chanced
using his master key to open the door. Dennis lay in the far corner, a
shadow on the floor. The cell was very dark and smelled strongly of
urine. One of Ralph's jobs was to clean these rooms at the end of the
day, and lately, horrors had awaited him: crescents of broken nails and
smears of blood on the walls, puddles of shit in the corners, dabbled in
with bare hands.

Dennis didn't reply. He just lay there.

"Maybe you're thinking you can just stop living. I tried that, back
at Axis. You know, she still hasn't recognized me. I don't think she ever

will. She forgets the boys, after she's done. Unless they please her, and refuse to leave. Some get that way—like whipped puppies, always licking the face of their mistress. I saw that at Axis. Anyhow, I tried what you're doing right now. There is no winning, son, with what you're doing."

"What am I doing?" It came as a whisper from the floor.

"Giving up," Ralph said.

There was a noise down the hall. Ike Tressler was coming with another boy. They could hear him dragging him, the boy begging not to do holding time, and Ike cursing him. Just like the use of the isolation cells, all the goodness Martha had promised had slipped away, and what was left was worse than before.

"I'll come back," Ralph said. "I'm not giving up."

IT WAS VERY LATE, ONCE MORE, AND MARTHA WAS IN THE THERAPY room.

All Martha remembered of her childhood was her father's belt. He took it off after work and hung it over a chair at the dining room table, where her mother, worn to a nub by her father, would silently dish out the food, and he would bless it. Martha and her mother—and the ghosts of her mother's expectations—would wait for her father to try the soup, or the casserole, or the baked ham. That first taste was always a moment of held breath. Would he like it? What would he say?

If it was a good day, her father would grunt, and in that grunt, Martha would see her mother's shoulders collapse, and everything about the night would be okay—provided her father didn't lay into the beer too much. Eventually she would go to her twin bed in her room down the hall, crawl under the flowered bedspread, and try to fall asleep before she heard the creak of her father lying on top of her mother in the dark.

It was funny that it was the belt Martha thought of now. It had a holster for his service pistol, and the holes were worn where her father had gained weight over the years. The buckle was brass but long since tarnished. She didn't remember the shape of the buckle. All she remembered was the sound of his hands, rough as sandpaper, on the belt. Undoing it.

Later, during those heat-shot weeks when Sunday came too soon and lasted too long—an endless tunnel of time—Sheriff King, on his day off, would decide to take his daughter into the desert. Mother never disagreed. Mother never disagreed with anything Father had to say. She stayed back in her kitchen, endlessly puzzling over what to cook her husband that he would finally like.

Martha thought of that now, too, with another dead boy in her arms. It kept happening, and she didn't know why. It had kept happening in Axis, and she had thought coming here—leaving the sleeping giants behind—would stop it. But instead, it was getting worse. She left the boys in the therapy room. She went on a break or to her office, and somehow a curtain fell over her and she dream-walked through the rest of the day or evening without even thinking of them. Then all of a sudden, it would come over her, and she'd come rushing back.

To find this.

Maybe you want to do this, she thought, cradling the boy's body. Maybe there is something inside you that wants—

She pushed the thought away. It was an accident. Holding time was risky therapy. Everyone knew that. In Colorado, a girl named Candace Newmaker had died after being wrapped in a flannel sheet. She suffocated after vomiting and defecating on herself. There had been other children in other centers, too, ones who never got publicity. The only reason people knew about Candace, Martha reflected, was because her therapists had called an ambulance. They had not been smart, like she and others were. In some instances, therapists had been able to claim that such deaths were therapeutic accidents.

But there were only so many times you could have a therapeutic accident. Once, maybe twice. Not as many times as Martha King. She had been forced to hide them.

This was just a mistake, she told herself. Just like the others, buried in their desert graves in Arizona, the sound of the shovel wielded by her father strangely similar to the sound of his hands rasping on the belt. Those first years he had come willingly. Too willingly.

She looked down at the boy's face. It was very still. She was aware she had taped the rug very tightly around him. Why had she done that?

The last one here had been named Steven. This one was . . . Joey. The boy in her arms was named Joey.

She stroked the tape around the rug. She kept thinking of her father's belt hanging over the chair. She thought of the sound of her father's hands on the belt and wanted to think no more.

Soon she would make her call. She would wave for help like a sleeping giant on the desert floor, and no matter who answered, the man on the other end would always be the same—the one who put her there.

LATE THAT NIGHT, A FIGURE CREPT FROM THE CENTER.

He carried the second boy deep into the forest. This time he kept an eye out for Brett Jarvis. He dug quickly, turning the boy into the hole. He had thought of throwing the bodies over the cliff into the sea, but there was always a chance they would wash up, either whole or in pieces, torn apart by sharks. This was safer and cleaner. There could be a thousand corpses buried in the Oregon woods. There probably were.

He stopped, wiping sweat from his eyes with the stained bandanna he kept in his pocket. He put the bandanna back and refilled the hole. He covered the grave with mossy limbs and broken branches. That would keep animals from digging up the remains.

He sat down on a log for a breather. It was very late, and the air had a crystalline quality. It was the salt from the sea. The sky above him was pure darkness, roiling away in clouds he could not see.

Picking up the shovel, he returned to the center. Martha was gone by the time he got back, which annoyed him. He knew she wanted to be able to pin it on him, if she was ever caught. But he had his own secret.

27

AMANDA WAS UP EARLY THE NEXT MORNING, WAITING IN THE
Sleeping Giant hotel lobby for Larry, her backpack at her feet. She was
holding a report.

Larry entered the lobby, walking slowly due to his sore knees.

"Whatcha got there?" he asked, looking around for the coffee urn.
He poured himself a cup. From the other room came sounds of breakfast, but they needed to hit the road. He would grab a bagel, he decided.

"A child protective services report," she said.

"How did you get that?"

"Last night I met some people, at a pub. One put me in touch with a
local social worker. We met at a diner up the road. She gets up early too."

"Let me guess. Runaways?"

"I'm sure those exist, but no."

"What is it, then?"

She held it out.

It was an investigation into Sheriff King for the sexual abuse of his
daughter.

REGGIE DUPREE HAD DISCOVERED HOPE. IT WAS IN THE HOLLOW
of his lover's voice. It was in the brief sensation, like breaking through

rain, in the moments before orgasm. Once, when he was crying, he had felt it.

He held on to that memory as if it were a talisman.

He left the apartment, going down the stairs. He didn't use the elevator. He hated the elevator. He hated all enclosed spaces. They made him feel like he was choking. He hated the smell of gymnasiums and the color gray. He hated bald heads on men. He hated crimson lipstick. The world was full of pain.

But he had hope.

The stairs opened up onto a fetid and dank alleyway. Here the apartment manager piled the garbage he hoped the homeless would take, so he wouldn't have to pay for the removal. There were old couch cushions and a broken television stand. The dumpster nearby was crawling with rats.

Reggie no longer worked in a shop; now he had a job working festivals on the waterfront. He liked working outside. But he still remembered those first few years working with Jerry in his musty, incense-smelling antique shop as some of the best of his life.

He stopped as he was about to turn onto the street. There was a figure at the end of the alley.

All the hope inside him dried up then. He could feel the menace coming from the shape. He felt himself panicking. It could not be real. He was dreaming again. It was another nightmare from the past. He turned to run, but his legs felt as frozen as they had when he was a child, wrapped in the hard tube of a rug, the weight of Ike Tressler pressing down. Smiling at him and whispering in his ear, *Later*.

The shape was behind him, and then, somehow, the shape was inside him. There was a shock to his system, a feeling like an earthquake under his feet. He was falling. He felt the pendant of hope break against the dirty ground, and his face landed, hard, against the gritty pavement.

He closed his eyes. He really didn't want to see anymore. He was aware he was hurt inside, but he didn't want to think about it, or the vast feeling of wetness inside him, leaving his body.

In his last moments, he saw the tall windows of Brightwood on the day the transport van had pulled up. He remembered jumping out of the van as if life were a new adventure and whatever was about to happen to him could not quell the magic inside him, the hope he had carried with him all the time back then, despite foster parents and fears and prayers. The air had tasted of salt. He had seen the ocean on the drive, and he had every confidence he would see the ocean again. He had every belief that someday the world would understand him, and he wouldn't be forced to understand the world.

He felt his mind drift then. In his final thoughts, he was turning to Jerry. Jerry was behind him, calling his name.

"REGGIE IS DEAD," LARRY SAID.

They had just arrived back in Portland. Amanda was standing at the baggage carousel, where they were waiting for Larry's suitcase.

It took Amanda a moment to process. She had been looking at her phone while Larry had answered his own.

"That was Jerry. He could barely get the words out. Portland Police is there."

"But—how?"

"Murdered, in the alley behind their building. Reggie was found by a transient. Stabbed to death. They're combing the scene, but there isn't much to go on. No witnesses."

"Can we go? Comfort Jerry, at least."

"I'm sure he has his own friends to comfort him."

"We should tell the police there."

"About what, exactly?"

She held out her phone.

"You were right. It was this kind of knife."

SHARON GRAVELLE WAS A LARGE WOMAN WITH A COMMANDING build and a compelling gap-toothed smile. She and Larry went way back, to when they had both worked patrol. She had advanced into sex crimes—they always wanted to put women there, and keep them there—while he stayed on foot. Sometimes she teased him about it. Mostly she seemed puzzled.

"You made it to homicide," he said.

"Larry! How nice to see you. That's right, no keeping me out of my rightful position."

The homicide unit had historically been seen as a man's job, inside the bureau. No more, he thought.

"I thought you had retired," she said. "What brings you out?"

She was standing next to a dumpster that was smeared with blood. It looked like Reggie had died near where he had fallen. The body, a few feet away, was covered with a privacy sheet.

"We talked with the decedent a week or so ago," he said. "Me and that young lady standing over there. I told her to wait."

Sharon glanced at Amanda, then turned back to Larry, curious. Larry wasn't known for being overly friendly, and she wondered how he had made such a nice-looking friend. His voice had been positively paternal when he mentioned her.

"What did you talk to him about?" she asked, pulling out her notepad.

Larry told her. She took notes, including his current phone number.

"His partner called me," Larry said. "He said Reggie was stabbed."

"Maybe," she replied cautiously.

Jerry and his friends were at the end of the alley, being held back by patrol officers. Larry remembered having that job.

"You might want to have the medical examiner check the stab wounds to see if they match a knife like this."

Larry showed her the picture of a hunting knife with a gut hook.

"THEY MUST HAVE BURIED THIS REPORT," AMANDA SAID ON THE drive back to the coast. She was in the passenger seat, reading. Larry admired that. He always got sick trying to read in a car.

"What makes you say that?" he asked, keeping his eyes on the road. These mountains held a lot of risk-taking deer. He and Amanda had already passed a car totaled by one.

"Because they didn't do anything," she said, turning a page. "Martha was only ten at the time. Her gym teacher saw blood on her underwear. She called child protective services. Martha told them her dad took her into the desert every Sunday. She said she couldn't remember why. Her mother refused to talk. She had bruises on her neck."

"Sexual abuse is hard to prove."

"A doctor found evidence of sexual trauma."

Larry grunted.

"The police didn't seem to do anything," Amanda said.

"He *was* the police, remember?"

Amanda put the report in her lap. She closed her eyes. They drove in silence.

"Larry?"

"Yeah?"

"What made you want to become a cop?"

"Never gave it much thought, to be honest," he said. "I was eighteen, casting about for what I wanted to do. I checked out being a firefighter. It's got decent income. Steady work was what I was looking for. I decided on being a police officer because they had a hiring bonus back then. It's as simple as that."

"When did you get married?"

"Five years later. I met Marjorie on my beat, actually. She was the same age as me, working in a toy store."

"A toy store?"

"Yeah. Downtown. Called Finnegan's. Not far from where Reggie lives—lived—actually. I would walk by. Never went in, because why would I? Then one day I got called to this liquor store up the street, and Marjorie and I practically ran into each other on the sidewalk. As they say, she had me at hello." He was smiling. "What a girl. That's what I always called her. My girl."

"Did she always work at the toy store?"

"My goodness, no. She was finishing her nursing degree. That's what she did. She worked in the neonatal ward for a while." His voice faltered, and Amanda opened one eye. "She stopped doing that and went into the terminal ward. She did that for the rest of her life."

There was something he wasn't saying. Amanda could feel it. But she didn't press. Secrets were okay with her.

"We should see the constable as soon as we get back," she said.

"WHEN WE FIRST CAME TO YOU, YOU SAID YOU DIDN'T REMEMBER anyone from Brightwood," Larry said, entering the constable's office.

"That's not quite true," the constable said. "I recall saying I had to leave to patrol."

"But you know Ike Tressler, I bet."

Constable Roberts sat back in his chair.

"Yes," he said reluctantly.

"Why didn't you tell us about him?"

"It was a can of worms. I didn't want to bring it up because nothing ever came of it. A few complaints that led nowhere. Nothing substantiated." He looked at Amanda. "When you showed up, I was surprised to even learn Dennis had a sister. I didn't want you to worry. There never was any indication of foul play in his death. I thought about telling you other stuff. Like how sad Dennis seemed, or about Martha and her treatments. But I didn't want to burden you with details when there was no proof anything criminal happened here."

"What if it did?" Larry asked.

"Like what, exactly?" the constable asked.

"Maybe Dennis was murdered. Same with the other missing boys."

"What missing boys?"

"Those other runaways sure never turned up."

"I told you, there were no runaways—"

Larry reached into the folder he had brought, and handed over the reports. Constable Roberts read, his face going pale. Here was the missing piece he had never found. He rubbed his forehead. He felt sick.

"I had no idea. I knew there was something going on there. I visited several times. I talked to Ralph. He kept coming to me. Brett Jarvis came in too. But when I talked to Martha, she acted like everything was fine."

"You still could have told us," Amanda said.

"Look. At a certain point, if a case gets dropped, it gets dropped." He looked at the reports, shaking his head. "This number at the bottom?"

"Arizona."

"Figures. That's where Martha came from, right?"

"Her dad was a sheriff there."

Amanda held out the picture of the knife on her phone.

"We think the same guy who chased me with a knife like this stabbed a man named Reggie Dupree, who was also at Brightwood. Reggie told us Ike Tressler sexually assaulted him."

The constable sighed, still rubbing his forehead.

"I missed it. Goddamn it. I missed it."

"Do you know where Ike lives? We looked in the directory, but we can't find him."

"If he hasn't moved, I sure do. Come on," Constable Roberts said, grabbing his hat. "I want you there," he said to Amanda. "Maybe you can identify him."

THE ONCE PRISTINE, COZY CABIN NEAR THE NEHALEM RIVER WAS now a broken-down mess. Torn curtains hung in the windows, and the front yard was a swale of mud. The river, swollen with spring, ran by, and the constable saw where Ike had built an illegal fish trap. The river's edge was littered with trash and fish spines.

The house appeared empty. The windows were dark, and Ike's truck was missing from the front yard.

The constable approached with care, signaling for Larry and Amanda to stay back. The porch was swarming with dark flies. One landed on Larry's ear. He cried out, swatting at it.

"Deerflies," Amanda said. "They take bites out of you." She knew all about biting insects from the zoo. The keepers had to be vigilant about keeping the bugs down.

The constable knocked. There was no answer. Larry peered inside the front porch window. The inside of the cabin was piled with trash.

"Are you sure he still lives here?" Larry asked.

"No, but some of this garbage looks recent."

"There's no car out front," Amanda said, trying the front door.

"We don't have a search warrant," the constable said.

"I'm not a police officer," Amanda said.

"I can't let you—"

The door opened, and the smell billowed out. It was the stench of rotting food and raw blood from animals slaughtered and then cooked in the open fireplace. Amanda reached for a light switch and discovered there was no power. The place was in darkness. The sound of the flies was loud.

"He's not here," the constable said.

Amanda peered into the mess. The kitchen counter, covered in old copies of the local paper, had been used for butchering. The papers were dark with dried blood.

"Maybe we can find the knife," she said.

"Stop," Larry said. "If you find it, they'll never let it into court, because the search wasn't done properly. Come on now. Out of there."

She retreated. Larry closed the door, and the constable looked relieved.

"It's weird he left it unlocked," Amanda said.

"I grew up on the coast," the constable said. "We never lock our doors."

They walked to the shed out back. Years of spent blood darkened its walls. A rotting deer carcass hung inside. The smell about knocked Amanda over.

"Why would he hang meat like that and leave it?" Larry asked, holding his sleeve over his nose. His bitten ear was still bleeding.

"Alcohol," the constable said. "Probably killed the deer, gutted it, and forgot about it."

"Or he had a trip to make, to Portland," Amanda said.

They walked back to the constable's car, almost slipping in the mud.

"What's next?" Amanda asked as they drove away.

"I'll find him," the constable said. "He's probably out for a hunt—I didn't see any rifles or binoculars inside—and when he turns up, I'll bring him in for questioning."

"You got cause?" Larry asked, holding a handkerchief to his ear.

"I don't think a man like him will ask," the constable said.

"DO YOU WANT ME TO MAKE UP THE GUEST BED?" LARRY ASKED Amanda that evening as they finished a simple supper in front of the fire. Larry had made scrambled eggs and toast. Amanda's car was parked down the road. She had said she would feel safer staying with him.

"That would be nice," she said. "I'm only staying tonight. I have something to do tomorrow."

"Really? What's that?"

"I'm going up to Seaside to see a friend. I might be gone a few days. It has to do with Molly."

Amanda left the edges of her toast on the plate, as usual. Curious, Larry decided to ask her about it.

"How come you do that?" he asked, pointing.

"I just don't like edges, that's all." Her cheeks burned with embarrassment, but she held steady. It's not a crime, she told herself.

"Really?" Larry looked curious. "Why's that?"

"I don't know. I've always been this way. If something has a corner or edge, I can't finish it. It's not just food. At work, I set up all my tasks in a circle. That way I'm not at the end of a grid, with a corner left, because then I'd have to leave that task."

He was watching her, his face friendly. He looked intrigued.

"How interesting," he said. There was no judgment in his face.

"No one has ever been able to explain it to me. I used to get into terrible trouble at school. You should have seen it at recess when they made us play four square."

He laughed, and Amanda relaxed.

"You know, I always wanted a daughter like you," he said.

It had just slipped out.

"I mean, a child," he said, quickly. "Marjorie and I talked about it. What kind of interesting things would they do? How would they make us laugh? She used to say having children would be like a magical trip you take to a destination that will be revealed to you, step by step, over time. She said it would be like going to a museum where the paintings changed every day, and you got to interact with the artist. Marjorie loved kids. She wanted them so bad."

"You didn't have any?" she asked.

"We tried. None of them made it."

"I'm sorry," she said.

He could tell she meant it.

"It's been my greatest regret. Not the fact that it didn't happen. That's life. It was how I handled it. Or more like how I didn't handle it. I was a cop. That's what I told myself. I said, Larry, you put things away. You handle crises. I acted like Marjorie's pain was some goddamn case I could close." He shook his head, his eyes sober. "That's not how it works."

"You never thought of adopting? Kids like me?"

"By the time we gave up on having babies, it felt too late. The last one was stillborn, and Marjorie was never the same after that. Of course, I wasn't expecting her to be. But she needed me to help her out of the wilderness, and I was just not there."

Larry got up with his plate. Amanda wondered if she should hug him and decided not to. He didn't seem like a hugger.

When he came back for her plate, she had arranged all the toast ends to make a shape. "Here," she said.

It was a smile.

Larry laughed. It was a good laugh.

"See? I told you," he said. "Like every day is a surprise."

THE MAN WATCHED FROM OUTSIDE THE CABIN AS LARRY AND Amanda did the dishes, then turned off the kitchen light. It was too bad Amanda had not gone back to the hotel. He didn't want to have to try to kill them together.

One at a time was easier. That was what Martha had said.

He had planned to kill Amanda that night he'd chased her. But she had gotten away, and he'd felt like breaking down her hotel room door might attract attention. Then she and Larry had left town, and he'd had Reggie to take care of.

Now they were back, and Martha had said it had to be done right away. It was already almost too late.

He watched as Larry stirred the fire, killing it. Amanda used the bathroom—the light in there was turned on, then off. He could hear running water. Finally, all the lights inside the cabin were turned off. The plume of smoke from the chimney died. All was quiet.

He waited. It was a strangely windless night. He could hear Larry snoring in his bed. In the woods, he knew, the boys were asleep in their graves. Dennis was in the ocean, his bones worn down to glass.

Time passed. The moon grew fat and full. He crept slowly to the outer walls of the cabin. He felt the soft dander under his feet.

He thought of Martha. From his earliest memories, it was her face he saw. When he had crawled out from that rug back in Colorado, as one of her very first patients, he had felt reborn. All his past memories—the abuse, the abandonment—had been stripped away, leaving in their wake only her face and the pure sweet taste of milk, dripped from a bottle. She was like a mother to him.

He would do anything for her.

But he had discovered, as the years passed, there was a cost to losing his memories this way. He no longer knew why he did what he did. He was as untethered to the past as the moon was to the earth. He was unable to form any other attachments. In a place inside him he could barely recognize, he feared the next person he loved would smother him too.

He dragged a can of gasoline from the woods. Working quietly, he poured it around the edges of the cabin. He wondered if he should torch their cars, too, and decided to let nature take its course. He was hoping the whole dune would go up, so that by the time fire trucks arrived all the way from Seaside, the cabin would be burnt along with the surrounding woods, and no one would be able to figure out how it all had started. Larry and Amanda would just be two more corpses in an unsolved wildfire. He knew all about wildfires, because after he was finally discharged from the Colorado clinic, he had been transferred to a youth facility where the boys worked on fire crews. He had written Martha regularly during those years.

Later, when he moved to the Oregon Coast, they had stayed in touch. She had even helped him out. He had been happy when she took the job at Brightwood. She had told him their relationship needed to stay secret. It was smart thinking, he knew, with all that had happened. She had needed him. No one had ever needed him before. He could not explain to himself why this troubled him so much, why there was a part of him that hurt so bad.

The cabin walls were now soaked with accelerant.

Stepping back, he wiped his hands carefully and set down the empty can. He reached for a book of matches, and set the world on fire.

28

IT WAS VERY EARLY WHEN RALPH SHOWED UP TO WORK. THE nightmares of his youth had returned. He woke up with his heart beating so hard he thought it might explode. Unable to sleep, he had taken to coming to work earlier and earlier.

He reached the custodian closet, shrugging off his jacket.

He stopped.

The shovel had been moved. He was pretty sure he had left it in the corner. He put all his gardening tools there. The shears and rose clippers were on a shelf, and the lawn edger leaned against the wall. The shovel was usually there next to it, its handle worn smooth by his hand.

Now it was a couple of inches away. Not far, but far enough that he thought, That cannot have been me.

Puzzled, Ralph ran his hand through his unruly hair. His hair was always dry because he used bar soap on it. At the center, they had used the cheapest soaps, never any shampoo. He didn't know any better.

He looked around the closet, at the cleansers lined up on the shelves and the mop bucket on the floor. He kept the closet locked, of course. The stuff inside would be dangerous for the boys. The lock could be opened with the master key all the staff carried. It worked in every door except that of the treatment room. Only Martha had the key to that door, and she guarded it carefully.

Shaking his head, Ralph changed into his work jacket and checked the clipboard by the door, where the staff wrote down everything that needed to be fixed. There was a clogged sink in the boys' shower. He picked up his plumbing snake.

But first, he needed coffee.

HE STOPPED IN THE KITCHEN, WHERE THE COOK WAS ALREADY AT work, making biscuits she would serve with country gravy. Ralph's mouth watered at the smell. It was the one good thing about working at the center. You got to eat the same meals as the boys, and they were good, in his estimation.

The cook looked up. She had a smear of flour on her face.

"Coffee's hot," she said.

Ralph poured himself a cup. It was still early, and the boys had yet to awaken. The night watchman was pulling candy wrappers from his desk, getting ready to leave.

The cook saw the snake in Ralph's basket of tools.

"Another clogged line?" she asked, making a face, tucking a sheet pan of biscuits into the massive oven. Two more sheets were cooling on the counter.

"Not the toilet, at least, this time. Got a note from last night."

"You musta heard what happened."

"No. What?"

"Another boy run off. Joey. You know him? Sweet little tyke, but he has a mouth on him. Sure hope he's okay. I never heard what happened with the last one, did you? Martha said once they catch them, they send them on to another place. She was here earlier but went home, upset."

Ralph drank his coffee. He had heard about Steven. It happened in places like this, he had figured. But then again, it hadn't happened before in all his time at Brightwood.

"How did he get out?"

"Back door was unlocked when I got here."

Ralph set down the coffee and went to check the back door. The lock hadn't been broken. It had just been left unlatched.

"Doors are supposed to be locked every night," he said, coming back into the warm kitchen.

"Don't I know it," she said. "Night watchman swore it was locked. Personally, I think he goes outside on his shifts, heaven knows why. He raids the kitchen too. Don't tell anyone I said so."

Ralph picked his coffee back up. It was lukewarm. He gulped it, eager to be awake.

"Maybe the boys are getting ahold of his keys," the cook said, rolling out another batch of biscuits. The dough was so light, it sprung in her hands. She patted it lovingly. In a pot on the stove behind her, the thick white gravy bubbled.

"What makes you think that?"

"He's always sleeping. Thinks no one knows, but I'm here at the crack of dawn, and more times than not, that man is just waking up. He puts his keys right there on the desk in front of him." She shook her head, and went to stir the gravy.

"More coffee?"

"Not now," Ralph said.

RALPH FOUND DENNIS ASLEEP IN HIS ROOM. HE WAS VERY SWEATY, and the custodian knew he was having bad dreams too.

The custodian put his broad, cool hand on the boy's brow. He felt the thoughts rushing there. The boy's breath quickened, and then calmed. He twitched and fell back to sleep. Hopefully, this time his dreams would be better.

"Ralph?" Dennis said when he was almost out of the room.

The custodian stopped.

"Yes?"

"Are you okay?"

"Why do you ask, son?"

They could hear cars arriving outside, including Martha's. It changed the air in the entire center. Dennis never knew when it would be a holding time day. Sometimes days passed and Martha didn't call for him. Then, suddenly, a week came where it was every day. The uncertainty was part of the cure. You never knew when the monsters were coming.

"I don't know. You don't seem right."

"I suppose I'm not. Get out of bed, try to have a good day. There's biscuits and gravy."

"I don't like biscuits and gravy. They hurt my stomach."

That's because that woman presses on you, Ralph thought.

"Guess I'll have to eat your share, then."

He was rewarded with a rare giggle. It sounded nothing like an honest giggle, and it hurt his heart to hear it. Dennis turned over in his bed, seeing the morning light coming in the window. He remembered in that moment, and the respite from pain was gone. The rabbit was gone.

But Ralph was here.

"Okay," Dennis said.

DENNIS ATE HIS BISCUITS AFTER ALL, AND RALPH AND THE OTHER staff members ate after the boys were done, the last of the gravy spooned over their plates. They ate quickly, before going back to work. Only Ike lazed around, trying to shoot the bull with the cook, who wanted him out of her kitchen.

"Get on now," she said, shooing him out. "Unless you want to do dishes."

In the hallway, Ike ran into Ralph, who had finished unclogging the drain and was now carrying hedge clippers outside.

"Get out of my way," Ike growled. He had no use for Ralph.

The custodian stepped aside.

"Hey," Ralph said as the man passed. Ike stopped.

"Someone was in my utility closet," Ralph said. "Any idea who that would have been?"

There was no expression on Ike's face except for annoyance.

"Do I look like a fucking custodian? Why would I be in your dumb closet?"

WINTER ARRIVED IN A FURY, BATTERING THE AREA WITH STORMS. So many trees fell in the forest, they sounded like gunshots echoing through the center. Boys hid under their blankets and cried, and Ike Tressler made fun of those who did. He called them sissies. Sissies and pansies.

Dennis turned nine. Reggie was thirteen.

Martha said nothing. She had stopped having trainings. She no longer cared about the fake flowers on the dining room tables, and when the cook tried to interest her in a more nutritious meal plan—suggesting that maybe they could even start a vegetable garden with the boys—the director was silent, and then walked away.

Maybe she didn't like it at the coast, the cook thought. Not everyone did. It was cold and wet.

"It's almost spring," the cook said, following the woman down the hall. "If we plan now, I can buy some seed at the feed store in Wheel Stone."

"I'll consider it," Martha said, closing her office door.

She closed her door a lot now, the cook thought. For hours, days, and even weeks, it felt, the director disappeared with boys into the treatment room. She left the rest of the staff to take care of things. It was okay. They had been doing it before she came. Still, the cook was disappointed. She'd had such high hopes for the place when Martha King arrived.

Day after day, week after week, month after month, boys were taken to the holding time room. Sometimes it was Reggie; other times, other boys. Martha was picking on them, Ralph decided. There were certain ones she seemed fixated on. The homosexual boys, for sure. But also boys like him and Dennis. Boys with a tender side, and a fighting one too. There was something about that combination—like the rabbit— that she found intolerable.

For some boys, there never would be a cure, he realized. No matter how much they gave in, it would never be enough for Martha.

The latest boy was named Angel. Sure enough, a few months after his intensive treatment began, Angel, too, went missing.

"ANOTHER RUNAWAY," THE COOK SAID.

Ralph was in the kitchen with a cup of coffee, and a sense of déjà vu swept over him so strongly that he felt weak at the knees and wanted to sit down.

The cook was boiling a ham. She'd wanted to start it early for lunch. Breakfast this morning was a big pot of old-fashioned cornmeal mush boiling at the back of the stove, slowly turning into a thick golden soup. The boys would be given brown sugar and milk to pour over it at the table. The next morning, the cook would make patties out of the leftovers and fry them in margarine, which was even better.

Ralph liked cornmeal mush, but this morning he wanted nothing.

"That's three," he said, drinking his coffee.

"You okay?" She looked over from where she was poking the ham with a large fork.

"You ever think anything of this place?" he asked.

"Not sure what you mean," she said. She put a lid on the simmering ham. "It's a job, and we both care about the boys."

"What about Martha King?"

The cook set the fork down and leaned against the counter. "I don't know what's wrong with her now. Maybe she feels bad about the boys getting out. It's not her to blame, though."

"No. I'm sure it's not." Ralph poured his coffee into the empty sink. He didn't want it anymore.

"You off to work?"

"Gonna go check my shovel."

"Excuse me?"

"Nothing."

"I JUST WANT YOU TO BE SAFE," RALPH SAID.

Dennis lay in his bed. He turned away from the custodian, staring at the wall. He was tired of the custodian telling him he cared. Martha kept taking him to the treatment room, and nothing ever changed. Ralph had turned out to be a liar too. They all were. They all said they loved you and let others hurt you.

Ralph was even worse than the rest of them. He had made Dennis love him, and now look. He couldn't even save a rabbit.

"I hate you," Dennis said.

Ralph understood.

"They're saying the missing boys took the keys from the watchman," Ralph said. "I don't believe it."

Dennis rolled over in bed. "Is that possible?"

"I guess."

Dennis rolled back.

"What do you think happened?" Dennis asked the wall.

"I don't even want to say."

"Maybe Martha is doing them a favor," Dennis said.

Ralph rubbed his face. He had dandruff in his eyebrows.

"But I hope Reggie doesn't disappear," Dennis said. "I like him."

"It's you I'm worried about right now," Ralph said.

"Well, there's nothing you can do. Right?"

Ralph looked sad, and sick.

"Maybe it would be for the best," Dennis said, after a bit.

"What?"

"If she made me disappear too. Then it would be like I was never born."

"No, son."

"Why not?"

The center was waking up around them. Ralph knew he had better go before he got caught, because Martha would take it out on Dennis if she saw them together. It would be more evidence of their "unhealthy attachment."

"Ralph?" Dennis asked. His voice was calmer.

"Yes, son?"

"Do you remember what you told me, back when we met?"

"What was that?"

"About the ocean. You said it was like this place. Nice on the outside. But dangerous."

"It is. Don't do anything, son."

Dennis did not answer.

29

LARRY AWOKE TO THE SMELL OF GASOLINE. IN HIS DREAMS, Marjorie was saying it was good they had updated to an electric car, because she really hated this smell. Larry had never bought an electric car in his life—he knew it would garner ribbing from his colleagues, though now he wasn't sure why—and this comment puzzled him greatly. He turned over in bed and sat right up.

It was outside. There was a flicker of light outside his windows. A fire.

He jumped out of bed and ran to the guest room. In moments, he had Amanda standing, without even knowing how. The flames were climbing the cabin walls around them, shining through the windows.

Amanda blinked, still half asleep in the flickering light, and then she was awake.

"La—"

"Move," he said, and grabbed her hand, only dimly aware she was dressed in yoga pants and a sleeping shirt. They ran into the living room, where the flames illuminated the dead fireplace. The fire was growing quickly but not quickly enough, Larry thought. Whoever had set it hadn't thought about the wet conditions. Even with an accelerant, the fire was finding the damp cabin hard to catch. The soft duff on the forest floor caught with little blazes that turned to char that Larry could smell.

Amanda reached for the front door. Larry looked at the closed windows.

"Hold on!" he yelled.

He ran to the kitchen sink, turning on the cold-water tap. "Amanda!" he screamed, and when she turned around, he sprayed her. She turned in the cold water, gasping, understanding intuitively what he was doing. When she was soaking wet, he doused himself, then soaked a dish towel. He threw it over her wet hair.

"Careful," he said, and then reached for the front door.

He opened it with a yank, the hot doorknob burning his hand. The flames roared into the room. Larry knew in that moment that all his belongings might be destroyed, and he looked over his shoulder at the urn on the mantel, realizing it was too late to get it.

"Now!" he yelled.

They ran through the open door. The flames leapt around them but seemed to retreat from their wet clothes. Outside, Larry spun Amanda around, using his hands to put out any fires. There were none. He slapped his own head, afraid of what little hair he had left burning.

They turned to look at the cabin. All the walls were on fire now, and the fire was licking over the mossy roof. This went up with a blaze. The woods began to catch, the fire burning resentfully at the fresh pine trees.

"We have to let someone know."

They both looked down. Both were in socks.

"Do you have your phone?"

She shook her head.

He backed away from the flames. A burning shingle fell, and in the forest, a dead bush went up like a torch. The air was filled with the smell of burning moss.

IN TOWN, GERTRUDE SMELLED THE FIRE FIRST. SHE WENT TO WAKE Aspire, and called the fire station, then the constable. Flashing lights filled the sky. They reflected over the ocean, which was indifferent. The sea lions, back on their rock, watched the burning hill, the fire reflected in their small, black, interested eyes.

The fire stopped at the cemetery. The sand there smoldered. By then the sun was coming up, and the fire trucks had arrived, pumping seawater with vast fat lines flung in the water. The burnt hill looked like a naked black sore against the fresh green of the forest. The fire had burned downward, toward the coast, which was odd, the constable said, because usually, the winds would push it inland. They had been lucky the night had been so quiet. The other homes on the dune were spared, and so were Larry's and Amanda's cars.

The locals turned out, as they did for any disaster. The fisherman brought a pair of boots and an old oilskin for Larry. Others donated other clothes. The firefighters were able to salvage Larry's wallet from the ruins, and the urn with his wife's ashes. Most of his clothes, along with Amanda's parka and all the clothes in her backpack, had been ruined by the smoke and water. Amanda's driver's license was smudged and half melted.

The bear tooth, in its glass case, was scorched but okay. Their phones, plugged in in the kitchen to charge, had fallen under a table and been protected from the worst of the flames and wet.

Larry and Amanda stood by their cars, looking at what remained of the cabin. The burnt trees dripped salt water. A faint rain began falling, and then it turned into a heavier rain, putting out any remaining stragglers, the fire chief said.

Everyone went home, except for Amanda and Larry, who were given free rooms at the hotel until Larry could figure out what to do.

In her room, Amanda took a deep breath, and made the call. She figured her parents might hear about the fire—for all she knew, her mother was watching any news coming from Eagle Cove.

Her mother answered.

"Hi, Mom. There was a fire, but I'm okay," Amanda said.

"I'M SORRY ABOUT WHAT HAPPENED TO YOU," CHARLIE SAID, FETCH-ing extra towels and a bedspread. Larry sat on the edge of the lumpy mattress. He hadn't really cared about the cabin. What he did care about was the urn containing Marjorie's ashes—which was now safely in a corner of the hotel room—and the value of the property. He had already been in touch with his insurance agent and discovered he would get what he had paid for it.

"I guess I'm a free agent now," he told the hotel owner.

There was a knock on the wall beside him. Amanda was in the adjoining room. Larry had asked to be put next to her. Whoever had tried to kill her had now tried to kill them both. He was worried about her.

"At least you got your car, right? You can go wherever you want," Charlie said.

"If only it was that easy."

Larry picked up his phone, called Amanda. "Everything okay?"

The hotel owner stood listening. Larry waved him away. Charlie left, smiling, closing the door softly behind him.

"They gave me clothes," Amanda said. Her voice was hoarse, and she sounded upset. "These are not the kind of clothes I would ever wear, Larry."

"Why's that?"

"You'll see."

"Everything else okay?"

"Gertrude sent more food than I could ever eat." She paused.

"I called my parents. They might call you. They're weird like that. I told them it wasn't your fault. And that we're working with the police down here."

He looked down at his own care package. For him, Gertrude had included a bottle of whiskey. "I'd be happy to talk to them, if you like. Of course they are worried. Of course they are."

"They still treat me like a kid. A special-education kid."

She had never said those words before.

"Any parent would worry in this situation," he told her. "It's been twice now someone has tried to hurt you."

"I didn't tell them about the first time."

"Oh. Okay." He didn't press. She was right—she was an adult. But still, he wished she had told them.

"My hair feels strange too. Like plastic."

"It probably got a little singed. We can find a way to get you a cut." She yawned, and he could hear her jaw cracking.

"I'm going to take a nap now," she said.

"I'll be right next door."

A FEW HOURS LATER, LARRY MET THE CONSTABLE IN THE FRONT office. All the little dings and scrapes and burns that hadn't been apparent earlier were now. His face was ruddy with heat exposure, making his sunburn from Arizona even worse. Most of his hair had been singed off, it turned out.

"I'm going to find Ike Tressler. He's our primary suspect," the constable said.

"You have more than one?" Larry asked, drinking the vile coffee Charlie provided.

"Well, not really." It was raining. The hotel appeared to be empty, as usual. Some things never changed. The constable looked out the office window. "Shit. That newspaperman is here. You going to talk to him, Larry?"

"I have a feeling that article is what sparked this in the first place," Larry said. "So to speak."

Amanda came in, her hair wet from the shower. Charlie had given her a pair of scissors to cut off the burnt ends. She had done a fairly remarkable job of trimming her hair herself. It now swung above her shoulders, in a shorter bob.

Larry thought of her dad, who had called him after Larry and Amanda had talked earlier. The man had a high-pitched, imperious voice, but under the academic pretense, Larry could hear his worry. Amanda's parents loved her. It was clear from the first moment the man spoke.

Larry had told him he would do his best to protect their daughter, but no, he could not make her return home. The conversation had ended on a sour note.

Amanda looked at Dwight Bowman, who was parking in the lot.

"I really don't want to talk to him, Larry."

"Then you don't have to," Larry said. "It's probably better for the constable at this point if we don't. Open case and all."

"Yeah," Constable Roberts said, putting his own notebook away. "Though at this point, I feel like enough of a fuckup to not judge anything you do."

Larry was surprised to hear that.

"You didn't know we would open a can of worms," he said.

"It makes you think, doesn't it?" the constable asked. "How many graves are there across the world, holding secrets?"

"Empty graves, full of secrets," Amanda said.

Larry glanced at her. Sometimes Amanda said things that astonished him.

"Yes," Larry said. "Empty graves, full of secrets."

Amanda poured a cup of the awful coffee, sniffed it, then dumped in a bunch of the old creamer powder. It was so old, it made greasy globules on the surface. She gave Charlie a polite smile so she wouldn't hurt his feelings.

"I'm going to head out," she said. "I'm late for a trip I'm going to take."

"You're still leaving?" Larry looked surprised.

"Why not?" She looked at Larry. "Do you need me? My car is still working. I'm going to Seaside. I'll be back in a few days."

"We'll be fine," Larry said. "Big-boy pants and all that."

"I mean, for the investigation." She looked pointedly at the constable.

"I can get your statement later," Constable Roberts said. He dumped the last of his own coffee in the trash and zipped up his rain jacket. They watched Dwight approach the office. "I'm going to get to work. I'll be in touch."

"You'll be okay?" Larry asked Amanda, worried.

She smiled at him, her blond hair damp at the tips. "Just a trip up the coast, with someone I know is safe."

"Leave his number, at least."

"I'll text you."

Amanda passed Dwight as she left. When he spoke, she shook her head. Larry, too, declined to be interviewed, so all Dwight had in the end was grinning Charlie, trying to interest him in an article about the hotel.

THE CONSTABLE WALKED THROUGH THE BURNT WOODS BY THE cabin. He had strung up police tape earlier, and the wind had already blown it down. He stopped to lift up a section, then dropped it.

Between the rain and the fire trucks, he didn't expect to find much. That's what made arson so hard to solve. Fire burned evidence, and then the firefighters poured water on it, turning everything into sludge.

What he was looking for was the trail that began where the fire damage ended. He walked back down the dune road, where a local might have come from—the fire trucks had taken the main road—and inspected the steep sandy road. There were no tracks he could see. At the cemetery, he stopped to wander among the graves a bit, just thinking. Where the memorial to Dennis stood, a fine view of the ocean unfolded, from cape to cape. He looked at the cliff where Brett Jarvis had taken his life years before.

There were shells piled around the memorial. He knew of the sea tradition. The shells were for warding off angry ghosts, left for eternity in the sea. He knelt, picking one up. It was a mussel shell. A recent addition. He could tell by the fresh barnacles. All the sand dollars were whole. That was important. Broken sand dollars were bad luck. Whoever had left these shells had taken care to find just the right ones.

"Someone is afraid of you coming back, buddy," the constable said, feeling the memorial stone with his hand. It was warm to the touch, despite the cold weather. At least the rain had stopped.

"I failed you before," he said. "I'm not going to fail you again."

30

"RALPH."

It was the night watchman, running up to him.

"Yes?" Ralph jumped from his truck. The sun had yet to rise, and his truck was the only one in the lot, except for the watchman's. The cook hadn't even shown up yet. Ralph had found sleep impossible.

"Another one of the boys got out."

Ralph felt his heart constrict.

"Which one?"

"Dennis Owen."

"Where—"

"He took my keys. This time I know it happened. I woke up, and the back door was open and my key ring had been moved."

RALPH RAN OUT THE BACK DOOR. SMALL SHOE PRINTS WERE STILL visible in the dew-frosted grass. They led directly into the brambly woods. He followed them until the prints were lost in the trees.

Dennis was heading directly toward the ocean.

Ralph ran back to the center. "How long ago?" he asked the night watchman, his throat aching.

"I dunno. Could have been hours."

"I'm going after him," Ralph said.

"You want me to tell the boss?"

But the custodian was gone, jumping in his truck and barreling back out of the gates, down the mountain road.

The watchman felt tired, and hoped he wouldn't get in trouble. Martha hadn't blamed him for the other boys, but for some reason, he felt sure she would blame him for this one.

THE SUN WAS JUST PEEKING ABOVE THE TREES WHEN DENNIS MADE it through the woods.

For the first time since Martha had come, Dennis felt at peace. He had made the right choice. It was better to die out here than to die in the center. He knew now he was going to die, one way or the other. At least this way, Ralph could quit the center and leave, and he could have a good life. He would remember Dennis. It was a good plan, Dennis thought.

He walked onto a road covered with sand. There were cliffs to his right, and in front of him was a dazzling scene he could never have imagined.

The ocean.

For a minute, Dennis had no words, not even for himself. Never had he thought anything could be so beautiful. The waves rose and spun in a strange harmony with each other, crashing against the shore. He could smell the wet sand. He could feel the force of the waves.

Dennis breathed deeply. He thought of all the homes he had been in before Brightwood, and of the day he had met Ralph. Now here he was. He would die in something beautiful.

His institutional shoes were covered with burrs, his gray pants smeared with mud and fir needles. Thorns had caught his hands. He crossed the road, marveling at how the wind tugged at his pants. He reached the white sand and stumbled over it, gaining his footing. He looked at the ocean and began to walk toward it. There was no hesitation in him.

The sea stretched on for eternity. Soon he would be part of that eternity.

There was the sound of a familiar engine in the distance. He turned to see Ralph's truck racing down the road behind him.

Oh, Ralph, Dennis thought. You shouldn't have come.

The truck came to a screeching stop. Ralph flung open the door. And Dennis began to run.

CONSTABLE ROBERTS CAME AS SOON AS HE GOT THE CALL. THE CUS-todian was soaking wet and covered with sand, shivering on the bench in the store. He held the boy's wet shirt in his hands. His eyes, catching the constable's, said one thing: *This is your fault. And mine.*

"What happened?" the constable asked.

"I tried to catch him," Ralph croaked. He coughed, water still coming up from his lungs.

The constable took the shirt. *Dennis Owen*, said the label on the back. Gertrude and the others saw it, which was how they were later able to tell the newspaperman the boy's name.

"We need to form a search party," the constable said, turning to the others.

"Sure thing," Charlie said. More people were gathering, including the fisherman and his wife. Some carried thermoses filled with sugary hot chocolate or coffee, and blankets for one another, and for the boy, if he was found.

"Who has the walkie-talkies?"

"Me," said Gertrude, pulling open the drawer behind the counter.

"Okay." Charlie took charge. "Come on, we'll divide up the beach."

"I want to help," Ralph coughed.

"You nearly drowned," the constable said. "Do you want someone to drive you to the hospital?"

"I'll be okay," the custodian said, wiping his face. "We need to find him before it's too late."

The searchers looked at one another. No one was going to say the obvious. They all hoped too. That's why they carried the blankets.

The constable put a hand on Ralph's wet shoulder. "Go home for now. I'll be in touch. Don't leave town until the investigation is done."

Ralph nodded, miserable.

THE LOCALS SPENT TWO ARDUOUS DAYS SEARCHING, TAKING RISKS themselves. Brett Jarvis, sober for a change, climbed the rocks by the cliffs to see if the body had washed up there. Others walked the surf, examining the deep waves, and a few took their fishing boats out beyond the rocks, just in case the boy was floating out there.

There was nothing. The boy's body could be tumbling along the ocean floor miles away by now, fifty or a hundred feet under. It could be bobbing alongside an ocean liner or tossed up on a remote beach halfway across the globe.

On the second day, Martha King paid the constable a visit. She sat across from him, smiling at the quaint decor. She had worn lipstick for the meeting.

"Tell me what happened," he said.

She told him how Dennis Owen had taken the keys. He had unlocked the back door, replaced the keys, and run. She had fired the night watchman and would be hiring someone who didn't sleep on the job. That was it.

"What will you do?" he asked.

"What else? Keep working."

"Any idea why he ran?"

"No," she said, then smiled. "He was very disturbed."

She rose to go. The constable was thinking of the boy standing at the window. He was gone now and never coming back.

"I wanted to remind you," Martha said, "that state law prohibits us from sharing anything related to the boys with the press or anyone else. We are both bound by confidentiality."

Constable Roberts understood exactly what she was saying. If he talked, she would get him fired.

"HERE TO GIVE NOTICE?" MARTHA ASKED RALPH AS HE ENTERED her office.

Two weeks had passed. The constable had officially closed the case. The local paper had run an article, and the town had put up the memorial, which concerned Martha. But neither seemed to get any attention. The caseworker for Dennis had closed his file and moved on.

Martha knew she should be relieved. It was over. But the boys buried in the woods told her it was not.

"The constable says I'm free to go," Ralph said.

"Well, then. Going to give me time to find someone else?"

Ralph looked around at her diploma-covered walls, and the cards on her desk from grateful parents, and even a few from boys like him.

"No," he said.

"Figures. I owe you a final paycheck." She went searching for her account book.

Ralph picked up one of the cards from her desk. This was so sacrilegious, she gasped.

"Put that down," she said. She didn't know what had gotten into him, and she didn't like it. It was good he was leaving.

He put it down, and she exhaled. She wondered at herself. Why did she even have all those thank-you cards out? Some were dangerous. She vowed to hide them as soon as he left.

"I was wondering if he would write you," Ralph said.

"Who?" She glanced up, filling out his check. It wasn't for much money, and she didn't care.

"Your father."

"My dad?"

"Tough old man. Mean, actually. Everyone thought he was great, cleaning up the streets of Sleeping Giant. No one asked if the streets needing cleaning."

"You know my dad?"

She looked up at Ralph and frowned, as if seeing him for the first time.

"It made sense. Perfect your whole life, from what I heard. Graduated magna cum whatever. Director of the Axis Treatment Center. Helping boys. That's what they always said. Her dad keeps the town clean, and Martha keeps the boys' hearts clean. Two good souls, doing a lot of good work."

"You were at Axis?"

"I was there. One of your boys. That's what you always said. 'My boys.' Like you owned us." He stopped, trying to restrain his emotions before they broke loose all over her office. She didn't deserve them. "You know what I think? I think you did something to some of those boys. Just like here. You made them disappear too. But I don't have any proof. The constable here won't listen to me, and I tried. But I know you. I used to look in your eyes when I was just a child. I could see that you were the one who needed help."

Martha King felt frozen in time and space. She was inside one of those sleeping giants, screaming at the sky to just make it stop.

She spoke deliberately, her lips tight.

"What are you going to do?"

"What is there to do? Like I said, I have no proof. I could dig up every inch of forest from here to Seaside, look over every cliff, and still not find those boys. So I'll make you a deal. You close down this place and stop working. I move away. Someday you'll die, and then I'll be at peace."

Martha thought about it. He was right. It was time to retire. She could stop taking risks and having accidents. She could leave this all behind and be thankful for all she had accomplished. Maybe she could even write a book.

She looked up, hope in her face.

"Did I help you at all?"

He breathed in at the temerity of it.

"No," he said.

31

AMANDA MET PETE ASHOONA AT THE SEASIDE AIRPORT. IT WASN'T a commercial airport but a small landing strip outside of town with a helicopter pad advertising tourist rides. Pete had a friend who was willing to loan him his little plane to fly to Alaska.

"Anger Bay, here we come," Pete said. He was wearing the same plaid shirt as before, only this time under a heavy parka. His long gray hair coiled down his back. He carried a flight bag over one shoulder.

"Is it big enough?" Amanda asked, looking askance at the plane.

"We don't need to fly high. Just well," Pete said. "It will be a rocky ride, anyhow. Hope you're okay with that."

"I've never been in such a small plane," Amanda said, climbing in. The plane smelled of old rubber and oil. The leather seats were cracked, and someone had spilled what looked like Goldfish cracker crumbs across the floor.

"I've got sick bags. I'll take it easy, over the mountains."

"Which ones?"

"All of them. Say, you okay? I heard there was a big fire last night in Eagle Cove."

"Yeah. There was." Amanda didn't want to talk about it. He glanced at her, then turned the engine over. Amanda had brought the bear tooth in a bag from the market. Its presence reassured her.

"Wait till you see the ocean from the air," he said. "It is something else."

Amanda took a deep breath, steadied herself, and buckled in.

She looked out the window as the plane took off and was startled at how much she could feel the air outside. She was part of that air, now. She was part of the Pacific Ocean they flew out to and over, to cross Canada to the northernmost US state.

THE SEA ICE BEGAN FAR BEFORE THEY REACHED ANGER BAY, AS THEY flew over the Chukchi Sea. Amanda was by now thoroughly chilled and wishing she had found a better pair of boots before she left. Hers had been loaned to her by Aspire, and while they fit, they were far from warm. Her borrowed jacket was also not made for real cold, and she shivered inside it.

"We'll get you in better gear when we touch down!" Pete yelled at her over the sound of wind. Little bits of ice hit the windshield. Amanda looked down over the frozen sea. It *was* something else—she could see the shape of waves. The ice was a hard, smooth blue where the wind had worn away the snow.

"Should have done that before!" he yelled.

They had been flying for four hours, and Amanda had been sick twice. It was good her stomach was empty, she thought. The plane swayed as they made their final descent, over the frozen sea toward a narrow landing strip dusted with snow. A single blinking light let them know where they were. Amanda peered out the frozen windows. All she could see was snow and more snow. Here and there were dark humps that might have been roofs.

"Hold on." Pete took his time lowering the plane and crab-walking it up the landing strip. "We're here. Wait a sec."

They rolled into a completely deserted airport. The few other planes on the tarmac were covered with snow. Pete jumped out, testing his feet on the ice. He went around and got Amanda, opening her door and looking sympathetically into her green face.

"Welcome to Anger Bay."

PETE PUNCHED A CODE INTO THE AIRPORT DOOR'S KEYPAD AND LET Amanda inside. It was very cold in the building. Amanda took in a tiny snack bar, with a turned-off light above it, and a single waiting room. There was a metal detector pushed to one side.

"This place never gets used anymore," Pete said. "Once the station was closed, that was it. No more visiting scientists. Now it's just us locals, flying in and out. There aren't any roads, of course. Too much snow."

"How did people travel before planes?" Amanda asked.

He laughed. "By sled, of course."

Amanda knew from her research that there was a small village near the research station. She wondered if that was where Pete was from, originally. She didn't want to be intrusive and ask.

"We'll spend the night in the village and head out in the morning. But first, I need to get you into something warm. You'll freeze to death otherwise. Stupid of me to not even think of it before we left."

In a dark airport closet, Pete dug through boxes of old flight gear and came up with an oil-stained orange snowsuit and a pair of men's snow boots. Amanda put on the snowsuit, feeling like an odd, bulky bear. The boots were too big, but warm. She felt instant relief.

"Next stop, home."

"How do we get there?"

"Snowmobile."

He led her across a gritty, icy parking lot to a metal shed that banged with the wind. Their plane was already covered with a sheet of ice. Amanda wondered if they would be able to leave as planned, in two days. The sky was whirling with fresh snow.

Pete unlocked the shed and rolled out a snowmobile. After checking the tank, he made sure there was an extra can of fuel and safety gear in the back. Pete handed her a helmet and put on his own. Amanda took her seat, putting her arms around his waist, and they took off into the snow and wind.

Everywhere Amanda looked, from inside her drawn hood, was white. The snow blew in sharp gusts around her, and she tasted it. It tasted different from other snow. She reminded herself to take a video to send to the zoo, so they could share it with Molly. She wondered how the bear was reacting to the videos she had sent so far. She had been too shy to reach out to Sean and ask.

They rode for what seemed like a long time, but the hazy sun in the distance never changed. It hung like a yellow halo in a sea of silver white. Lights appeared in the distance. Amanda peered at them. They were coming from windows, in houses nearly buried in snow. There was no woodsmoke—they would have no wood to burn, she thought. What appeared to be large oilcans were buried in yards.

Pete stopped, the snowmobile sputtering. He got off, stretching.

"Come on," he said. Amanda followed him, the snow gusting around them. In a few crunching steps, they were at a door.

It opened.

"Pete! You old dog. Come say hello to your mother."

INSIDE WAS ALL WARMTH, LIGHT, AND NOISE. A TELEVISION WAS blasting in the living room, and the smell of something rich and warm came from the kitchen.

"Amanda, this is my little sister, Samantha."

Pete's sister was maybe in her thirties, with a wide, friendly face. A little boy clung to her leg, excited about the newcomer.

"Hello," a voice called, and that was Pete's mother, perched on the couch.

"Mom." Pete leaned forward to kiss her cheeks.

"Missed you."

"Said I'd be back soon, didn't I? Taking Amanda here on a bit of an outing. Say, I'm hungry. We flew all day. No time for lunch, of course."

"Made you stew. Your favorite."

"Now that," Pete told Amanda, "is a joke."

He set down his bag, and the boy stared at Amanda from behind his mother's legs.

"Didn't you bring a bag?" the boy asked Amanda.

She didn't want to say almost everything she had brought to Eagle Cove from Portland had been destroyed in a fire, so she just smiled.

"Maybe she likes to travel light," Pete's sister said.

"Get out of that snowsuit, or you'll be drenched in sweat," Pete said.

Amanda nodded, and started to strip off the snowsuit, feeling self-conscious. She was aware of the loaned clothes she was wearing, especially the sweatshirt from Aspire that said *Fancy* across the front. She tried to hide it under the jacket, but Pete reached out to take the jacket too.

"You can use the bathroom if you want. Wash up."

Amanda did, feeling better once she'd splashed her face with cold water and scrubbed her teeth with her finger and a swipe of toothpaste. Her toothbrush had been lost in the fire, and she hadn't thought to get a new one before meeting Pete. She wished her brain worked better.

Samantha was already setting the table. Pete was sitting next to his mother on the couch. His mom was back to watching her television show. The little boy was perched on a dining room chair, his eyes watching the food as it traveled from stove to plate.

"Here," Samantha said, handing Amanda a tub of margarine. She set it on the table, next to a stack of white bread. There was a bowl of what looked like preserved kumquats.

"Dinner," Samantha announced, and Amanda realized she was very hungry.

The stew was full of meat and potatoes and carrots.

"It's delicious," Amanda said, tasting the gravy.

Tentatively, she poked a piece of meat, trying to figure out what it was. She didn't want to be rude.

"You don't like meat?" Pete's mother asked.

"I like it," she said hurriedly, cutting the soft meat with her spoon. "I like it cooked soft, like this. Just like this."

"It's caribou," the little boy said.

"It's tasty," Amanda said, eating the meat.

AMANDA SLEPT ON THE COUCH, AND PETE SLEPT ON THE FLOOR. IN the morning, she woke up early, stumbling over him on the way to the bathroom. He was awake by the time she returned, yawning hugely.

"Breakfast," he said, and got up and made pancakes studded with nuts, and eaten with swaths of butter and syrup. His sister left her bedroom, where her little boy still slept, a huddle of warmth in the blankets. Pete's mother was in her room, snoring mightily. It reminded Amanda of Larry. He had been snoring like that the night of the fire. It didn't seem like that had been only two nights before, and that the man had chased her less than a week before that.

"You heading out?" Samantha asked.

Her brother nodded, eating the last of the pancakes. He signaled with his fork at Amanda's plate.

"Those are nuts," he said.

Amanda picked one up, chewed.

"I always tell him not to put weird shit in his pancakes. People like them plain," his sister said, coming back with an armful of clothing for Amanda. She dumped it on the couch.

"Here, wear these," she said.

Soon Amanda was dressed in a delightfully warm pair of pants and a thick, pillowy-soft parka lined with fur. Her boots were as light as air. She was amazed at how airy everything was, and yet so completely warm. The parka had a drawstring hood and came with a pair of warm gloves, attached to the sleeves so she wouldn't lose them.

"All right, let's go," Pete said, pushing back from the table. He left his dishes for his sister, who gave him the stink eye.

Pete grabbed a rifle from near the door.

"Get my bag, will ya?"

Amanda complied, carrying the bag behind him to the snow-mobile, which was now half buried in snow. He set it on the back with the rifle, and Amanda helped him push and rock the machine out of the drift.

"This is good weather. We're lucky," he said. "Last chance to use a real bathroom. For the rest of the day, you'll be leaving droppings in the snow."

"I'm fine. I just went."

"Good. All aboard. Let's go."

They rode off, past more houses buried in snow. In the strange pale light, Amanda could see how small the village was.

"Where we are going, my people usually don't go. It is the place of the bears," Pete said, calling into the wind. "We don't hunt there. The bears do. We leave them alone, and they leave us alone."

They left the town for the white hills. Eventually, Pete stopped on a rise. Below them, the frozen ocean stretched out, all blue and white ice, jumbled from chaotic waves. A soft wind moaned over the frozen sea. Even at a distance, Amanda could hear the ice expanding and complaining.

"Don't stare too long. You'll get snow blindness," Pete said. He reached into a compartment and handed her a pair of sunglasses. He started the snowmobile again and they kept driving, over the ridges. He drove down into what looked like a small valley. Amanda realized they were crossing a lake, frozen solid underneath them. The snowmobile treads creaked over the snow.

Pete pointed as they drove.

"The station is up there," he called.

Amanda looked up. The old research station was on top of a hill overlooking the sea. She could see the wooden boards. The warning light had long since broken off.

"No point in going up there," he said. "Sometimes male bears den in abandoned buildings. We don't want to mess with them. They're not what we're looking for, anyhow."

He kept driving, taking them deep into the hills, next to the frozen sea. The crevasses between the hills became nearly impassable, with giant hunks of ice and snow-covered rocks.

Pete stopped the machine.

"From here, we go on foot," he said.

He went around the back and grabbed the rifle. This he put over his shoulder, and then he grabbed a long ice chisel, for testing the snow. He made sure Amanda was safely bundled into her parka, and carrying his bag.

"Walk directly behind me," he said.

The snow squealed with delight as they walked. Amanda noticed the pale sun cast no shadow.

PETE WALKED CAREFULLY, USING THE CHISEL TO CHECK THE SNOW ahead of them. Every now and then he stopped, looking around. His eyes scanned the surrounding hills as if looking for danger.

Amanda could see nothing. But then, she knew a bear would see them long before they would see it. A polar bear motionless in the snow was nearly invisible. By the time you saw it, it was often too late. It could outrun you too.

Polar bears were not afraid of humans. They could and would attack, especially if they were hungry. Or if you were near their den. Or just because they didn't want you around. Especially if you were in their range, and they were a nesting female bear. Those were the most dangerous of all.

Amanda began to speak. Pete shook his head. He pointed at the steep snow-covered hills around them. Noise could cause an avalanche. It could also attract a bear.

Amanda nodded, feeling snow on her lashes. She had never been to any place like this—she and her parents had never traveled much when she was a child, and then only on family trips where they did everything for her, and the entire experience felt curated, supervised, and controlled. This was different. Now she was out on her own.

Despite the dangers, Amanda felt calm and peaceful. It had been the same after the fire, she realized, and even after being chased. She felt filled with a warm glow of excitement and pure joy in life. Out here, in the snow, she was, finally, just Amanda.

Pete's chisel suddenly broke the snow in front of him. He jumped back, pushing her back with one arm.

With a soft thud, the snow in front of them collapsed. A large dark hole appeared.

Pete lifted his rifle and waited.

Nothing came out of the hole. Pete crept forward, peeking. He put the rifle back over his shoulder.

"Come see," he whispered.

Amanda came forward and looked into one of the marvels of nature: an abandoned polar bear den.

It was like a small snow cave, she thought. The den was large enough for an adult bear, which meant it was several feet across. The snow had been melted by the bear's breath and body heat, and then refrozen, forming an airtight, warm seal against the weather. The bottom was littered with tangles of shedded hair.

"This is a sleeping den," Pete said quietly, kneeling to look.

"How do you know? Size?" Amanda asked.

"Yes. And a maternity den would have baby poop in it."

"How do I get down there?"

"With my help. Hurry. If there is a den here, there is probably another one close by, and that one might contain a bear."

He helped Amanda lower herself into the hole. Crouching, she quickly combed up bits of fur with her gloved hands. She put these into the baggies from Pete's testing kit, which was in the bag she had carried. The plastic was so cold, it was crisp.

Pete kept an eye out. He remembered the researchers coming here against his advice, talking, barely paying attention to their ice picks. He had warned them. He took no pleasure in knowing he had been right.

Amanda crawled out of the hole with his help. She put the baggies back into the bag, her hands shaking. He looked into her face. The shaking was from excitement and pleasure, he saw, not fear.

"Ready," she whispered.

They traced their steps back to the snowmobile. The sun never seemed to move position. As she walked, Amanda took a video of the endless white hills, for Molly. Bears had genetic memories. Molly would instinctually know her ancestral lands.

"Hurry," Pete urged.

Amanda caught up.

"You ever worry about Molly charging you?" he asked.

"Of course," she said. Molly was a wild creature, just like her. Both were unpredictable.

"That's good. You sound like you know her."

They were out of the hills and closer to the snowmobile. Pete had relaxed now that the risk of avalanche and bears was retreating behind them. "People talk about anthropomorphizing animals, but I think it's more like infantilizing them. Listen to how people talk to their pets, in baby voices."

Amanda had noticed this. It had always made her slightly uncomfortable, but she figured this was because of how teachers had talked to her. Like she was a baby. One had explained that her IQ made her younger. Amanda didn't think so. Having a hard time learning some things didn't make her less mature than the other kids. If anything, she thought having to work harder than many of the kids might have made her more mature. It was all very confusing.

"They think an animal is like a child, an infant," Pete said as they reached the snowmobile. He kept the rifle over his shoulder. They put on their helmets, and Amanda got behind him. The land of the bears receded from them as he turned and headed back toward the town.

"We don't understand the languages of others," Amanda said.

"That is true," Pete said.

PETE AND AMANDA WERE IN HIS RESEARCH LABORATORY ABOVE the aquarium. The small, damp room was filled with cross sections of whale bones, scraps of animal hide, samples of soil, and more.

Amanda picked up a vial filled with what looked like dried blood. They had flown back that morning, and now were—suddenly, it felt—back in Oregon. Amanda felt strangely naked being back in the clothes Aspire had loaned her. She would miss those pants and parka, but they belonged in Alaska.

"That's from one of the seals," he said. "I'm researching how they handle the stress of captivity."

"I thought they lived longer in captivity. Like bears."

"Yeah, but that doesn't mean they live happily."

He finished putting the samples Amanda had taken into vials, then tucked them into an overnight envelope, along with a DNA order form.

Amanda took the heavy polar bear tooth out of the bag.

"Can we have this tested too?"

"Hey. You got that?" he asked. He took the fire-smudged case from her. "What happened to it?"

"It was in a fire."

"You mean—"

"Would it have DNA as well?"

"Possibly. We can try."

He put on a fresh pair of gloves and took the tooth out of its case. He took samples from the interior, where the root had been.

"How long will it take?" she asked.

"A few days, at the most. Why didn't you tell me you were in the fire?"

The newspaper had been sitting on the front counter when they returned. The cover said, "Fire Destroys Eagle Cove Residence. Arson Suspected." Amanda's and Larry's names were right there, but neither Amanda nor Pete had read the article yet.

"I didn't feel like talking about it."

"Fair enough. Want to talk now?"

"No. I have a hard time focusing on more than one thing at a time. Right now I'm thinking of Molly. Then I'll go get my car, drive back to Eagle Cove, and see how Larry is doing. I'll think of that there."

He thought of the stew. Amanda liked things clear, he thought.

"I'll let you know the results," he said, turning back to his desk.

AMANDA WAS ON HER WAY DOWN THE STREET OUTSIDE WHEN SHE ran into Patty, who was parking her motorcycle. The social worker was shaking out her long hair, much to the admiration of an older gentleman on the boardwalk.

"Hey, just who I was planning to call," Patty said.

Amanda was eager to get back to Eagle Cove. She wanted to change out of the strange clothes. Then she remembered she didn't have any of her own clothes anymore. Not with her, at least.

"Can I talk to you for a minute?" Patty asked.

"Maybe later? I'm tired."

"We'll make it quick. Coffee?"

Amanda looked at the rainy sky. Her stomach was still upset from the plane ride back that morning. "Tea would be better."

Patty bought her a cup in a nearby café, bringing it to where Amanda stood at the window counter. "Here. Peppermint, just like you wanted. I heard about the fire. Are you okay?"

"I'm fine."

"You're a tough girl."

Amanda thought about what Pete had said, and her own experiences with teachers who called their special-education students kiddos. They were never just students.

"I'm not a girl."

"Sorry. I should know better," Patty said. "Want to sit?"

"I'd rather get going, if that's okay."

"I don't know a good way to bring this up, Amanda, but when we met before, I noticed a few things about you."

Amanda said nothing. She took a sip of her tea and wondered if it would be okay to just walk out. It had started to rain in earnest. Maybe Patty was the not-so-smart one, to take her motorcycle out in the rain.

"I wondered if you were diagnosed with anything."

"No."

"Have you had a lot of different struggles?"

"When I was little, my mother always had to comb the back of my hair. If I couldn't see it, it didn't exist."

"What else?"

"Why?"

Amanda was angry at herself for saying anything at all. She wasn't required to tell this woman her life story. She picked up her cup to go.

"Are you familiar with fetal alcohol spectrum disorders?"

Amanda stopped.

"You mean the kids with funny faces?"

"The media has gotten it so wrong. Most people with fetal alcohol don't have the features. They don't even know they have it. It's a spectrum disorder, like autism."

Amanda looked out the window. She could see every raindrop on the motorcycle.

"Most teachers don't know about it, and specialists rarely test for it."

"You think that's what's wrong with me?"

"You'd have to get evaluated."

"Did Dennis have it?"

Patty was touched that this was where Amanda went.

"Possibly. It's very common in institutionalized children. It's often mistaken for other issues. Like attachment disorders."

"So he got sent to Brightwood for the wrong reason."

"Unfortunately, many people confuse disability with defiance."

"Teachers used to say I was lazy."

"See?"

"Okay. I'm going now," Amanda said. She felt sick from exhaustion and travel and being chased and murders and fires and everything else, and now this woman was telling her she had a dreaded disabling condition that no one had ever even mentioned. Dating had been hard enough before. What was she supposed to tell guys? What about Sean? He would never like her now. No one would like her.

"Amanda, this is good news."

"How so?"

"You can get treatment."

Amanda was silent.

"I've seen it. Occupational therapy that was pioneered with stroke victims. It uses exercises to strengthen the parts of the brain that were damaged."

"I could get better?"

"You might never be a math genius, but I've seen some pretty amazing results."

Amanda put her hands on her face, as if feeling that she was still there. She let out a deep breath.

"I wish Dennis were still alive."

"Why is that?"

"So we could do it together."

AMANDA FOUND LARRY PICKING THROUGH THE REMAINS OF HIS cabin. Despite the rain, he was wearing a short-sleeve shirt, probably because he didn't want to ruin a loaned sweater. His arms were stained with soot. Outside, lurid strands of police tape hung on black branches. The woods behind the cabin were decimated.

Through the remains of the trees, Amanda could now see the beach.

"You're back," he said, happy to see her. He picked up a scorched plate and set it down. "Don't come in. It's a mess. The constable gave me the all clear to salvage what I could. Case closed."

"Really? He caught who did it?"

"Well, almost closed. He found Ike Tressler. Drunk as a skunk in his filthy cabin. So drunk, in fact, he confessed to molesting Reggie and a few of the other boys. Not Dennis, he said."

"What about chasing me? Murdering Reggie? Setting the fire? Did he confess to all that?"

"Not yet. Apparently, he passed out in the back of his car after puking all over the seats. It happens more often than you want to know. The constable will get back to it when the man awakens."

"What about the knife?"

"He probably threw it away. Same with whatever gasoline can he used. But the constable can test his hands for accelerant. Gasoline doesn't just wash off right away. There will be other evidence too."

Larry sounded calm, and relatively happy. Amanda looked into the dripping mess. She saw the fireplace, still standing, and felt sad. Never again would she sit in front of it, eating nuts or drinking coffee with Larry.

But Larry didn't look concerned. He even looked animated, as if the fire had given him a new lease on life. Amanda wondered if part of him was relieved to get rid of the cabin his dead wife had wanted. Maybe now it would be easier to grieve.

He went into his bedroom and came out with a scorched metal box.

"Almost forgot to look for this," he said, putting it down outside, next to a pile of other salvaged items.

"What is it?"

"Stuff from my service. How was your trip?"

"It was great. Ran into Patty in Seaside."

"She have any news for us?"

"Not for us. I want to go home, Larry."

"Don't blame you. Life is a bit hazardous here, isn't it? A madman chasing you down the beach and setting my cabin on fire. Never a dull moment in Eagle Cove, apparently." He stopped joking and smiled at her. It was a tender smile. "Of course you want to go home."

"Will the constable need me?"

"Not right away. If Ike confesses, you won't be needed until a trial, and if he pleads guilty, you might not be needed at all."

"Martha never spoke to us."

"She's clever, that one."

"Do you think we'll ever know exactly what happened?"

"Ike might tell."

"Okay." She stood there awkwardly.

"I'd hug you, but I'm all dirty."

"It's all right."

"I'll call you as soon as I hear anything."

She turned toward her car. "Bye for now."

"Bye."

He watched her walk to her car, and back it carefully away from the burn scene. He could imagine her stopping in Wheel Stone for gas, and then heading into the mountains. He imagined rain pouring down, and then the sky opening the way it did in the ranges, where it seemed you were driving right up into the clouds. Then the slow descent back into the city, and her home there.

Larry went back to picking through his stuff.

32

BRIGHTWOOD CLOSED, AND THE YEARS PASSED. BRETT JARVIS HAD a brief, wonderful stint of sobriety after his daughter, Aspire, was born. It ended with a drunken rage during which he broke every one of his wife's precious plates, inherited from her family, and left her huddled on the floor with the baby, sobbing.

Stumbling down the beach, Brett saw dead bodies with sea stars growing out of their faces, climbing from wet graves in the woods. They followed him, and he screamed. The constable found him the next day, and was able to talk a judge into putting a two-week hold on Brett. He was taken to the hospital in Seaside to dry out. In the hospital, Brett spit bright red blood into plastic trays. He told the doctors about his visions. He saw ghosts in the windows, luminescent shadows as bright as the northern lights. He talked incessantly about the murderous Sasquatch who had stolen at least one boy from Brightwood.

The doctors said his liver was failing. He would die now no matter what he did. Sobriety could no longer save him. Nothing could save him.

They discharged him. He stayed in bed for a week, pissing himself, then broke the lock Gertrude had put on the beer cooler, drank himself into a stupor, and stumbled out once more to the beach, cursing at her from below. This time Gertrude didn't call the constable. She let him go.

The beach was awash in moonlight. It bathed the sand with white light. Brett stumbled all the way to the cliffs. The tide was far out. He could see and feel the ocean, as dark as the night.

He was a bit more sober by the time he reached the cliffs. He began to climb. He was an expert at climbing these rocks. He climbed until the rocks ended and steep forested land began. The trees grew almost vertically from the cliff face. He pulled up from one after another, feeling his aching liver.

The top of the mountain was very cold. He spit out a wad of fresh blood. It looked like black tar on the ground.

He walked out to the very point. The trees here bent backward until they tried no more. He stood on the edge of the cliff.

Someone walked out from the woods behind him.

"Sasquatch?" he asked.

The figure was wearing what seemed like a heavy jacket. He must have seen Brett climbing, Brett figured, and come through the woods. That's what he should have done, instead of climbing the cliff.

Sasquatch stepped closer. The moon caught his face.

"Oh, it's you," Brett said, and then felt puzzled.

"You thought I was Sasquatch?"

"Well, what else?"

"Heard you were talking at the hospital. Someday someone might listen. So I followed you here, to make sure no one ever will."

Brett nodded. It made perfect sense.

"I didn't leave a note," he said. "I should go back, leave a note. For Aspire."

"Too late."

"Really?"

"Leave your jacket, so they know."

"Good idea." Brett stripped off his jacket and stood there, shivering, in a short-sleeve shirt. He didn't know why he hadn't put on a sweater. He wasn't thinking right anymore. Heck, he hadn't been thinking right for a long time.

"What about Aspire?"

"She'll be better off without you."

The wind felt cold and sweet on his naked arms. His lungs felt filled with fluid. He knew his skin was a pale yellow, his eyeballs stained the color of piss. He coughed again, and tasted blood.

"I wish I had left her a note," he said.

The visions were returning. Brett saw tall shapes in the trees. All the ghosts of the past were returning. They were stumbling from wet graves in the woods, coming toward him, asking why he hadn't done more.

"Why did you do it?" he asked Sasquatch, who had stopped being a man he knew and returned to what he had been all along: half man, half monster.

"She asked me to," he said.

"Who?" Brett asked, afraid.

"You know," the man whispered.

Brett took a step back.

The man felt bad. In a way, it was like saying goodbye to an old friend. Brett had been part of this story for a long time, and it was hard to see him go.

"Goodbye, Brett," he said.

Brett turned to face the moonlit sky. The air was breathtaking, and the sea huge. The horizon was a single black line, but everywhere else there were dark waves, cresting over the glittering black sea. He wondered what it would feel like to plunge into that water, to feel the icicle shock of cold before the waves smashed him against the rocks.

"You don't have to—" Brett said.

The man stepped closer, and pushed. Brett felt himself falling, into open air. He felt his arms stick out, as if he were embracing the air, but his mind was a jumble of thoughts, and the primary one was that he didn't have more time to think. He wanted to put things in order. He wanted—

He fell, hard, into the water, plunging so deep he lost consciousness, and the waves crashed him against the rocks, and he was sucked back with great force, and someplace in all that greatness, the life left Brett Jarvis.

All was silence again. The man stepped back. He took his time, erasing any trace of his boots from the thick dander of the mountaintop.

He left the jacket for the constable to find.

AT FIRST, EVERY FEW MONTHS TO A YEAR, THE CONSTABLE WOULD drive to the abandoned center, just to check on things. He felt as if he had unfinished business there. Metal scrappers stripped the place of every cot leg and stray bit of metal they could remove, even the wires in the walls. The plaster began to reek of mold and decay. The constable bolted NO TRESPASSING signs on the gate and a DANGER sign on the door.

Still, he kept returning, and sometimes he paused on the second floor, looked into the silent array of trees, and wondered.

He often thought of the boy in the well. Sometimes you had to let things go. He felt he had failed. Years later, he would hire a secretary, and she would indeed purge many of his old reports, and by then he would feel he would rather not know if he had made a mistake, after all.

IN THE TOWN, ASPIRE GREW. WHEN SHE WAS OLD ENOUGH TO HOLD a spoon, she was put to work in the kitchen with her mother. It was clear that this was more for Gertrude's benefit than the child's. The town tried to intervene, gently, by making sure the girl got to school.

The memorial aged, but the stone had been well cut. Everyone aged.

The coast was a place where you got older, like the sturdy pines facing away from the wind. If you look closely at their needles, they are flat on the wind side, bulging with promise on the lee.

The constable's children grew up. Like most coastal kids, they left and didn't come back. His wife stayed. The bartender died in a freak accident when a keg he was keeping on a rack rolled off and fell on him. The cook got the job at the nursing home. Ike Tressler vanished into the woods, and eventually, the constable almost forgot about him. Just as they all nearly forgot about Ralph, the kindly custodian who had disappeared soon after the boy died.

Charlie ran his hotel, and on good days, the locals would see him out on the dunes, studying the sea. The crowds never did come.

33

"YOU'RE BACK!" AMANDA'S BOSS SAID.

"I still have two more days," she said. "But I brought something for you."

"It'll be great to have you back. Hey, I heard Molly loves your videos. Sean hooked up a television outside her sleeping quarters. She goes in there, watches you. The one you just sent, from Alaska? He said she stood straight up."

Amanda wasn't sure that was good, but she smiled at him. He got up, and celebrated her return by popping a gumball in his mouth. Today he wore a ratty shirt that said *Blue Gallery*. The back said *ART MUSIC BEER*.

She handed over a file.

"For me?"

"Open it," she said.

Inside was a printout of a DNA profile. On one side was Molly. On the other side were three other bears.

"What's this all about?" he asked.

Amanda stood next to him and pointed. "This one is Molly. This next one is from the tooth that was supposedly taken from her mother. The rescuers found the body on the ice, a week after taking Molly."

"It's not a match."

"Because it wasn't her mother."

"Okay. Fill me in here."

"This other bear here, this one is her mother." Amanda pointed. "I got the DNA from hair I took from a sleeping den in Anger Bay, Alaska." His eyes jumped to her, full of alarm and amusement. "One of the former researchers at the station, Pete Ashoona, took me there. I found Pete after I started looking into what happened to Molly. I had questions, and he had answers."

Her boss stopped smiling. His face had become very serious.

"So her mother is alive."

"Polar bears can live up to thirty years in the wild. They start having babies around age four or five. She's probably not fertile anymore, but yes, she's still there, in the same territory."

"Okay. Tell me more."

"Pete Ashoona told me what really happened. He said the men were out in an area known for bears. One of the researchers fell through the snow into a maternity den. The mother was inside. She charged at them. They shot at her. They thought she was hit—she took off running. They took Molly, thinking it was for the best. When they found the remains of a female bear on the ice, they assumed it was the dead mother."

"What happened to the real mother?"

"She came back a few weeks later. She tracked them to the station and hung outside for weeks, charging at them. Trying to kill them. She knew they had taken her babies."

"Hold up here. You just said 'babies.'"

"There was more than one. There were two cubs in that den, and they took both. This is the second one." Amanda pointed at the final bear. "See the match?"

"Holy shit. Excuse me. There was another cub?"

"They left that unsavory detail out of their reports. By the time the real mother had shown up, it was too late. The cubs were gone. They didn't name the second one, because she ended up being sold on the black market."

"What's her name?"

"Nova. She lives in a really horrible little private zoo in Singapore. I got the zookeeper there to send me pictures."

"Same issues as Molly?"

"Worse."

He handed her back the file and stood at his window. He couldn't see the polar bear habitat from here, but he could see the path down to it. A peacock strutted on the sidewalk, fanning its feathers.

"I know what you're thinking, but there's no reason to believe Molly would accept her sister. It's been, what, fifteen years?"

"In the wild, polar bear sisters and their mother live in overlapping territories. Had Molly and Nova not been taken, they would still be there."

"It's a lot of money and effort to ship a polar bear here from Singapore. And there's no reason to believe they will let her go."

"They will let her go," Amanda said.

AMANDA WALKED DOWN TO THE POLAR BEAR HABITAT. SHE STOOD at a distance, admiring Molly in the sun. She was rolling in the grass on the top of the hill. Amanda didn't want the bear to see her until she was back for good.

Sean saw her, and waved. He looked happy to see her.

"Hey." He came at a trot.

"Hi," Amanda said.

"You're a sight for sore eyes."

Amanda knew this one. He was saying he was glad to see her, not that his eyes were sore.

"So are you."

The sun caught his dark hair. She wondered if she had made a mistake saying that. But he smiled at her, and she felt good all over.

"Did you have fun on your trips?" he asked innocently.

"Kind of. I'm going to miss Larry."

"Who is Larry?" He looked concerned.

"He's a friend of mine. Older. Like, you know—a father figure."

"Oh. I was worried there, for a minute."

He was still smiling at her, directly. He didn't look at all ashamed of what he had just said.

"Why did you say that?"

Now he looked nervous. "You know I like you, right?"

"I couldn't tell. I'm sorry."

"Don't apologize. Just say you'll go on a date with me." His cheeks had turned a deep crimson red.

"Yes."

It was that easy, Amanda thought. It had been that easy, and that hard, all along.

She felt the heat in her own cheeks.

"I'm hot," he said, then blushed some more. "I mean, warm. Nervous. I have a break. Want some ice cream? As long as we're acting like kids."

Amanda walked with him to the ice cream stand near the popcorn kiosk. Kids milled around, coming up to their waists. Sean got vanilla, and she got rocky road, her favorite. She remembered how as a kid she had once dissected a cone, asking her mother for the name of every ingredient, so she could safely guess what they were once they were in her mouth. Here, this was a nut. A mini marshmallow. All safe in her mouth.

Sean and Amanda sat near the primate habitat, suddenly shy around each other. Their thighs touched. The sun melted her ice cream, but Amanda was too nervous to taste it.

"What should we do on our date?" Sean asked.

"What do you want to do?" Amanda was scared of dates. She hadn't gone on many, and most had been total disasters.

She looked at his shiny hair and realized Sean might have issues too. She had never asked about his past, but maybe there was a reason he had also gone to work at the zoo and not to college. Not that everyone smart went to college.

"I like to go for long walks. My mom got me into it. Sometimes I go to the track for the car races, but to be honest, that's more for my dad." He ate his ice cream, thinking about it. "Whatever you want. Maybe you could tell me more about Molly. We could do something fun. How about a movie?"

"Not the loud ones," Amanda said. "I don't like the loud ones."

"Me either. Hey, have you ever played miniature golf? It's really fun."

Amanda thought about it. "I might get it wrong."

"Who cares?"

"Okay, then." They finished their cones.

"This weekend?" he asked as they both carefully wiped their hands and dropped the napkins in the trash.

"Yes, please," she said, and he held her hand all the way back to the gates.

WHILE AMANDA WAS GEARING UP FOR WORK—AND POSSIBLY love—Larry was walking the beach, once again. His feet felt different on the sand, like he was going someplace. He was staying at the hotel until he decided next steps. Maybe he'd buy a little place in Seaside. Something more modern than the cabin, like a condo.

Stomping his feet like a local, he entered the market.

Gertrude was in the back, but this time she waved at him. Aspire was at the counter, looking bored.

"Did Amanda give you those clothes I loaned her?" the teen girl asked.

"She's going to send them back, all nice and laundered, now that she's home."

Larry poured himself a cup of coffee. "You give any thought to what we talked about? Maybe striking out on your own somewhere?"

"Where would I go? What would I do?"

"I don't know. What would you like to do?"

Larry noticed her mother was listening. She looked sad but receptive, from the shape of her head.

"I like anime. And books. Not much to do with that."

"There's a ton you can do with that. Why not look for a job in a bookstore or library? Rent is expensive, but you could get a place in shared housing, with young people like yourself. Safety in numbers, and some of them might turn out to be friends."

Aspire looked away, her eyes filled with boredom.

"Maybe," she said.

"You should," her mother said, stepping from her doorway. She wore mismatched socks. "Get out of here, go live your life."

You could say that in a nicer way, Larry thought, but he gave her credit for saying it at all—it had probably taken all she had.

"Maybe," Aspire repeated.

"Talk to the constable. I bet he has lots of ideas," Larry said.

"Or the man at the paper," her mother said. "He knows people."

"I can even drive you in to interviews," Larry said.

"You'd do that?" her mother asked.

"Sure. Why not? I've got things to do in the city."

Aspire smiled, suddenly more cheerful.

Larry drank his coffee. The door behind him jangled, and one of the old men came to take his seat on the bench. He pulled out a container

of chaw and moved the wastebasket closer, so he could spit. Gertrude
brought him a cup of coffee.

"You could take your father's car if you move," she told her daughter.
"We'll get it fixed up first."

Aspire's face lit up. She could have a piece of the past with her.

"You haven't bought any spaghetti bake for a long time," Gertrude
told Larry.

"Guess I'll have to fix that," he said.

LARRY WAS ALMOST BACK AT THE HOTEL, CRADLING THE WARM
package, when the idea came to him. He unlocked his hotel room door,
set down his food, and took the phone out of his pocket.

"Yeah, Larry here. Hey, can you check something for me? It occurred to me that Ralph Higgins may be in his fifties, but he probably
lived a hard life. Maybe he filed for disability at some point."

He waited, listening.

His friend came back.

"Thank you," Larry said.

He wrote down the address he had been given.

AMANDA WAS BACK IN HER APARTMENT, LOOKING AT HERSELF IN
the bathroom mirror, when Larry called.

"We found Ralph Higgins," Larry said. "He recently filed for disability for a bad back. He lives way out in the boonies—out past the
gorge. I'm looking at his address right now."

"Can we go?" Amanda asked.

"Looks like about a four- to five-hour drive from your place."

"What about Ike?"

"The constable said he's now denying everything except the

molestation. It's how it works. The constable swabbed his hands for accelerant and sent it to the state lab. We'll get him, don't worry."

"Okay," she said.

"I'll pick you up bright and early."

After they hung up, Amanda found a new bag to pack, and Larry sat in his hotel room with his stocking feet on the metal box.

CONSTABLE ROBERTS STOOD OUTSIDE HIS ONLY JAIL CELL. IT WAS rare that he held anyone here, unless it was a drunk tourist needing a dry-out. Most prisoners went on to the county jail, up the coast.

But not Ike. He had been stumbling drunk when he was taken in, and the constable worried that his confession wouldn't hold. Now Ike was in the corner of his cell, having a little snooze. Like a lot of drunks, he preferred the cold floor to the cot. Constable Roberts, who drank very little, never understood that.

"Ike," he said.

The man groaned and stretched, then fell back to sleep. He scratched his groin.

The constable studied him. The worn boots. The filthy trousers— they might have been khaki once but were gray now. The thin flannel shirt under all the jackets. His neck was stained with dirt.

"You've been sleeping long enough. Time to get up," the constable said.

"Why?" Ike muttered thickly.

"I need to know where they are," the constable said. Sometimes it was best to get right back into it.

"Who?" The man turned over, bubbling in his sleep.

"The boys. The runaway reports Martha filed, back in the day. I think we all know now those boys didn't run away."

"Sure they did."

"I figure you made them disappear because you were afraid of them telling on you."

"What?" Ike opened one eye. It looked like a poached egg with red veins. "You're drunk."

"No. Though I think you have been."

"I already told you what I did to those boys, all right? Not all of them. Just a few. Ain't proud of it. You're the only one who knows, except I think Brett might have suspected it, and he's dead now. They're all dead."

"Including the boys. Including Reggie."

"Really?" The drunk man looked upset. He sat up on the concrete floor. "Reggie. I remember that boy." He had a little smile that made the constable sick. "You say he's dead now?"

"You killed him. You should know."

"I should? I didn't kill anyone. Not that I remember, anyhow." He scratched his scaly scalp, then looked at his dirty fingernails. "Fuck, I feel like shit. It's funny, you start not being able to hold your liquor."

"That's a sign of liver failure, Ike."

"Ain't that what happened to Brett?"

"It's what happens to a lot of us, when we don't stop in time."

"You sound like fucking AA, Constable."

"All right." The constable tapped on the bars with his class ring. "Come on. I'll get you something to eat. What do you want?"

"Some fish-and-chips would be nice."

"All right, I'll go get some, be back."

"You gonna let me out of here?"

"You're under arrest, Ike."

"What for?"

"Attempted murder. Murder. Arson."

"Get out! All because of what I told you? Those boys were long ago. I haven't touched anyone since. Just looked at a few. You know, through windows."

"You're a Peeping Tom then too."

"Ain't there a statute of limitations?"

"On the sexual abuse back then, yes, unfortunately. Not on the rest."

"I ain't done anything," Ike said, scratching his head and grumbling. "Go get me some food, you pig."

Liver failure, the constable thought. It had given poor Brett visions, at the end. But some of those visions turned out to be true. Now Ike, Brett's onetime drinking buddy and a former staff member at Brightwood, was eating up his visions and spitting them out, saying no, no, and no again.

The constable left to get the fish-and-chips. He felt troubled. He had already searched Ike's cabin, with the then-drunk man's permission. He had found no matching knife. He had found no evidence of any of the crimes.

34

THE COLUMBIA RIVER WAS SO IMPOSSIBLY BIG THAT AMANDA COULD not take it all in at once. Windsurfers, out on a gusty spring day, rocked across the waves, so tiny they looked like flying dots.

From the city, they had driven up the gorge. From there, they crossed into high rocky lands that turned into vast farms combed with tractors, and tiny ranches in the distance that grew bigger as you got close. These became patchy pine hills, and soon theirs was the only car on the road. They passed a sign that said PRAYER VALLEY MUSTANG RESCUE, and Amanda peered down a rocky road that seemed to lead nowhere. She could see what looked like wild horses grazing on the hills.

"Getting close now," Larry said. They had made the drive in record time. It was barely afternoon.

Larry glanced at the map he had screenshotted—in case their phones went out, which they did—and followed the river road until the next turnoff, which was up a dirt road. He watched for potholes.

"I don't see many people out here," Amanda said, looking over the parched land.

"Drought chased most of them out. Not that there were many to begin with," Larry said.

THE TRAILER IN THE CLEARING LOOKED RUN-DOWN BUT COZY. OLD sheets hung on a line outside, catching the breeze off the river. An ancient truck was parked in front, its wheels collapsed in the dirt. Behind it was another truck, this one in slightly better condition. It was still ticking and warm.

"He might have a visitor," Larry said.

They approached, Larry's hand under his jacket. There was laughter coming from inside the house. Something inside Amanda shifted.

Larry knocked, firmly, then stepped back into a defensive posture.

The door opened. The man was the custodian in the picture from long ago, but very aged. His eyes were dewlapped with skin, his ears mottled with sun. His hair had receded, showing a sun-damaged scalp. The last of his hair hung by his ears.

He looked down, curious, at the man at his door and the young woman by his side. His gaze lingered on Amanda.

"Who is it, Ralph?" A young man stepped into the doorway. His skin was tanned a deep honey brown, his blond hair bleached white at the tips. His dark blue eyes looked friendly.

Amanda felt her heart knock in her chest. It knocked so loud it was painful.

"Dennis," she said.

THEY SAT AROUND THE EMPTY FIREPIT OUTSIDE, IN GREEN CANVAS lawn chairs that sagged, so their bottoms were nearly touching the earth.

Amanda could not stop staring at her brother. She felt she could spend the rest of her life just savoring this moment. You are alive, she thought. You are really alive.

"Maybe you can tell us what happened," Larry said.

"Ralph saved me," Dennis said. "He caught me after I went under, and dragged me to the beach. He hid me in his truck and went to the market and told everyone I had been swept away."

"You planned this?" Larry asked.

Ralph shook his head. "I didn't know what I was going to do until it happened. I remember thinking, I can't take him back there. Not to her. I thought, I'll lie. I'll save him. I'll say he drowned, and when it's all over, I'll take him far away. So that's what I did. After I went to the market, I hid him in the woods behind my place and took care of him. When the constable closed the case, we left in the middle of the night. We never looked back."

"How did you survive?" Larry asked.

"We stayed on the road, working the migrant farms. I told everyone Dennis was my nephew. Eventually, I got him a fake ID. We used it as the name on this place. We didn't stop for the longest time."

"I healed, on the road," Dennis said.

"Do you live here?" Amanda asked.

"Naw. I live and work at a wild mustang rescue. You probably passed it on the way here. I'm not so good with numbers, but I like animals."

"Me too," Amanda began.

Larry's phone buzzed. He got up to answer it, walking a distance away.

When he came back, looking puzzled, Amanda and Dennis were deep in conversation, talking about their mother, Brightwood, and their lives. Dennis was telling her about the horses, and she was telling him about Molly. Larry had never seen Amanda so animated, so happy.

"Who was that?" Amanda asked. She knew Larry wouldn't have taken the call if it wasn't important.

"Constable Roberts. Ike Tressler tested clean for accelerant. The constable isn't finding any evidence of the other crimes at all. There's something else too."

"What?" Amanda asked.

"Apparently, the old truck Ike has barely drives. It would have been hard for him to make it to the city."

"He could have borrowed a car."

"Ike Tressler?" Dennis asked. "That brings back memories."

Ralph looked worried, like ghosts were coming back.

"There's a lot we want to talk to you about," Larry said.

Amanda didn't really care about anything else at that moment. She just wanted to sit there, in the dappled sun, and look at her brother.

"Those other boys," Larry began.

A shot rang out, and Ralph fell backward in his chair.

LARRY IMMEDIATELY SCRAMBLED TO THE GROUND.

"Get down!" he screamed, shielding Amanda. Another bullet whistled past, taking a piece of his ear. Amanda dropped to the ground and tried to scramble away. Dennis was already halfway across the lot toward the trailer when he was hit in the leg. He fell over, landing in the dirt. He turned back to see that Ralph was down, lying on the ground.

Larry whipped into position. There were things you never forget. He crouched above Amanda, protecting her, and he had the service weapon from the holster under his arm in his hand without thinking, his finger on the safety. He had already seen where the shots were coming from. Decades of experience told him everything he needed to know. The bushes shook, and he could see the shape of a man hiding in them.

Larry took careful aim, and fired.

"ASSHOLE," THE MAN WHEEZED AS LARRY STOOD OVER HIM.

Larry had started running as soon as he saw the target was hit. It was important to take him out of commission. A mortally injured man could still fire on others. It wasn't like in the movies. Even after being shot in the head, it could take a person several minutes to die.

The man on the forest floor looked at home there. He lay behind the trees where he had hidden, after parking up the road. He had followed Larry and Amanda here. It wasn't hard. He had put a tracker on Larry's car that day outside the hotel when he'd commented on how the sand followed him everywhere.

Even now, there was sand in his ears. He reached for it, and realized he was bleeding, and badly. That was why he was on his back, he thought. He couldn't figure it out until now. One minute he was shooting. The next he was shot.

"Amanda said you didn't have a gun anymore," he said.

"How would she know?" Larry asked. He holstered the gun he had taken from his safety box that morning.

Amanda came running.

"Careful," Larry said. He stepped on the man's wrist before taking the rifle out of his grip. The man stared up at the rifle as if he had never seen it before. There was a knife at his belt.

Amanda looked down at the man who had chased her through the rain, and thought of everything she had overlooked until now—how he had always known where she was, how he had told her a friend had helped him purchase the hotel, how inept he had seemed at life. The bullet had taken the top of his skull off, and it was hard to look at.

"Charlie," she said.

CHARLIE BLINKED. IT WAS GETTING HARDER TO THINK, AND THE top of his head hurt. He realized his hands were not working so well anymore. He still wanted to kill them—it was just getting harder to move. He felt like a fish, out of the sea and pinned to the sand. Left flopping there.

"You were one of her boys too," Amanda said.

"Hero," he bubbled. "She gave me . . . holding time."

"And never let go."

"Owe her." He breathed. "She helped me buy . . . the hotel."

"Did you kill Reggie too? In case he had seen something?"

Charlie blinked. Yes.

"The shells," Amanda said, everything falling together. "You're the one who hung the shells. Hoping the past, and the pain, would just go away."

"He's dying now," Larry said. There was no emotion in his voice. He stood up, wiping his hands on his pants. To the man on the forest floor, he seemed very tall indeed.

IN THE CLEARING BEHIND THEM, DENNIS WAS CHANTING RALPH'S name. He had crawled back, bleeding, and was now leaning over the prone man, begging and pleading with him not to die.

Ralph opened his eyes to look at him.

He was remembering.

THE LONG SHADOW OF THE MAN CHASED AFTER THE BOY RUNNING across the wet gray sand. Ralph stumbled over the soft white sand before gaining his footing. He found the hard, packed sand, and the run turned into a sprint.

Dennis! he screamed.

There was only the flat, implacable beach and the angry, torrential waves. They slammed so hard on the beach, Ralph could feel them shaking the ground under his feet.

The boy ran directly into the ocean.

Without hesitation, Ralph did too.

The first wave drenched him, and the third knocked him over. He felt his feet slip out from under him. Dennis had disappeared in the waves. For a moment, Ralph couldn't see anything. Scrambling, he regained his footing, only to be knocked down again.

Dennis! he screamed, over and over again. *Dennis!*

The ground beneath him disappeared. Ralph gasped for air, sputtering salt water. He had stepped off a ledge into much deeper water. His legs churned below him, helpless. He had never learned to swim. Dennis had vanished, and Ralph couldn't see anything but sea-foam scudding across the waves. The water was icy cold, and already his legs were growing numb.

Dennis! he tried to yell, but his mouth filled with seawater, and he coughed. I'm going to drown, he thought as another wave crested over his head. He bobbed again, gasping. It might already be too late to turn back. Water covered his mouth.

Something hard hit his legs. For a wild moment, he thought it was a shark. Then he saw, down through the swirling water.

It was Dennis.

Ralph grabbed, hard, and felt Dennis in his grasp. His skin was slippery, but Ralph managed to hold on under his arms, pulling the limp boy toward his chest. Another wave washed over them. Ralph kicked hard, feeling the ocean suck at his boots. It was astonishing how strong the undercurrent was. He could feel it trying to pull them under.

He kicked even harder, gasping for breath. The shore was frighteningly far away. He grasped the boy tightly in his arms. Wave after wave crested over them. He could not think or see. Water ran over his eyes in a film.

The sea pulled them down. He felt himself looking up, through the water, at the miracle of the sky.

Suddenly, a large wave swelled underneath them. It was a different temperature, even colder than the rest of the ocean. It was a sneaker wave, and in a rare stroke of luck, they were on the right side of it. The massive wave drove everything to the beach, including them, on a current so swift and strong the custodian was shocked at its power. He felt their helpless bodies rushed far up the beach, past piles of driftwood, and then, just as quickly, the water began sucking it all back. Ralph found his footing and fought hard to stay on the sand. The wave rushed backward, clawing and sucking at his legs as it went.

Stumbling and gasping, Ralph dragged Dennis out of the surf. Dennis slipped from his hands, falling hard against the packed sand. He convulsed. Water poured from his lungs, as pure as blue glass.

The custodian dragged the unconscious boy farther up the beach. Water ran from the boy's mouth. His skin was very cold. The wind whipped against them. Ralph was freezing. He picked up Dennis, holding him in his arms. They were both covered in wet sand.

"Help," he croaked.

The beach road looked so far away. His truck, the door still open, seemed so small in the distance.

"Help us," he whispered.

The beach was empty. The market was a mile down the road, hidden in the trees. No one had seen them. No one was coming.

The idea came to him then. It came back to him now, in the final moments of his life, as he lay on his back in the clearing outside the trailer where he had spent his last, contented years, knowing he had done at least one small good thing in his life. Blood trickled from the wound in his chest. He could feel it, but it didn't matter. All that mattered was the memory.

Let them think he's dead.

On that wet and cold beach, Ralph had stopped.

Tell them he died in the waves.

Shivering, he had cradled the wet boy in his arms and stumbled to his truck. He stripped Dennis out of his wet shirt and then wrapped him in warm blankets, his head safely out, and covered him lightly with a tarp, hiding him on the floor. He parked the truck where no one would find it, and walked the rest of the way to the market.

Twenty years later, a gunshot wound to his chest, Ralph looked up. The boy, now grown, was above him. He was talking. Ralph blinked, drowsy. He felt very tired from going in the waves. It was time to rest. He saw that Dennis was holding the rabbit. That was good. Dennis put the rabbit down, and she sat next to the older man. Ralph could feel her by his side. She wanted to tell him something.

He turned his face, away from Dennis, so he might hear.

35

IT WAS FALL, AND THE RAIN REMINDED AMANDA OF THE BEACH.

A large travel crate sat on the concrete floor inside the habitat.

In the shadows, a small crowd watched. Pete was there. Amanda had made sure he would lead all the research into the reunion. Next to Pete was Patty, who seemed quite enamored with him. On the other side was Pete's sister, whom he had flown down from Anger Bay. She wanted to take back a blanket imprinted with the smells of both of the sisters, to reassure their mother back in Anger Bay that her daughters were still alive.

"Now," Amanda said, and the door of the crate was lifted. A dirty, malnourished polar bear stuck out her snout, sniffing. Patches of her fur were worn away. Her black eyes were filled with fear.

Larry stood in the back, next to Dennis. He had bought a small condo in Seaside, where he had hung out his shingle as a private investigator. Dennis had moved to Portland; he was attending occupational therapy with Amanda, and they were slowly getting to know each other. Dennis had discovered he had a knack for politics, and was working to pass a bill against holding time. He called it Reggie's Law.

The door of the travel crate opened directly into the enclosure where Nova would live, beside her sister, until her quarantine had ended. If all went well—and it never had before with Molly—the bears would live in the habitat together. Nova could heal and get treatment in the presence of her sister.

Molly was currently outside, napping at the top of the hill. She did not know another bear had arrived.

IN HIS HOTEL OFFICE, THEY HAD FOUND CHARLIE'S SECRET. HE HAD filled a notebook about Martha King and how she had been his therapist in Colorado, at the beginning of her career. He wrote about buying the hotel with her help, and having her reappear in his life, only to enlist him in covering up the murders of the boys. He even wrote about pushing Brett off the cliff out of fear that someday he would realize Charlie was the one he had seen in the woods. Under the notebook was a tape machine that had been attached to his hotel phone, where he had recorded Martha calling in the middle of the night, asking him to bury bodies. It had been enough to convict her of several charges of murder. She was unrepentant to the end, saying the only thing she had ever done wrong was care for children. She now lived in prison, surrounded by her thank-you cards.

After a long, fruitless search, the constable had given up trying to find the missing boys buried in the woods. Ike Tressler died of liver failure soon after his release from jail. He was never charged with the sexual abuse of boys at Brightwood. Justice, Amanda was learning, was a concept, not a cure. People looked for the easy answers, when there were none.

SLOWLY, NOVA CAME OUT OF THE CRATE. SHE ENTERED THE CON-crete enclosure and sniffed.

"You can close the gate," Amanda said, and Sean closed the door behind the bear, smiling at Amanda. The floor of the enclosure was bare, except for a pile of hay in the corner, for sleeping. Nova sniffed around the corners.

From outside came a sudden long, moaning call.

Molly had smelled her sister.

"Here she comes," Amanda said.

Molly came running into her enclosure, shrouded with rain. They could smell it on her. She stopped, looking around. On the other side of the bars, Nova lifted her long, sinuous neck.

Both she and Molly swiveled their heads to look at each other.

Molly rose to standing. At the same time, so did Nova. Both bears stood and stared at each other through the bars.

Molly was the first to drop to all fours. She approached the bars carefully, and sniffed. Her sister dropped, too, and came closer, to smell Molly.

They inhaled deeply, as if in ecstasy.

"Would you look at that," Pete said.

The two bears stood again, belly to belly, at the bars dividing them. Their long necks wove and danced. Molly clawed at the bars, as if she had waited her whole life for this moment and would not be denied.

ADDENDUM, FROM THE *ALASKAN GAZETTE*:

A female polar bear has been photographed outside the closed research station in Anger Bay, Alaska. She has been carrying a blanket in her mouth. Locals say the bear carries the blanket everywhere she goes.

ACKNOWLEDGMENTS

—

I WAS A YOUNG FOSTER MOTHER WHEN I FIRST HEARD OF HOLDING time. A therapist suggested it for one of my children, who was struggling with an attachment disorder. Despite there being zero scientific evidence in support of the theory or its methods, holding time was very popular at the time, celebrated in mainstream media as well as in foster and adoption circles.

When I learned more about the treatment I was horrified. I knew intuitively, as a trauma survivor myself, that to allow anyone to violate my child's body and mind in such a way would be a terrible betrayal. I said no and fired the therapist.

That child is now a healthy, responsible, and successful young adult. What he needed was love and constancy, not cruelty masquerading as therapy. Holding time was eventually exposed as dangerous, after at least six children died as a result of the methods. But it was never outlawed. It is still used today, against some of our most vulnerable children.

In writing about holding time, I wanted to explore something I've learned in years of justice work. Harsh cures—whether mass incarceration or draconian treatments like holding time—often say more about the unexamined motives of those pushing the cure than they do the cure itself. The character of Martha King represents many people I've met in my work who believe they are doing the right thing, even as they commit the worst harms.

But even as we are capable of terrible violence to each other, we are also capable of tremendous good, and I wanted this story to capture that too.

My thanks go to my amazing kids, Lulu, Dontonio, and Markel, the lovely Lihn and grandbaby Aria, as well as all those I am honored to consider family and friends, including Tamira, Bill, Casey, Keddy, Anna, Gemma, Liz, Cece, Dianah, Leah, Monica, Jen, Kelly, Jane, Julie, Alice, Heidi, Mary, Stephanie, Cate, Andrea, Elizabeth, Rhonda, Alia, Cheryl, Lidia, Carmel, Parag, Debby, Stephen, Laura, Gigi, Luisa, Chris, Amy, Skip, Donald, Mo, Teresa, Jordan, Nastashia, Ronni, Bob, Jeannie, Elisa, Michele, Eric, Jo, Sara, Wendy, Ellen, Tracy, Elle, Owen, Maggie, Heidi, Shawn, and Shannon.

Any mistakes in this book are mine alone, and not the fault of those who graciously helped me with additional research.

An extra-special thanks goes to my agent, Richard Pine, who has shown me immeasurable patience over the years. I'd also like to thank my editor, Sarah Stein, for her amazing feedback, and the stellar teams at Harper, including publicity, marketing, and copyediting. I am lucky to have such support.

My final thanks go to my readers. It was books that saved my own life as a child. In books I found understanding, hope, and belonging. I hope you find understanding in this book, dear reader. I hope you find love.

RENE DENFELD is an internationally bestselling author, journalist, and licensed public death row investigator. She is the author of the critically acclaimed novels *The Child Finder*, *The Enchanted*, and *The Butterfly Girl*. She lives in Portland, Oregon, where she is the happy mother to children from foster care.